SEASIDE AMBUSH

I stood on the farthest rock. Swells rose out of the dark, passed over my feet, swept behind me toward the beach. I didn't hear Sylvus until he was nearly to the end of the jetty. I turned and saw him, a bulky dark silhouette between the rocks. Even then I didn't realize who it was until I smelled the beer on his breath, felt the sharp metal of the shotgun as it knocked me over, saw the pasty-white face illuminated with hatred. He could have shot me then, but he paused to catch his breath.

I shouted for help. It was a waste of breath. The shout was swallowed up in the hiss and slap of the sea. I grabbed the barrel of the gun and it went off, taking a chunk of my side with it. The pain was sharp and terrible. We grappled for the gun, the two of us slipping and sliding on the rocks in the blood pouring out of my side.

We held the gun between us. The muzzle was pointed at my chest. Sylvus clawed at the handle to get to the trigger and fired again....

A NICE LITTLE BEACH TOWN

E.C. WARD

ST. MARTIN'S PAPERBACKS

A NICE LITTLE BEACH TOWN

Copyright © 1989 by Elizabeth C. Ward.

Cover art copyright © 1990 by Marc X. Witz.

All rights reserved. No part of this book may be used or reproduced in any manner whatsoever without written permission except in the case of brief quotations embodied in critical articles or reviews. For information address St. Martin's Press, 175 Fifth Avenue, New York, N.Y. 10010.

Library of Congress Catalog Card Number: 88-29874

ISBN: 0-312-92230-2

Printed in the United States of America

St. Martin's Press hardcover edition published 1989
St. Martin's Paperbacks edition/July 1990

10 9 8 7 6 5 4 3 2 1

For Sean

Ducks. Thousands of them, along with the wild geese, herons, coots, jacksnipe, plover, pelicans, gulls. Rising out of the dark waters, up out of the reeds, gray between the willows, wings flapping against the silence like canvas sheetings, a great billowing tent of them expanding upward against the gray dawn sky. The great mass of them wheeling, moving over the bay to the west toward the cliffs, stirring the still night air, disappearing finally into the mists out over the sea.

Old Sven's eyes, blue, were clear as an hourglass. Nothing stirred in them but the birds. An old man remembering back sixty years. Twelve years old, he had lain in the duck blind hand-fashioned out of reeds at the edge of Duck Island, cradling the gun in his arms. He aimed the barrel out over the bay, the water trembling in a thousand wakes, the mists breathing out of the reeds, up into the sky. Aimed at the last few straggling up out of the darkness. Shot. A single bird plummeted, dead weight, into the bay.

The old man stopped talking. We were hunched together, the two of us, Old Sven and me, over the table in his kitchen like conspirators in a Dostoevski novel. Sven talking. Me half listening. Humoring the old man. Listening to stories I had heard before. The ducks. His fishing boat, the *Anna Louise*. The first time he saw his wife. Each time he told it just a little differently. Broke the rhythm with something new to catch me out. Rushed on when he had my attention again.

But tonight something was on the old man's mind.

Sven was small, wiry, with nervous hands that plucked and pulled at the oilcloth on the old plank table, brushed crumbs onto his napkin, rose to dump them in the sink, rinse them down the drain. Everything neat as a pin. Sink scrubbed down to the grain. Pots hanging in the same place they'd been for half a century. Orderly as a lifetime spent on an albacore fishing boat would make a man. Everything nailed down. Secured in place. As though at any moment the sea outside, a hundred yards across the beach, would come crashing through the front window and sweep it all away.

I waited for the next part of the story. But the old man seemed distracted. He got up, restless, crossed to the window and looked out. The beach was nothing but a mound of shadows, shadows heaped up out of the dunes to where the sea ran black beyond it.

A truck rumbled down the peninsula under cover of darkness. We heard it long before it got to the alley behind the house. Gears grinding. Brakes going on and off like steam boilers. It navigated the corner of the alley, inched its way between the back fences. The house vibrated as it passed. The earth shifted beneath the asphalt. Sent tremors up through the loose-packed sand, rattled the windows, shook the walls.

Sven swore. Rose again to stare out over the yard at the dark shape of machinery atop the flatbed truck. Swore as it rumbled past with all the noise of a battalion of tanks moving up to the front. Took up its post in the dark.

The engine was shut off at the end of the alley. We listened in silence to the squeal and clank of metal as first one bulldozer and then another one were unloaded by a driver in a hurry to get rid of his burden before anyone could stop him. Then, weightless, the empty flatbed rattled past again and made its escape up the peninsula.

Sven swore again and then fell silent. Usually the old man would talk for hours. Follow me into the next room, out into the yard. Stand at the foot of the stairs and shout up as I unlocked the door over the garage. Wait for me in the alley when I came home from work, follow me up to the apartment I rented from him. Catch me when I tried to sneak in. Watch by the window and see me creep past like a naughty kid, bent below the level of the hedge. Come out on the kitchen steps and start talking. He drove me crazy with his stories of the sea. Talked nonstop as though he had to hurry before time ran out on him.

Something stirred on the sand outside. Sven rapped on the window to chase it away.

He'd had a visitor the night before. I'd heard them arguing in the kitchen. A man's voice. And Sven's, high as a fishmonger's. Shouting. Sven threw him out. I heard the kitchen door open and someone retreating across the yard. By the time I got to the window he was gone.

"Sven? Are you all right?"

I could see the old man framed in the light of the door. For the first time I could ever remember, he had not answered me. Had closed and locked the door and gone to bed.

"I gotta go, Sven. Class tomorrow at eight. AP English. My brightest kids."

Sven didn't seem to hear me. He peered out again, old eyes staring into darkness.

I threw my beer can at the trash basket and missed. Sven came back automatically and picked it up. Dropped it into the trash. Wiped the spot up off the floor.

We were an odd couple if ever there was one. Me, his tenant. Past forty. Aging by fits and starts and mad as hell about it. Inflexible. Bull-headed. Cranky. Bellowing, most days, like a bear with a sore paw at a world gone sour.

And Sven. In his seventies. Built like a banty cock. Feisty. Strong. All nerve and muscle except the eyes. Sea-blue. Set in deep Viking bones. Blond hair turned white. Lots of it. Hands too big for his body. Calloused. Tough as leather. Gentle as cat's fur.

"I'm going out. Into the estuary. Want to come?"

"Tonight?"

"I want to show you something."

"Some other night."

The puppy in the basket in the corner stirred. Sven went over and quieted it. Thrust his hand down into the pup's bed, against the muzzle. The pup sighed and went back to sleep. Sven kept his hand there.

He started talking again. Nervous. Almost by rote. As though he was circling around what he wanted to say. Postponing the moment when I'd leave him and he'd be alone again.

I heard him out. Most of it I'd heard before. He threw in bits and pieces that were new, but he didn't have his heart in it. I gave him plenty of time. Had another beer. Threw out a line or two and let him take the bait or not as he chose. But he circled, nervous as a bride. Skirting the thing that was on his mind. I let him talk. Finally around ten o'clock he ran down and I rose to go.

"Sure you won't go with me? We'll be home by midnight."

I shook my head.

"Another time. This weekend, maybe."

He followed me out onto the kitchen stoop and watched while I crossed the yard to the garage and climbed the stairs to my apartment on the top.

I heard him go out about midnight. I was already asleep. Heard the garage door creaking and groaning as the old wood protested at being pulled back. Felt the vibrations as he untied the pulley and let the boat down onto the gurney. Lifted the oars off their hooks and placed them in the boat. Pulled the whole thing across the cement floor into the alley. Felt the old door being heaved back into place. The squeak of wheels as the gurney bore its burden up the alley to the corner, then turned left toward the bay for the solitary journey up to the estuary.

I should have gone with him. Listened to him talk until my eardrums were raw. Taken the oars for him at the head of the bay where it crossed under the bridge and flowed silently up onto the marshes. Sat with him in the darkness listening to the sounds of the wildlife around us, heard whatever secrets he needed to tell me. Or, barring that, gone down to help the old man load the skiff onto the gurney, shut the garage door after him, given him a hug and told him I loved him. But I didn't. I never got another chance.

They found him adrift out near Duck Island, the boat floating slowly down through the marshes with the tide. The sound of the bulldozer woke me. I heard the engine straining, a high whining noise and then the wrench and groan as the house at the end of the alley tore loose from its foundation and collapsed onto the sand. It was 6 A.M. Not yet fully light. I expected Sven to come cursing out of the house to rail at the workmen and the new owners who always stood nearby taking photos, but the kitchen door remained closed. No one stirred. I heard the puppy whining while I shaved but I didn't go down to investigate. It wasn't until I went to get my bike out of the garage that I realized the boat and the gurney were still out. It wasn't like Sven to leave it overnight on the beach but I checked anyway. The gurney was there. The boat was missing. Sven didn't answer the door when I knocked.

It was too early to get the ferry, so I drove all the way back along the peninsula and then south along the mainland to the one-lane road that skirts the back bay. The tide was flowing out, just barely moving between the reeds, carrying twigs and bits of leaves along the surface. The sound of my motor frightened a pair of nesters, sent quail scurrying across the road. The estuary itself stretched gray and smooth, like an inland sea, between the bluffs.

The little cluster of White's Bay police and firemen were at the head of the estuary, with half a dozen joggers as onlookers. The harbor patrol had sent a small motorboat up from the harbor and it was just pulling Sven's boat to shore when I got there.

The oars were still in the locks. Sven was slumped down inside the boat against the prow. The hunting gun was propped between his legs, pointing up at the place where his chin had been. A brace of ducks lay on the floor beside him. The top of his head was still intact. The white hair, unruly, shifted gently in the air. The deep-set eyes, blue, were wide open, blinded for good. One of his hands trailed in the water, the sleeve of his old faded wool shirt sopping wet to the elbow.

I waded out into the mud and the muck that make up the bottom of the estuary. No one tried to stop me. I lifted his hand out of the water and laid it carefully down along the oar. The body beneath the shirt seemed so fragile suddenly, like that of a puppet. His bones dangled loosely inside the cloth.

I stood there in the mud and the cold water up around my waist while they lifted him out and laid him on the ground and took some more pictures. One man could have slipped him into the body bag and hauled him away. I gave the cops his name and told them what time he'd left home.

The sun came up then over the east bluff. No cloud of ducks rose into the sky or went wheeling out over the bay toward the sea. The estuary was gray and empty and cold. The cortege moved back along the road to Coast Highway. After a while I followed them home.

"Name?"

"James Chandler Cairns."

Lieutenant Lawrence of the White's Bay Police Department typed it carefully into the slot provided for it on the form.

"Occupation?"

"Teacher. South Coast Unified School District."

He didn't look like a cop. He was too handsome in a

7

pretty way. Eyelashes long as a girl's. His uniform looked hand-tailored.

"English."

He looked up at me blankly.

"I teach English. At the high school."

He back-spaced and typed it in.

"Married?"

"Once. Briefly." It was the first time that morning that I'd thought of Kate. Someone would have to tell her. I supposed the job fell to me. I felt numb. As though I had died instead of Sven.

"Your relation to the deceased?"

"Friend. Or tenant."

"Which?"

"Both."

The young man typed neatly and quickly.

"When did you last see the deceased?"

"Sven. His name was Thorvald Svennson." I didn't mean to sound so angry.

"Sorry." He gave me an apologetic smile. It was about as genuine as a four-carat piece of glass. "It was midnight when you last saw Mr. Svennson?"

"More like ten o'clock. We'd been in his kitchen having a beer together. He was telling stories. Marking time until he went out."

"Was there anything about his behavior that seemed unusual?"

I jerked my mind back from that frail body slumped in the boat. Tried to reconstruct the feisty little man who had moved restlessly around the kitchen only a few hours earlier, peered out into the dark, talked nervously of this and that.

"He was . . . anxious."

"Anxious?"

"He kept looking out the window. As though he were afraid someone was out there."

"And was there?"

"No. I don't think so. Just shadows."

"Anything else?"

"He'd had a visitor the night before. They had an argument. Sven threw him out."

"Did you see him?"

"No."

"Do you know what they were arguing about?"

I shook my head. "It wasn't like him."

"What wasn't?"

"To throw someone out. It never happened before."

"Did Mr. Svennson tell you he was going out in his boat?"

Grief jammed itself up tight in my chest like a pile of stones.

"Yes."

"Was it something he did often?"

"Not every night. No."

"On occasion?"

"Sometimes he just rowed up the bay to the Fun Zone or the cannery where his fishing boat used to be docked, looking at the lights, sitting out there in the middle rocking back and forth in the wash of the ferry. I went with him a couple of times. He had a lot of friends. They called to him from the piers. Off the tackle boats. He liked to go late when there wasn't anyone around."

"Did he ask you to go with him last night?"

It was the question I'd hoped he wouldn't ask. Lawrence kept his eyes on his typewriter. He gave me plenty of time.

"He did. Yes."

"And you didn't go with him?"

"No. I said I had to get ready for an eight-o'clock class. But I didn't really need to. It was the last thing I wanted to do. Go rowing up the bay listening to the old man's stories. I'd heard them all before. I knew them by heart. I wanted to go to bed."

Lawrence typed something in at the bottom of the paper.

"I should have gone with him."

Guilt rose up in my throat like bile. I tried to swallow it and failed.

Lawrence looked at me sharply, started to say something and then thought better of it. He finished the page, took it out of the typewriter, inserted it again.

There were a few more questions. They were already calling it an accident. Possible suicide. I gave Lawrence the names and addresses of the children. Sven had a daughter in Costa Mesa. The boy worked for a charter-boat firm. I'd let the police tell them. Neither of them gave a tinker's damn for the old man. I didn't mention Kate. Lawrence asked me to keep in touch and let me go.

T he dog was whining in the kitchen where Sven had shut him in the night before. I let myself in with the key Sven left hanging on the hook in the garage. The puppy fled through my legs out the door into the yard.

The house was quiet as death. Already the smell of damp and that thin odor of methane gas that seeps up through the sand made the air foul and stagnant. A couple of puddles stood on the linoleum where the puppy had left them. I threw a handful of paper towels down on top of them.

I looked for a note. A sealed envelope. Anything to tell me what had happened. Or, at least, why. The obvious place was the kitchen table. It was wiped clean, the salt and pepper standing neatly side by side, paper napkins in the wire holder. A clean coffee mug was set out on the stove for breakfast. The sink was spotless. Nothing out of place. The puppy had rummaged in the trash and one of the beer cans was in the middle of the rug, dented where his sharp teeth had chewed on it.

The curtains were drawn in the living room and the door locked from the inside. All the switches had been turned off. Sven's car keys lay next to the phone on the sideboard with his wallet.

God damn the old man! Silent. Nervous. Keeping his secrets to himself. What was it he'd been looking for out there in the darkness? Why hadn't he told me? Shared his fears? He'd locked the door and gone to bed. What had he been afraid of? Harmless, good-hearted old man. What trouble could touch him out here on the peninsula at the end of his life?

The gun was not in its rack by the fireplace. Sven took it down and oiled it every once in a while but he never used it. Hadn't used it since they'd banned duck hunting in the back bay. Twenty years ago? Thirty? It was the one that had killed him. I'd recognized it, pointed upward. Wet and slick where the blood had come pouring out of the hole, muzzle cradled in his hand, between his knees.

I rummaged around in the little desk he kept beside the front door and where he made out his bills, laboriously, with the handwriting of an obedient schoolboy. There were no notes. No diary. His bills were neatly stacked with a big X on the ones he'd paid. Letters from his wife bundled in rubber bands. Photographs of Sven as a young man. The children,

11

chubby little tots playing on a big swing he'd built for them. A calendar. No dates marked in it.

I went upstairs. Everything was in order. Toothbrush dry in its glass. The bed neatly made, coverlet pulled up over the pillows. Shoes tucked away in the closet. His wife's picture on the dresser.

In the picture she was young, the way he'd remembered her. A quiet, strong Swedish girl, he'd told me, whom he'd married and bedded, built this house for, and been gifted by her in return with children. I'd met her once. Shrunken-up old lady. Pain-racked with cancer. Bundled up on the couch.

They'd spent their wedding night in this room. "She was beautiful," he'd said, and his lips drew out the word as though to include all of her in its tone. "I'd lie out there at sea, at night, the ship creaking and the bunks plowing up and down like horses trying to buck us off onto the floor, and dream about her, about coming home. We'd go up the coast, past Mendocino, clear up to British Columbia sometimes. Six weeks, more. And then, finally, when we'd run into the big catch and the holds were filled with albacore, we'd come back home and she'd be waiting. It was like a honeymoon, every time. We'd go in our little house, this little house, and lock the door. I'd carry her into the bedroom and we'd make love for two days, three. Oh, she was beautiful . . ." His hands, outsized, strong, had pawed helplessly in the air and then, not finding what they sought, dropped back to his side.

From the window beside their bed I could look down on the beach, and beyond that, to the sea. The tide was out. A couple of waves lapped dispiritedly against the steep slope of the sand. Farther down, by the wedge, a surfer waited for a wave that wasn't going to come.

I knew that I shouldn't be there. I felt like a voyeur. Looking on his nightstand and in the drawer underneath. Opening the dresser, one drawer at a time. Feeling between the books, behind the photographs. Running my hand under the pillow, between the sheets, for a piece of paper, a note, something addressed to the police. Or to his children. Something to get me off the hook. Relieve the guilt.

The telephone rang. It echoed up from below. Someone insistent. Eight rings. Ten. The sound vibrated hollowly against the shades, still pulled down to the sills, the light yellow behind them. Finally it stopped. I wondered how soon the police would be here.

It was on my way out that I found what I had been looking for. I almost missed it. The puppy's dish. It was empty. No food. The water bowl was bone-dry. I looked on the sink for the dog food, the special formula that Sven bought from the vet, where he might have left it for me to feed the dog. It wasn't there. I found it under the sink, the ten-pound sack, the top neatly rolled down. There was no note pinned to it telling me how much to feed the dog. No extra bowl set out in case I should not come until nightfall.

And I knew. I knew with absolute certainty that whatever dark things Sven might have hidden in his heart, whatever secret pain or remorse or fear overwhelmed him, he would never have left that puppy closed inside the kitchen with no extra food, no pan of water, if he had suspected that he would not be coming back before morning. The guilt, some of it, lifted, and the grief poured into its place.

I called the dog in and put the food in his bowl. He circled the kitchen, sniffing the table, the legs of the chairs, the doorway into the living room, for Sven. I filled the pan with water and stuck it outside on the stoop and moved his basket under the porch in the shade. And when he began to cry for Sven I sat with him on the grass and held him until the police came and it was time to go and find Kate.

They were up at Geisler Park huddled together like a small band of pilgrims under a tree. The lawns rolled away in all directions, utterly deserted this gray morning except for this odd group of citizens. Someone had brought a bowl of salad. A plate of sandwiches lay covered with Saran on the picnic table. Kate was struggling to set a blackboard upright against the trunk of the tree.

I felt the same pang of regret that came every time I saw her. An unwelcome reminder that I had once basked in the glow of that warm, astonishingly alive creature. It was something I chose not to think about, just as I refused to dream of being an astronaut or solving the riddle of gravity. These were things beyond my reach. It came, anyway, when I least expected it. A glimpse into the past. That rich, happy time when I, already middle-aged, set beyond changing, had been the recipient of all those gifts: the laughter that came as easily as running water; the singular honesty that drove me to distraction; that taste of Eden when I'd been angered and exasperated and driven wild by nothing more than the way she ran ahead of me on the beach, served my coffee, turned to me in bed.

Now, catching sight of me approaching across the lawn, she smiled. The joy on her face shot across the space and caught me like a warm burst of sunlight. I suppose I scowled because she gave me a wave and an amused look. It confirmed that she did not yet know about Sven. I wished that I did not have to be the one to tell her.

The crowd was the usual one. Friends of the Bay they called themselves. The mean age was sixty. Many of them had graying hair. Intelligent faces. Wrinkled from all those years of living out in the sun. Provocative. Graduates of Bryn Mawr and Mount Holyoke and Stanford in a day when only the elite went to college. They were an interesting group. Opinionated. Individualists. Writers of letters. Citizens who hauled themselves up out of deathbeds to vote. Oddballs, all of them. Hated by the business community. Embracing lost causes for no better reason than that they believed them to be the right ones. Among the long list of the bay and estuary's protected species, they were the most endangered.

The blackboard had a list of committees and empty spaces for the names of chairpeople. Kate was scratching names and phone numbers in the columns, assigning precincts to canvassers.

"It's the recall election," Fiona confided in the stage whisper she affected at all public events. "I trust you're going to write another letter to the *Times*."

Kate straightened and faced her little band, smudges of chalk dust on her cheeks where she had rubbed them with the backs of her hands. The group turned to her expectantly.

"They're fighting us every step of the way," Kate began. The gray heads nodded vigorously. One of the old-timers gave a derisive hoot.

"Who is?" I whispered to Fiona.

"Rancho Pacifica."

"Ah. The enemy."

From the park I could look out over the hills up and down the coast. The sea was a huge blur that made everything else seem miniature. The bay was still as glass. It wound back between the islands, reflecting them like the silver backing of an antique mirror. You could see where Rancho Pacifica began as clearly as though some architect had drawn the curving lines with his protractor. Seaward, along the tide line, the old town of White's Bay clung to the sandspits, the peninsula, and the islands. It was a cheerful jumble of beach shacks and summer cottages, surrounded by sea walls and a lively clutter of docks. Inland, where the Rancho Pacifica lands began, an entire city had been laid out with the corporate sameness that bedeviled all planned communities. Monotonous curving roads. Long, sleek, look-alike houses without trees. Characterless, it spread outward along the foothills, covering them like a thick layer of plastic.

"This may be our last chance to save White's Bay from the developers. To keep this lovely little beach town from becoming another Westwood. Another Los Angeles. To keep the bay from being buried in smog and noise and pollution and crime."

I'd heard it all before. For ten years Kate and her gallant little band had been tilting at the behemoth windmills of the developers. I couldn't remember that they had stopped a single building from being built, or a highway from being constructed, or saved a square foot of beach from the developers' maws.

Still, they never gave up. Kate was incredible. She had a gift with people. A quick mind. A rich intensity poured out of her. The unfashionable conviction that people should act on their beliefs. She was strong and fine-bodied. But what I saw, standing there on the fringe of that ill-assorted group, was the vulnerability.

The copper hair curling around a sensitive face. Freckles parading across perpetually sunburned skin. Lovely green eyes undecided whether to laugh or to cry at the human condition.

The city councilman was holding forth. He'd brought some charts showing what he called the demographics of White's Bay. The gray heads nodded solemnly. As far as I could see, the charts were meaningless.

I waited until Kate had finished organizing her band into little groups and passed out the petitions and the lists of voters, until the sandwiches had been passed out and the little band stood around gossiping about peregrine falcons, the war in Nicaragua, and the need for aid to unwed mothers, before I beckoned Kate aside and told her about Sven.

For a moment she did not seem to take in what I had to say, and then, surprisingly, she accepted it. The green eyes filled with tears and I knew, without asking, that they were for me as well as for Sven. She moved close, put her arms around me and held me tight against the grief that flooded over us. Her body, once part of mine, comforted me. Instinctively lessened the pain by sharing it, crying over Sven who had loved us both. We stood that way without speaking, separated from the others, until the worst of it was over. Then we let go of each other as we had done too many times before. Gradually. Carefully. Withdrawing into ourselves slowly so that neither one should leave the other off-balance.

Her cheeks glistened with tears. I fumbled in my pocket for a handkerchief. She dried her face and then gave it back to me, gripping my hand, clinging to it for a moment, fiercely, as though she were protecting me and not the other way around. And then she was gone, back to her flock under the tree and their

17

sad, valiant attempt to keep the world from self-destructing.

By the time I got home the police had gone. The dog was still out in the yard crying for Sven. I took him upstairs with me and put his basket next to the bed. For a long time I hung my arm over the side with my hand spread on his belly, as I had seen Sven do. It didn't fool him for a minute. He knew I wasn't Old Sven. He shivered and whimpered. Twice I took him outside but he just growled into the darkness and refused to leave my side. Finally I gave in and took him into bed with me. He curled up next to me, wet nose jammed up against my armpit, sighed and dropped into a coma.

We might have made it through the night except that the damned garage door needed oiling; it creaked like an arthritic drawbridge when it was opened. Only half awake, I thought it was Sven coming home from his night out with the Scandinavian Club, and then I remembered that Sven, what was left of him, was on a table in the morgue and wasn't ever going anywhere again. I waited until whoever it was had bumped into the ladder and extricated the key from beneath the fuse box before I crossed the floor to the window and looked out. A shadow, about the size and shape of a packing crate, crossed the yard. I saw the kitchen door open and close. A flashlight moved past the window, over the cabinets, and down onto the floor.

I climbed into a pair of pants and went down to the yard. I armed myself with a heavy wood oar that still

18

leaned against the house where Sven had left it and let myself into the kitchen. By now the man was in the front room, opening and closing drawers, moving the light stand, dragging the couch away from the wall. He was clumsy, maybe drunk. I reached around the corner of the wall and flipped the light on.

He straightened up and hurled a lamp in my direction. It hit the wall beside me and broke into a million pieces of purple glass. I recognized him immediately. It was Sven's son-in-law. His name was Sylvus. It didn't fit him. He was certain to be a disappointment to the mother who had given him that fancy name. Sylvus was a slob. His belly hung out below a Tecate Beer T-shirt that didn't quite cover it. His beefy face had two expressions, which consisted of complete blankness and snarl. It was the latter he turned toward me.

"Hold it," I said, "I'm Cairns. I live over the garage."

He reached out and grabbed the second of the pair of lamps and held it shoulder-high. I held the oar out in front of me. I hoped he'd take it as a gesture of peace.

"I thought it was a burglar." The way I said it didn't quite exonerate him from that category.

"The old man's dead. This is my house now." His voice had a belligerent cadence. It came to him naturally. "So fuck off."

"What are you looking for? Anything in particular?"

"None of your business." He strung a line of the usual obscenities together. Nothing very imaginative. I could tell this was not going to turn into a casual exchange of pleasantries.

"Does Sheila know you're here?"

He snarled again. It didn't mean yes. It didn't mean no. I don't think Sheila meant anything more to him than the Pop Tarts he probably wolfed down for breakfast. I couldn't quite decide if he was mentally

19

retarded or just mean and stupid. In either case, he wasn't anyone I particularly wanted to get to know.

"I got it made now. Half of all this is mine now." He started pawing under the cushions on the couch. He threw them onto the floor and ran his hand down the back of the sofa. It came up empty.

"Oh?"

"State of California. Common-property law." I wondered if someone had been talking to him or if he'd found it out on his own. If so, he hadn't read the small print. Common property didn't automatically apply to an inheritance left to one spouse. I decided to let someone else enlighten him.

Sven had hated the kid. Called him a redneck from one of those other places. California was full of them. "Brought their meanness with them," Sven said. "When I came here, there was nothing but miles and miles of orange groves and the old prejudices didn't take root. Just dried up and evaporated in all that sunshine and open space. It's different now. Comes over the state line. Not only survives but flourishes in the housing tracts and the smog and the noise."

The kid pulled the grandfather clock away from the wall and yanked open the back. I couldn't stand to watch anymore. He gave me the finger and I left.

I took the oar up into the apartment with me and locked the door. He was after Sven's secret stash of money. The old man had a couple of thousand dollars hidden away. "In case the banks fail." It was an item of faith with him that whatever had happened before could happen again. I could have told Sylvus where it was but I didn't. It was the least I could do for Sven. He'd have gotten a kick out of that. Sooner or later it would be found and turned over to the estate and he'd get his big ugly hands on it. Meantime he could just sweat it out.

I stood for maybe half an hour at the window and watched him make his way through the house, tearing it apart room by room. He didn't even try to hide his presence anymore. The sounds got louder as he got madder. Finally I got tired of watching and crawled into bed with the dog. We slept, exhausted, for the rest of the night.

The service was held the following week. Sven would have hated it. The daughter had made the arrangements. It was held in a pseudo chapel, the back rooms of which were the embalming rooms. Plate-glass windows along the aisle looked out on a huge asphalt parking lot, empty except for a gleaming black hearse standing, doors open, in the center of it.

The preacher came with the cremation. He was slick and phony-sounding and had probably done his apprenticeship as an encyclopedia salesman. He hadn't had the privilege of knowing the deceased, he said, and then proceeded to prove it. Sven was enshrined in a fake silver urn with a purple bow that looked like a perfume bottle. It sat on a folding table in front of the altar. A photograph of Sven was propped against it. Someone had sent flowers. They were orange and purple and looked as if they'd been appropriated at the last minute off the casket, which was now being wheeled out across the parking lot on a strange-looking apparatus, like a pair of tongs on wheels, and loaded into the limousine.

The daughter was there, a vacant-faced young

woman, with four empty-eyed kids in the first row. She was pale and obese, like someone who'd given up long ago and just goes through the motions of being alive. She had her mother's blond hair. It hung limply around her shoulders. If there were any of Sven's genes there, they were buried beneath all that flesh. She had fixed herself up for the occasion in a black dress that was about ten years out of style and several sizes too small. Sylvus slouched beside her and looked resentfully at the insignificant amount that remained of Sven.

Kate slid in next to me and put her arm through mine. I could feel her through the sleeve of her jacket, fine-boned and strong. She brought, as she always did, some dignity to the place. I was grateful for her presence.

Sven's son came in late. He was a handsome, blue-eyed, bleached-blond kid who lived alone on a boat in the bay and crewed for charters in and out of the harbor. As far as I know he hadn't been near Old Sven for eight years except to borrow money that never got paid back. I don't think he even pretended to try. Sven called him the bottomless pit. It cost money to put a notice of the funeral in the paper so it had not been there. No one had bothered to notify the Scandinavian Club or any of his other friends. There were only two other mourners. One of them was a fierce-looking old man. I recognized him as Ernie Davidson, old-time real estate developer and patriarch of the bay. He turned once and gave me a look of anger across the church, as though I were responsible for this ridiculous way to mourn an honest old man. His grandson was with him. David was a student of mine. One of my best. Had come to the house one day and met Sven. The two of them, rich kid and old fisherman, had become, most improbably, fast friends. David was fascinated with the stories. Sat at the kitchen table with Sven, wolfing down submarine sandwiches that the old man kept fixing for him. They went fishing together. Took mysterious trips up and down the coast in Sven's old Chevrolet. David didn't even look in my direction. He sat pale and serious in the fourth pew.

The preacher read a couple of inspirational passages from the *Reader's Digest* and something about a rose climbing over the wall to the other side. When the canned organ music slipped into a medley of Frank Sinatra favorites, Davidson gave me another murderous look and stormed out.

The whole thing was over in about twenty minutes. The family, after some prompting by the mortician, stood in front of the card table with the ersatz urn and the tinted-up photo of Sven and waited for us to come and pay our respects. The son didn't seem to know who we were. Kate said the service was very nice, which I thought was valiant of her. The daughter shot her a suspicious look. She avoided my eyes. Sylvus was already gathering up the flowers. The one who seemed to be taking it the hardest was Davidson's grandson. But when I turned around to speak to him, he was gone.

Kate had a basket with a bottle of wine and a couple of sandwiches in the car. We drove down to the jetty and ate there on the rocks. Afterward we sat together in silence while the waves rolled in and out again until the tawdry little service had been washed away and we had remanded the memory of Sven back to the sea where he had been at home. Just before dusk two dredging barges made their way down the coast from Long Beach and anchored just outside the mouth of the channel. They squatted there, dark and ugly against the sea. We turned out backs on them and went home.

T he eviction notice was taped to the door when I got home. It was a Xerox copy of those legal documents you buy at a stationery store. Sylvus had filled in the blanks with a big oversize scrawl that was hardly legible. But I got the message. I had been paying Sven $200 a month for nearly fifteen years. The rent was being raised to $1800 a month until June, when it would climb to that much every week for the duration of the summer. It was more than a year's salary for a teacher. I gave the pup a bowl of milk and went to bed.

S ven's daughter lived in a house he had bought for her in Costa Mesa. It was a cheap tract house, but it had been new when he put the 20 percent down on it and assumed the mortgage for her. The two of us had gone together to install the washing machine and fix the garage door so that it would open and close. In the six years since then the only thing they'd done to the place was to stick a TV antenna up on the roof. The rest of it was falling apart. Paint was chipping off the windowsills, plaster eroding on both sides of the garage where someone had banged it with the car and left it for someone else to fix. They hadn't gotten around to planting a lawn, so the front yard was the same weed-filled plot it had been when they moved in. It wasn't much worse than their neighbors'. The lethargy seeped over onto the whole block like spurge in a lawn. A truck from Beach Liquor on Coast Highway was sitting at the curb in front of the house. It was the favored source of spirits for parties thrown on private yachts and in waterfront homes and I didn't think it had come here to make a delivery.

The door was open. I could hear the voices of Sheila and Sylvus quarreling. It had the sound of just one more bout in a long-standing fight between a husband and wife who didn't have anything better to do. A half-eaten bowl of cat food sat on the doorstep. A television set was tuned to the soaps.

Sheila finally answered the door. She was barefooted, dressed in stretch pants and a shapeless top that probably came from K Mart. She'd been a pretty little thing once. I'd seen pictures of her as a toddler—blond, curly hair fastened with pink bows, sitting astride Sven's back while he galloped around the living room with her.

I gave her my written notice. She didn't seem to know what it was. Sven's son-in-law appeared in the doorway behind her. He gave me a big ugly smile and and took the envelope from Sheila. Then he turned and went back into the house. Sheila went in after him. I guess I was expected to follow.

The living room was like the inside of a lot of other tract houses built in the first flush of construction throughout the county before the developers realized how much more money they could make and upgraded them out of the reach of people like Sheila and Sylvus. It had cheap matching furniture that they'd bought in a set and were probably still paying off in monthly installments. The dark tweed-patterned carpet had long ago stopped hiding the stains. A baby clad only in a soiled diaper crawled across it. The television was new. The box it had come in was on the floor beside it, the packing material scattered around the room. The baby stuffed one of the Styrofoam bits into its mouth and started chewing. No one seemed to notice.

Sylvus threw himself down on the couch and helped himself to a can of beer out of a Beach Liquor box. He pulled the tab and popped it back into the can. He drank most of it without stopping. I wondered what else he did in his spare time, when he wasn't busy ransacking the house of a dead man.

Sheila looked at me questioningly.

"That's my notice. I'm moving out."

"Oh." She didn't know what to say.

"I raised the rent." Sylvus grinned up at me. "The old man was giving it to him."

I didn't expect her to come to my aid and she didn't. She was as vacuous as an overstuffed chair. Or the soap opera that flowed around us. No one else was going to do it, so I bent down and took the Styrofoam out of the baby's mouth before he choked on it. The baby let out a howl. Sheila picked him up and propped him against her hip.

"Anything else?"

I considered telling Sheila what her husband had been doing the night after Sven died. But it would only have made him mad at her. In the end she would have paid for it, not he.

Sheila followed me out to the front door. I stepped over a couple of dolls that had been subjected to whatever abuse they call it when you do it to a doll, and a battered walkie-talkie.

"Did he say anything . . ." She spoke in a low voice, as though she didn't want Sylvus to overhear.

"Who?"

"My father. He took the boat out. But you were with him. Before, I mean. Did he say why?"

"You mean why he would kill himself?"

She flinched. It was the first real sign of emotion I had seen from her. "Yes. I suppose that's what I mean."

"No."

"Or why he went?"

"Sheila!" The bully voice came in warning from the next room. Sheila shrank back from me as though I were the one who had threatened her. The son-in-law came through the hallway and brushed between us. He tossed his beer can onto the dirt in front of the house and hauled himself up into the truck. He started it, made a U-turn over his neighbor's curb, and roared back toward the beach.

"I'm sorry, you know." Sheila's eyes were clear and blue like her father's, only there was nothing behind them. Like mountain pools with nothing on the bottom. "Sylvus didn't like him. It made it hard." She was apologizing. I suppose it was for all the years when she hadn't bothered to call Sven. Had let him make all the house payments and never even invited him to dinner. If so, it was coming too late and to the wrong person.

She waited for me to say something but I didn't. She looked at me, a sad, frightened, blond-haired child hiding deep inside all that fat, where there was the illusion of safety. For a moment I thought she was going to tell me something else, something important, and then she moved back into the hallway and shut the door between us.

I walked back down the drive. In the dirt next to it a child's bucket and spade were upended. A couple of toy tanks had been left scattered in the weeds. A half dozen plastic soldiers had been buried up to their

27

necks. The fake silver urn lay on its side in the middle of them. The purple bow had come loose. A pile of ashes blew lazily in a long stream into the street.

The next day was Saturday. I thought of calling Lieutenant Lawrence and then decided against it. I spent most of the day trying to find another place to live. I started with the peninsula, around Sven's house, and then moved my search across to the island. I tried the Heights and finally Costa Mesa. By late afternoon I'd answered fifteen ads and seen eight real estate brokers. They were not the tight-corseted, overweight ladies I remembered from the sixties, with mouths that twitched like ferrets at the prospect of a commission. These newcomers were cold-eyed and handsome. Anorexic women in Italian silk and good-looking men in eight-hundred-dollar suits. A new breed. Self-assured. Sophisticated. Self-interest raised to a kind of patriotic duty.

Ms. Trueblood was seated behind a French Provincial writing desk. She was all gold and brown, with big oversized gold-rimmed glasses and bracelets to match. The dress was something out of *Town and Country*. Understated. Expensive. It was hard to tell whether she was a sales agent or whether she owned the place. She took me in in one disdainful glance. I was dressed up for the occasion. Teacher's uniform: tie, coat, dark loafers. Something about the outfit didn't come up to her standards. I asked if she had any apartments for rent. She pushed a form across the desk at me and asked me to fill out my name, bank, current address, profession, and salary. I should have refused. All I wanted was an apartment, not a goddamn loan. I filled it out dutifully and passed it back.

She didn't waste any time on small talk. "We have nothing in your price range in White's Bay, Mr. Cairns. You might try Costa Mesa." She sniffed disparagingly. "The west side. Or Santa Ana." She stood up and dismissed me curtly.

Twenty years ago, when I'd made the long trip down Coast Highway from LA with a portable typewriter thrown in the back seat of the car, a teaching credential, and a box of books, most people had never heard of White's Bay. Two hundred dollars had been the going rate for an apartment. The peninsula was damp and inconvenient. It was far away from all the amenities and comforts of the big city. A small beach town with nothing to recommend it but the sea and the harbor. Great stretches of rolling hills, green in winter, gold turning to brown in the summer, isolating it from the cities and the cultural revolution taking place inland.

The yearly invasion of teenagers to the island for Easter break lasted only a week. They crowded the beaches, California schoolgirls, pretty as a field of flowers, boys huddled together in packs, trying to get up the courage to speak to them. They eyed each other, indulged in short, impassioned romances, and then left, all at once, like a flock of swallows.

In summer the prominent old families of Pasadena and Bel Air came down to the islands, aired out the houses that had stood empty all winter, swam and sailed, turned the children loose on the beach, had cocktails at the Yacht Club, and departed the last weekend of August, leaving the town once again to the storms and the cold and the few natives who remained. The locals went about their usual lives.

Taught. Ran the market and the ferry. Organized fishing charters. Walked along the beaches. Bought a cup of coffee at the Goofoffers Club and swapped jokes with the monied men who hid their wealth under a thick layer of character. Snorted in derision at the foolish hordes who lived inland in the smog and the traffic and the press of urban living.

So the invasion caught them off-guard. In all those morning walks along the beach, the dog out ahead of them scattering gulls, they had neglected to look inland, across the bay, where, one by one, the hills were being terraced, gouged for freeways, the flora stripped from the earth. One morning they woke up and found they were surrounded. By then it was too late. White's Bay had been discovered by the ambitious, the upscale, by all the snobs who had scorned it before. And down they came en masse: land developers and businessmen, subdividers, young executives on the way up, with an army of architects and interior designers and fashion consultants to transform the beach town into a city just like the one they had left behind.

I didn't even stop to wonder if it had anything to do with the reason Sven was dead. I was too busy coming to terms with the fact that I was quite suddenly an alien, exiled perfunctorily from the town I had thought of as peculiarly my own.

Twelve of them. Smart-assed. Spoiled. Bright as hell. Ranged around the conference table gunning for me.

They slouch in their seats. Books stacked haphazardly in front of them. Pencils perched raffishly behind the ears. Essays typed. Double-spaced. Set neatly on top of notebooks waiting to be handed in.

McIan is the leader. Aggressive. Intense. Hostile almost. But elusive for all that. I'm never quite sure what to make of him. Takes nothing for granted. Is on me like a shark. Fights me every step of the way. Argues every sentence until all the facts fall out like teeth.

Today he is subdued. I wait until the bell rings. Another moment while they shuffle their books, find *Heart of Darkness*, then begin.

"Who wants to go first?"

No preliminaries. No "good morning" or small talk. There is no time for preambles. Roll. Nine months is all I have to teach these mentally undisciplined, snotty little preppies to read, write a clear paragraph, think for themselves. Become civilized. Part of the human race.

"I do."

It's Plaskett. Blond-haired. Freckled. An old man's dream. I haven't yet cured her of the awfulness of her romanticism.

We listen. It is a descriptive essay. Three photographs have been assigned from *The Family of Man*. She has chosen the one of the graveyard to write about. Her voice is high. Sweet. She has looked at the photo but not really seen it. Her graveyard is full of ghosts. They waft up from the ground and hover over the graves in vast hordes. There is no song of bird or distant hum of traffic. Only moans. Eerie whisperings. The smell of death. Decay. Fear. And, of course, in the concluding paragraph, life transcending all.

The students pounce on her like a pack of wolves. I

jump into the fray. Find myself defending her. Repel the attack before it gets started.

"Too many generalizations."

"Where's the point of view?"

"I don't see any ghosts in the photo."

She answers, quite rightly enough, "It's not your essay. It's mine."

Finally we come to the consensus that reality is not a requisite of the assignment. The ghosts are all right, but only if she gives more concrete evidence of them. A bent twig. A smell. The feel of something slithering past. She is desolate. "Leave out the ghosts," I advise.

We go on to McIan. David. Davidson's grandchild.

"You're not going to like it."

"Try me."

The kids snicker. Wait expectantly. It is the best game of the day. Catching Cairns out. Get him on the defensive.

"Let someone else go first."

It isn't like him. I let it go. Call on Campbell. He had chosen the same photo. It is a credible job. Unimaginative. Graves fallen and broken off in pieces. The boy crouching behind the tree. The kids are bored. We are waiting for David. I decide to get it over with.

"Mr. McIan."

He gives me a look, half guilt, half defiance, and plunges in.

The photo is clipped to the essay. He pulls it off and slides it down the center of the table toward me. Everyone stares. It is a news photo. We all recognize it. Black and white. Grainy. Creased where it has been folded. A police van stands at one side. Beyond it, the long stretch of the back bay and a cordon of onlookers, including me, at the edge of it, waiting for the boat and the slumped form, Sven's body, to be towed ashore.

"This is not the assignment."

"I know that." There is a hint of derision in his voice; a measure of uncertainty.

"Automatic F." That is Campbell. He knows, they all know that the first requirement of an essay is that it adhere to the assignment.

"You may proceed."

The essay is brilliant. The boy has caught the anger of that moment. The utter shocking violence of Sven's death against the background of the dull gray estuary. Without once mentioning the word, he has managed to convey death by the recitation of concrete detail, the sound of the mud as the police wade out into it, the tide flowing out through the reeds, the angry gaping hole of the wound. There is the gray morning, the stillness, the pathos of the small group of men waiting for the boat, the body slumped in the stern. And underneath the surface, like some nameless monster lurking there, a fury, an anger so personal that it frightens me, as though it were he, David, the writer, who has been violated, his own skull that has been exploded out over the marshes.

There is utter silence when he finishes. No one looks at me. They are embarrassed. Waiting to hear what I have to say. Afraid.

What does it mean? Was he there? I try to recall his face in the group of joggers as they trooped by and cannot. The essay merits either an A or an F. Nothing in between. I make no comment. Call instead on Heidi. The class breathes a collective sigh of relief. Or disappointment. We return to yet another graveyard scene.

When we break for second period I ask David to stop by my office during lunch. He is noncommittal. I wait for him from twelve-fifteen to one-thirty and after school. He never shows.

33

The traffic crawled to a stop just past the estuary. As I did every Tuesday afternoon, I took the Freeway north toward the mountains and then went along the foothills to Pasadena. My mother was the only family I had left. She lived, if you can call it that, in a bed in a semi-private room of a nursing home, with a window overlooking the lawn, a couple of orange trees, and, beyond that, on a rare day like today, when the Santa Ana had blown all the smog out to sea, the San Gabriel Mountains.

She did not recognize me. For several years now she had simply accepted me as a stranger who came every Tuesday, kissed her on the cheek, fed her her dinner and then left. Usually I talked to her about the Arroyo, about the old house, about the days when we were growing up and she was the sun around which we revolved. I told and retold the old King Kamehameha stories that she had made up for us, recounted the walks we had taken in the Arroyo, the trips across the contintent to her father's house in Berwyn, Maryland, the excitement of setting out in our little Ford on Route 66 for the great adventure.

I am not sure if she understood any of it. She listened soberly, without expression, this woman who had laughed with me, loved me fiercely, gone ahead of me, thrown down intellectual challenges, engaged me in combat over ethics and political theories. Who had read to me from Robert Louis Stevenson and Edgar Allan Poe and later played all the parts in *Hamlet* and *Cyrano*, except for the heroes, which she insisted I must play myself.

I forced myself to make the trip. Each time was as bad as the last. It was like opening a window, every Tuesday, on the past. A glimpse of Paradise once possessed, and then the long drive home in the night, the window slammed shut and only the future, smog-filled, lonely, ahead.

Tonight I told her about Sven. She listened gravely. Once, when I looked at her, I found she was weeping. For Sven? For me? For herself? I gathered the frail old body up in my arms and held her. I stroked the thin gray hair and wondered how something once so alive and generous could, in the end, be treated so shabbily by whatever god had programmed age and death as the final act to the sojourn of this once rare and once beloved creature.

It was nearly ten o'clock by the time I got home. The winds were still howling across the hillsides, the air was dry and hot as a summer night. Tumbleweeds, blown loose, rolled ahead of me on the freeway and plastered themselves by the hundreds against the chain-link fences. All the doors and windows in the row-on-row of condominiums at the edges of the city seemed open. People leaned against balcony railings, stared out across the valley toward the mountains, watched the headlights stream along the freeways, peered up into the sky.

I went upstairs just long enough to change into my bathing suit and then left the house. Sven's house was the last one on the peninsula. Beyond that was nothing but dunes. Tonight I left the sea behind and went to the bay side.

The water was warm even for October. I waded out and then sank into the darkness. It flowed around me like something alive. I swam out into the channel. A sailboat passed within a few feet of me, its on-board light winking across the water. I could feel the current beneath me moving out toward the sea. I drifted with it for a while, flowed into all that darkness as though I were part of it.

I swam over to Chinaman's Cove and sat there awhile, listening to the night sounds, dogs barking in the distance, television sets through open windows. The sea breathed in and out. Waves slapped gently against the rocks, slid up the sand in the dark and then out again.

From here I could see the lights of the houses winking like stars along the water's edge, and then, farther back, the headlights along Coast Highway. Above them all, silhouetted against the sky, Pacific Plaza, black, deserted, stood over the city.

The wind turned as suddenly as it had started. The first chill breeze came in off the ocean. I dived into the water and swam home.

I got home a little before midnight. I could see the light in my apartment from the corner. It went on for a quarter of a second and then blinked off. The gate was ajar.

He came out of the apartment with a rush, throwing the door open so that it knocked me against the rail. In the time it took me to recover, he was gone. The dog, quiet until now, started barking. I heard the

36

footsteps pounding against the cement walkway along the side of Sven's house and then nothing as they bounded into the sand.

I followed him along the beach toward the pier. For a while he kept to the sand. Sometimes he disappeared behind the dunes piled up along the house fronts. The waves banged and clattered to my left, out of sight.

Halfway up the peninsula he emerged onto the boardwalk and took off like a sprinter. It was impossible to get a good look at him. He was medium height, slim build, young. Around E Street he turned into the passageway between two houses and disappeared. I followed the sound of his shoes against the pavement in the alley. I knew the peninsula better than he did. Just before we got to the pier I took a shortcut. I caught up with him at the Pavilion. He sprinted past me down the boardwalk and leapt aboard the ferry just as it left the dock. He merged with the passengers and then the ferry moved out of the light and I lost sight of him.

I dived into the water and swam to the other side, just far enough behind to keep out of the backwash. Three quarters of the way across the channel the ferry stopped to allow the second ferry to leave the island side. In the minutes while it drifted I passed it in the darkness. I was waiting when it finally pulled into the dock.

The boy was gone. A Mercedes drove off with a middle-aged couple in it, along with a couple of bicyclers. The other passengers, about a dozen in all, were too fat or too short or not the right age. The attendant had collected twenty cents from everyone on board. He didn't remember any kid, slim, slight build, who was out of breath. The ferry took me back. I stared out over the channel for some sign of the boy who had slipped over the side into the dark. The lights from the Pavilion reflected out across the water in long, wavering gold lines. The places in between were black as death.

It didn't take a genius to figure out who had ransacked the apartment. Not much damage had been done. My briefcase had been opened and the contents dumped on the floor. The only other thing that had been touched were the essays I had left on the kitchen table. Someone had knocked them over in his haste to go through them. There were ninety of them. I checked them against my roll book. Only one of them was missing. It took about five minutes to figure out which one. They were all there. Except the one by David. The essay about Sven.

The two of them, David and Old Sven, hunched over the kitchen table, plotting together. Whispering. Excited.

I had come in the door grinning, expecting to be taken into their game of move and countermove.

They had looked up, startled. A blankness of face where I had expected invitation. David slid a sheet of paper under the table and held it there where I could not see it. There was an awkward silence while the two of them tried to think of something to say. Waited for me to state my business.

"I saw the light. Thought I'd see what was going on."

Reluctantly they asked me to stay.

Miffed, I had refused. Left them to their childish games.

I tried to sleep and failed. About two o'clock in the morning I pulled Old Sven's runabout outboard in from its mooring and motored up the bay. The moon had already set and the water was black. The islands were dark and peaceful, heavy under the weight of all those houses. Boats rose and fell against the stubby white docks. Out in the center of the channel a pair of osprey woke, flapped their wings in warning, and fell silent again. The awkward dark shapes of the ferries were tied, side by side, against the sea wall. The lights of the Pavilion had been turned off. The building rose out of the dark and squatted there like the giant shadow of a toad.

The two of them, Sven and the boy, had come here together. Motored up the bay. Seen something they shouldn't see. Found out something so terrible they were afraid to let me in on the secret. One of them was dead. The other had tried to warn me and then, in a moment of fear, taken that warning back.

I followed the big island around toward the turning basin. Sven must have come this way on the night he died. Bay Island was dark. The big yachts around Harbor Isle were locked tight. The houses behind the big plate-glass windows were dark. A party was winding down at the Bay Club. I could hear a loud drunken argument between a man and a woman on the deck of one of the smaller boats. Someone shouted down from a nearby balcony. There was the sound of a bottle crashing onto the dock and then silence. The boats rocked as I passed. Sleek and white. Powerful engines just sitting there inside all the fiberglass. Capable of going to Catalina or San Diego. Across the border to Mexico.

I circled the turning basin, motored back along the leeside of Harbor Isle. In the dark all the houses, packed close, looked alike. Who was it Sven had gone to meet? Or had someone followed him up the channel, past the islands and under the bridge, until the old man was alone and helpless at the far end of the estuary?

I cut the motor and let the boat drift. From somewhere farther up the bay a cruiser pulled out of its berth and came down toward me. It passed me in the dark without seeing me. Headed for the sea.

I waited until it cleared the channel between the island and the peninsula. After awhile I restarted the engine and went home.

David was in the school parking lot when I got there in the morning. He walked behind a row of cars on his way to class. The young face was troubled. Too serious for a kid of eighteen. I guessed he had been playing hooky. It wasn't like him.

He didn't see me until I called his name. He turned and stared at me, stricken. His face went white. He jammed his hands in his pockets and ran across the parking lot away from me, toward the Industrial Arts Building. The slim, frightened figure disappeared in the crush of students.

I let him go.

I found McIan on his boat. The *Mach 10* was tied up to the dock outside the Bay Club dining room. It was a sleek modern Italian cruiser with a price tag of well over a million dollars. The glossy white sides towered over the dock. It was all fiberglass and chrome, complete with half a ton of radar that sprouted from the top like fairy antennae. A crew of five was doing whatever it is that deckhands do on a class job like this one. They looked like an ad in *GQ* or undergraduates in the CIA school for spies. Masculine. Handsome in immaculate white shorts and T-shirts with the name of the boat stenciled elegantly across the pocket. I wondered if McIan rented them by the hour or if they came with the boat.

One of them took my name up to McIan. He glanced over the side of the boat at me and after a minute came down and invited me on board.

He wasn't a big man; he only gave that impression. He was in his early fifties with curly brownish hair going gray. Eyes the color of steel. Well built. Probably played tennis twice a week and swam forty laps every morning before breakfast. He fairly bristled with energy. It poured out of him in a constant stream, like electrically charged particles or his own brand of neutrinos.

"I'm Chandler Cairns."

He recognized the name. "David's English teacher?"

"Yes. I have to talk to you about your son."

He looked at me sharply. It was part curiosity and part the wariness of an adversary.

For a moment he stood there taking my measure. I could have presented no possible threat to him. I was everything he had spent his life avoiding. Unprepossessing. Middle class. I cut no handsome figure on the tennis courts. My net worth was about what he used for pocket money on a good weekend. We were about the same generation and sex. That was all we had in common.

The deckhands had stopped whatever they were doing and remained in suspended animation, ranged around us in a circle. I suppose they were waiting to see whether or not they were going to get to throw me off. McIan debated for a moment but curiosity won. He flicked his fingers at one of them. Four of them melted away into the interstices of the boat. The fifth leapt to the dock, ready to cast off. McIan nodded to me to come aboard.

The *Mach 10* had been designed and built to McIan's specifications. The inside looked like the presidential suite at the Ritz Carlton. Everything was done in muted colors. Mauve. Rose. Cream. Giant couches so low you had to be lowered into them. Cushions with sandpipers embroidered on them. There was a bar at one end of the saloon, glittering with crystal and silver decanters, all cleverly fastened to the paneling behind it so that if the ship rolled, the only thing that wasn't tied down was the passenger. One of the crew was tending bar. He flashed us a prep-school smile, friendly, eager, and calculated as a silicon chip. McIan asked for "the usual," which turned out to be a Perrier with a twist of lime. I took a Coke.

McIan led the way up to the pilot room. The control panel went from one side of the boat to the other. Behind reflective glass the display board was black with green lights. There were enough dials and numbers and little heat-sensitive switches to launch a shuttle. The radar and communication boxes took up a third of it. A big screen behind the wheel glowed with a computer-drawn map of the Catalina channel and the shoreline. A blinking white light marked the place where we sat at anchor in the harbor. McIan reached under the dash and flipped the switch.

Instantly, somewhere deep inside the boat the motor came to life, throttled down, dangerous. McIan backed the boat skillfully away from the dock into the channel. The water churned around the sides of the hull, forming the great glassy circles that indicate something powerful turning below the surface. He steered us away from the turning basin and down the bay. Harbor Isle passed to our right. The mainland, with Coast Highway snaking along it, slid by to the left.

It was Wednesday afternoon. The bay was deserted, the boats empty at their moorings, thousands of them tied up like fish caught on a line and abandoned. Already in mid-October they were collecting barnacles, gull droppings running down the sides in long white streaks. A pair of osprey perched atop the mast of a Coronado 30. The light was pale, slightly out of focus. It took about ten minutes to round the tip of Harbor Isle into the open bay.

It was my first audience with a developer. Next to Rancho Pacifica, McIan was small-time, only one in the pack of developers who had flocked into the county and were still dividing up the spoils. Maybe not being first was what gave McIan that edge. He was, according to his friends as well as his enemies, as competitive and hard-driven as a jackhammer.

McIan directed the conversation. He pointed out the marina he had just built and the yacht club started by Davidson in the forties and which he now owned outright.

"You know Ernie Davidson?"

I thought of the crusty old man, onetime friend of Sven's, who had glared at me at Sven's memorial service and then stomped out.

"I've met him."

"I married his daughter."

I tried to figure out what he meant by telling me that, or if he meant anything at all. He pointed up over the bay to Pacific Plaza, the city that had sprouted on a hill and then spread rapidly in all directions until now it crowded down to the edge of the bay, boxing it in.

"Rancho Pacifica," he said. "All of it. Fifty square miles. Owned by the Barkdahl family of Cleveland. I tried to get a job with them when I first came here. Told them I had some ideas. Old man Barkdahl didn't like me. Gave me five minutes and then kicked me out of the office." He paused.

"So I went to Davidson."

"You've done all right."

He laughed, a short, impatient laugh.

"Davidson was nothing. An old-fashioned California-style building contractor. A carpenter, really. Liked to see the wood frame going up. Hauling up the beams and joists. Jawing with the plumbers and bricklayers. It was the work he liked, not the wheeling and dealing."

"So why did you hook up with him? Why not start your own company?"

"I went up to the county assessor's office and spent a couple of days there looking through the records. And I found out something very interesting." He paused.

"What was that?"

"Rancho Pacifica, all those acres of ranchland that Barkdahl had just bought and was beginning to develop, went down to the bluffs. And then it stopped. Back in the early 1900s all this," he waved around him, "the islands, the peninsula, the coast below the cliffs up to the high tide line belonged to the state. Either the man who made the original map of the Spanish land grant neglected to put the tide lands in or else they hadn't been formed yet. Nobody wanted them. Why would they? They were nothing more than a couple of sandbars and marshland. You couldn't feed cattle on them or grow lima beans. Hell, the tides washed over all of it several times a year.

"A couple of people tried to develop the peninsula and the big island and went bust doing it. The land just sat there. Davidson's father started buying the lots in 1915 for about twenty-five dollars apiece. They just sat there until the thirties when Ernie inherited them and started putting up houses. He built them one at a time, he and a couple of carpenters, and sold each one for a small profit. Only—" McIan broke off and shook his head in admiration. "Here's the brilliant part. He didn't sell the lots. Sold the houses, got his profit from construction, and then leased the land under it."

"What kind of leases?"

"Twenty years. Most of them came up for renewal in the fifties and sixties before land prices had started to skyrocket. By then the people who lived in the houses had become attached to them and insisted on fifty-year leases. Davidson upped the rent and gave it to them. Later, of course, he regretted it. I looked at the price of comparable property. This was 1969 and already Davidson was worth millions. On paper, of course. Here he was living in that old house. Going out on construction jobs. Sitting on a goddamned gold mine."

"So you married his daughter."

He didn't answer. His hands moved restlessly on the helm. He fingered the throttle in a hurry to get out beyond the five-mile-per-hour limit.

"Barkdahl was already starting to plow the fields under. Pacific Plaza was under construction. Smug bastard. Owned everything around. The land. The police. The city council. Chamber of Commerce. Owned everything but the harbor and the islands: the jewel in the crown. I didn't like being kicked out of his office. I saw a way to get even.

"Davidson took me on as assistant." He laughed again. A hard, driving laugh. "I taught the old man a thing or two. How to borrow against assets. Squeeze a thousand units onto a parcel instead of the usual few dozen homes. Pour a hundred foundations in a day. Mass construction. Davidson hated it. Hated every minute of it. Did everything he could to stop me. But despite all that his construction company began giving Barkdahl a run for his money. Started taking contracts away from him. I was getting a good percentage of the profits."

"And Davidson?"

McIan grinned. "He tried to get rid of me but it was too late. I bought him out."

We passed along the end of the peninsula and turned south under the cliffs of Mesa del Mar. McIan turned the conversation to the price of oil and then to politics. He shifted gears as easily as a high-powered Rolls-Royce.

"Ever read the Warren Report, Cairns?"

I nodded.

"Now that was fascinating. All that evidence, thousands of hours of testimony, and they still aren't a hundred percent sure who did it. If it was a conspiracy or not." He paused. "I admired Kennedy."

A blast of wind came down the channel from the sea and ruffled his hair so that a lock fell across the broad tanned forehead. He threw his head back and gripped the helm with relish. It struck me suddenly, as I studied the man—the energy, the vitality, the arrogance and drive of the man, the restless ambition—that I had seen him before. That he was, that all those yuppies up on the hill were nothing more than make-believe Kennedys. They'd been in their teens and early twenties on the day the news came over the wire that the young, handsome President, his lovely wife beside him, had been killed. It was Kennedy's youth and vigor they emulated, the picture of the perfect family. The candlelit dinner parties in Georgetown and the White House, faithfully recreated in the Heights and University Park and up on the Hill. It was Kennedy, not Dylan or Lennon, who had become the role model to a whole generation. The style, if not the substance.

"I figured out how it could've been done."

"What?" I had lost track of the conversation.

"The assassination."

A wave passed over the end of the jetty and sent two fishermen scrambling up the rocks with their poles. Beyond them I could see the dunes and, farther along the beach, Sven's house. Assassination and murder seemed as out of place on this hazy fall afternoon as they must have seemed in Dallas in November 1963.

"Kennedy in Texas. Bobby in the Ambassador Hotel. Wallace in a shopping mall. Martin Luther King out on his balcony for a breath of night air. Tell me, Cairns, who were the assassins?"

I tried to recall the names. Oswald. Sirhan Sirhan. I couldn't remember the wretch who had crippled Wallace. I vaguely recalled James Earl Ray.

"What have they all got in common?"

I said I didn't know.

"Crazies. All of them were crazies. But what if one man was responsible for running all of them? I'm not saying it happened this way, only how it could have been done. One man could have done it. KGB. CIA. An ambitious politician. One insignificant paper-pushing FBI investigator could have been responsible."

I was amused. His theory was as bad in its way as that of the girl who had filled her graveyard essay with ghosts.

"How do you figure that?"

"Figure that at any one time there's dozens, maybe hundreds, of crazies out there who want to kill a public figure. They slink around with rifles they've ordered from mail catalogs. They call in to radio stations with threats. They follow their targets around from city to city and write it all down in lurid diaries. The FBI has files on thousands of them. When the President comes to town, they place the crazies all under surveillance, bring them in for questioning. Warn the Secret Service. Circulate photographs to the cops.

"All you need to do is to let one of them through the net. Neglect to make a file on him. Inform no one. Find him and then forget to report it. He's out there and nobody knows. That's what makes him dangerous. You don't have to do anything. Just sit back and wait for the poor son of a bitch to do it for you."

We passed between the two jetties and entered the open sea. The jolt of the first wave smacked the bow and sent up a spume of white spray. The horizon, until now steady and flat, began to move up and down. McIan waited until we were clear of the buoy and the surge and roll of the ocean were on all sides before he grasped the throttle and pulled it back as far as it would go.

The boat launched itself forward, the engine roaring beneath us like a holdful of lions. I was flung back against the cabin. McIan braced himself against the helm, legs apart, groin pressed against the bulkhead. The vibrations came up through the deck and coalesced around McIan as though all that energy were centered in him, flowing out, powering the boat. The boat became an extension of the man, rammed itself up against the waves, sliced the sea in half. Beneath us the water swelled and shifted, accommodated itself so that the hull could find the slot between, slip inside, drive forward into the furrows of the sea. McIan's face was closed down, without expression.

We made a run north and west up the coast, past the peninsula pier and the mouth of the Santa Ana River flowing weakly out over the sand. Finally, off Huntington Beach, he eased off a little. To our right the sea was dotted with surfers in their black wet suits. They bobbed up and down like seals in their mourning dress on the gray swells. The long flats of Bolsa Chica were coming up on our right. Long Beach and Los Angeles were somewhere ahead of us in the haze.

McIan slowed the boat. Stopped talking. I wondered if all the instruction about land development and the Kennedy assassination had been his way of postponing this moment when he would have to hear someone tell him something about his son that he might not want to hear. For a moment he looked vulnerable. I had an idea that the subject of David might be the only thing that could make him look that way. He wasn't the kind of man who had close friends. It was possible that David was, next to himself, the only person he really cared about.

"Well then, Cairns. What did you want to tell me?"

I hesitated.

McIan gazed off at the water ahead of us as though he were not fully engaged.

"David knows something about Thorvald Svennson's death."

For a moment it didn't register and then, when it did, he turned to face me in utter disbelief.

"You mean the old fisherman? The one who shot himself up on the estuary?"

I nodded.

"What in the hell could David possibly know about the old man?"

"They were friends."

It shocked him. I think if I had told him that David had killed the old man himself, he would not have been more startled. It was the fact of it, the friendship, that bothered him. I shot him a look of suspicion but the surprise was genuine. I wondered what else the boy had kept secret from his father.

"I don't believe you."

"David came to my house. He met Sven. The two of them took to each other. Sven taught him to bait a hook. The boy listened to his stories. Asked questions. They saw everything from different perspectives. The rich man's son. The old Norwegian fisherman. They made a good team."

The news upset him. I suppose he was wondering, as I was, why the boy had not told him about Sven. About the friendship.

"Okay. So the kid was a friend of the old man. What does that have to do with the old man's death? What are you trying to tell me?"

It wasn't a question exactly. More of a challenge. Hostility masked. The old bear instinctively erecting defenses around his son.

"David wrote an essay about Sven's death. It was brilliant. Too good. He'd got it all right. Almost as though he'd been there. He read it to the class. At least he read some of it. I think there was more. He broke into my house and stole it back before I could read it."

McIan spoke quietly. Every word was framed precisely as though he were reciting it in a courtroom.

"The boy wrote an essay. He was ashamed to be caught caring so much. You know how David is. Too damned sensitive. Thinks too much. He spilled his guts about the old man, a lot of idealistic garbage, and then wanted to take it back."

I started to protest and then stopped. He was looking at me. Not a muscle moved in his face. It was the kind of look he gave to his subordinates and the people he dealt with in the city council and the Chamber of Commerce. He would be, I thought, a formidable foe. But I wasn't afraid. We were on the same side.

"I think David was there."

"Bullshit." McIan's face was buttoned down. Hard. I wondered suddenly to what lengths this man would go to protect his son.

"Look, Mr. McIan, I'm not accusing your son of murder. David loved Sven as though . . ." I was about to say as though he were his own father but thought better of it. "As though he'd grown up knowing him. If Sven was in trouble, David would have gone to help him. Maybe he just met him somewhere. Went up the estuary with him. Just to keep him company. Talk things over. They did it often."

51

McIan gave a vicious turn to the wheel. The boat jerked and pulled back like a stallion suddenly reined.

"The date!"

For a moment I didn't know what he meant. He drummed impatiently on the helm. "The date of the old man's suicide."

"October third."

McIan didn't even stop to think.

"David was with me."

I didn't say anything. Waited to hear what story he would come up with.

"We were at the Arts Pavilion. The Moscow Ballet. My wife and I were hosts to the patrons' reception. David assisted. It was in the paper. You may have missed it." He was sneering. He knew I didn't read the social page. "Afterwards we went home together."

McIan had turned the motor off. The boat drifted with the current. We were about a mile out from the oil fields. Miniature black towers jerked up and down like wire horses trying to free themselves of their reins. A swell came out of nowhere. McIan shifted the wheel just enough to slide over it at an angle. The boat took it, easy as glass. Not far away another yacht steamed toward us. It came to within thirty yards and then turned south toward San Diego and the Mexican waters.

McIan dropped the helm and turned to face me. His eyes reflected the sea. "My son admires you." His face was hard with dislike. I wasn't quite sure what it was that we were fighting over.

"Leave David alone."

The warning went beyond Sven's death and his son's involvement in it. I wondered if he thought we were in competition for the boy's soul. Maybe I knew something he didn't. If David's written work told me anything, it was that the boy worshiped his father. There wasn't any contest.

"Don't mess with my son, Cairns." The voice was calm and deadly as an ice pick.

He switched the motor on again. The boat began to throb and hum and roar. It lifted out of the water and drove forward, smashing the waves, leaving an angry wake. Responding to some invisible signal, three of the deckhands ran up the stairs into the pilot room and stood behind McIan in a phalanx. A cold draft of air came with them. McIan didn't speak all the way down the coast.

I saw the two men as they emerged from the building, David and McIan, father and son. They bounded down the steps together. Vibrant. Full of masculine energy. A shared pride. The relationship was unmistakable. The son wore the same dark blazer in the same privileged, casual way. The sharp creases of the slacks broke at the same time. He matched his father's stride step by step, copied in his young, innocent way the arrogant tilt of the head, the athletic swing of arms.

The father uttered a confidence. The boy threw back his head and laughed. It could not have been important. A moment of male camaraderie between father and son, nothing more.

Three McIan Construction employees, two men and a woman, crossed the plaza and called out "good night" with that exaggerated cheerfulness of an employee to the man who owns the company. McIan waved good night. Anointed them. The boy basked in the glow of his father's importance.

The Ferrari was waiting for them in the place reserved for McIan. They swung down into the dark interior as one entity. Father and son. I felt a sudden brief pang of envy. The car streaked across the lot, stopped briefly at the street, and disappeared down the hill toward the winking lights of the city.

Lieutenant Lawrence was on the ferry when I made the crossing on my way to school. He was standing in the front of the boat eating a Winchell's doughnut and working on a cup of coffee. A bakery van and a VW drove down the ramp. I walked my bicycle to the front and stood there with him. The bay was gray. A thin film of oil covered the surface.

Lawrence looked as if he'd just come out of the shower. Even in all the damp and smell of salt, the shaving lotion surrounded him like an advertisement for Polo by Ralph Lauren.

"I got a message that you called."

The bicycle was between us. I took off my backpack and rested it on the wood plank seat. Beads of fog sat on the rail and ran down the slick gray-painted surfaces of the lockers underneath.

"Sven didn't kill himself and I don't think it was an accident."

If he was surprised he didn't show it. He raised an eyebrow.

"I'm listening."

I caught a glimpse of amusement behind the eyes. It was the same look I gave my students while I watched them wriggle as they tried to explain away something they had done wrong.

"Sven was out here on the bay all the time. Night. Morning. He knew it like a blind man knows the room in which he spends his days. It was his home. And he was sharp as flint. He didn't miss much. Anything out of the ordinary. A boat where it wasn't supposed to be. A person. I think he saw something he wasn't supposed to see."

Lawrence took a bite out of his doughnut. Wiped his lips with a paper napkin. I was sure he could tell I was lying, leaving something out: David. I started to sweat.

"What do you think he saw?"

"I don't know."

A third car thumped down the gangway and parked behind the other two. A kid in a windbreaker and shorts pulled down the big steel guard across the end and punched the button to let down the wooden gate. His pal blew a blast on the horn. A rush of water churned out against the dock and the ferry moved, slow and awkward as an oversized duck, away from the peninsula toward the island.

"It gets dark out here at night. Sven didn't usually carry a light. He didn't need to. Most of the time he was the only one on the bay. No motor. Just the slap of oars. No one sees him coming. Just an old man in a skiff. And then one night he comes up out of the night and stumbles onto something he's not supposed to see."

"Like what?"

He's watching to see how soon I'll hang myself, I thought. Bastard. If only I didn't feel so guilty.

I shrugged. "Murder? Drugs? You're the cop. You know more about what goes on than I do. I'm just a teacher, for God's sake. Anything bad happening, a scuffle, one man murdering another, Sven would have leapt right in. Shouted bloody murder. Wielded his oar like some latter-day Quixote."

"But he didn't tell you he'd seen anything, did he?"

I shook my head.

"He would have, wouldn't he?"

"I thought so. I thought he would. This time he didn't."

"Who else would he have told?"

"No one." I said it too quickly. Lawrence looked at me over the rim of his cup, took a long swallow, pretended not to notice my face flush.

The ferry chugged away underneath us. The vibrations came up through the deck. The kid made his way to the front of the ferry and collected twenty cents from each of us. It took about four minutes to make the crossing. We were more than halfway.

"We ran a check, Cairns." Lawrence looked north up the bay toward the turning basin and the commercial fishing docks. "We went over the records, everything reported along the bay for the last six months. Nothing came up. No murders. No unexplained thefts. Only a few drunken brawls. Nothing more."

"Drugs?"

He shrugged.

The ferry reversed motors, slowed as it plowed into the backwash. It slid into the dock and bumped against the loading platform. The kid slipped the hook over the stanchion and lifted the end bar. He punched the steam gate and the cars drove up the ramp. I wheeled my bike off onto the dock. Lawrence stayed on the ferry. I looked back when I got to the other side of the sea wall. The ferry was already moving out into the bay. Lawrence was the only passenger. He crumpled his Styrofoam cup and threw it over the side. Then he turned and looked back across the water at me. The shock of it hit me across the distance and the blurred gray light off the water. He thinks I killed Sven, I thought. And then the second thought came too quickly. Guilt turned against myself: I did.

Ninety descriptive essays waited to be graded on the kitchen table. I read each one of them twice. The first time I looked for the personal voice, the writer's sense of what he or she was trying to say. The second time I tried to help the student devise ways to make the statement as clear and forceful as possible. I did not presume to rewrite it. I tried to convey the idea that I took the author's attempt seriously. Sometimes my notes took up more room than the essay itself. At the very bottom, which is where I placed its importance, I added a grade.

Tonight I barely got through the first twenty. Half the time I got all the way to the end of a paragraph before I realized that I had not taken in a single word. Several times I got up from my work and went to stand by the window, staring down at the house. Expecting maybe to see the light go on and hear the sound of the old man singing as he did the dishes. Waiting for the kitchen door to open and Old Sven to emerge with a bag of trash in his hand and an excuse to yell up at me. But the house remained dark.

It was close to midnight when I put the puppy out into the yard and let myself into Sven's house. The old man's presence was beginning to fade away. The ship's clock had finally run down. The only

sound left was the impersonal faint hum of the refrigerator.

I slid the bottom drawer out from under the washboard of the kitchen sink where Sven had told me
it would be and emptied the clutter of gadgets onto
the table. It took a minute to find the right screw
and then another to lift the fake bottom out of the
drawer.

The message was there. Only I don't think Sven
ever expected that I would be the one to find it. I felt
sick. In beyond my depth. Behind me in the yard the
dog saw the light and heard me inside. Started
scratching on the screen door and letting out little
yelps of joy because he thought it was Sven come
back, that Sven hadn't deserted him after all.

In the drawer, packed as neatly as only Sven's hand
could do it, were about fifty little bags of white powder. Underneath, in an envelope, was his savings.
Two thousand dollars.

Poor dumb old man. Moving nervously about the
kitchen, staring into the dark. Feeding me can after
can of beer to keep me there. Company for what was
going to be a long, terrifying night. Hadn't confided
in me because he loved me. And then, finally, had
asked me to come along. Would he have told me if I'd
gone?

I snapped the lid down and replaced the screw. I
threw the pastry blender and the colander, a meat
thermometer, bag of cookie cutters, rolling pin back
into the drawer and slid it back under the sink.

I turned out the light and locked the door. I picked
up the pup, who was making small inconsolable
noises, and took him back upstairs with me. I called
the White's Bay Police Department and left an urgent
message for Lawrence. I told him to meet me here at
the house the following morning before seven, when I
had to leave for school. It was important.

Lawrence never showed. I tried to get him several times from school. The last time there was a message for me. Lawrence was tied up until the following day. He would meet me the next morning before I left home.

The Beach Liquor delivery truck was just pulling out of the alley when I got home. It squealed around the curve and nearly ran over me. The front wheel hit the bike and threw me up against the fence. I didn't see Sylvus' face but Sheila was there, staring down at me from the van with eyes that reflected nothing but pain. Red welts lay across her cheeks, big as hands. The van bore down on me and then at the last moment veered around the corner and roared off down the peninsula.

The front wheel of my bike was broken. I picked it up and carried it into the garage. I took my backpack upstairs. Then I went down to Sven's house to assess the damage.

The puppy had been locked inside. I supposed Sylvus had left the door open and the dog had slipped in behind him. I wondered if Sheila had told him where the secret drawer was or if he had had to beat it out of her. Sven would have shown it to Sheila when she was a child. Maybe she had watched him make it.

Everything lay where it had the night before. Except for the kitchen utensils. They were scattered where Sylvus had dumped them on the linoleum. The rolling pin had rolled across the floor and jammed up against the refrigerator. The drawer had been replaced.

I slid it out and placed it on the kitchen table. Unfastened the screw and took out the false bottom. A single rubber band lay on the piece of shelf paper with which Sven had lined it. Otherwise it was empty. I didn't know whether I was glad or sorry. I think mostly I was just scared.

By the time I got to Beach Liquor, the delivery van was parked alongside the back door. I pulled into the parking lot of the restaurant next door and waited. I made a quick call to the police department and left a message for Lawrence. At a quarter to five Sylvus rolled a couple of cases of liquor out of the storeroom and loaded them onto the truck. I followed him out onto Coast Highway and east a couple of blocks to the Bay Club. It stretched in a long thin line along some of the most valuable property on the bay. The guard standing in the little island in the drive waved the delivery truck through. I sat out on the highway behind the wall watching the Porsches and the Mercedes and BMWs go in and out. After about fifteen minutes the truck reappeared and returned to the store.

For a while after that the clerks were too busy to make deliveries. A steady stream of customers pulled in off the highway on their way home to pick up a six-pack or a couple of bottles of wine. I waited for it to get dark before I strolled over to the van and peered inside. I tried the handle but the doors were locked and a sticker warned that the alarm was set. A carton of Chivas Regal sat on the floor in front of the passenger seat. The delivery slip taped to the top was made out to a name and address that had been scrawled and was impossible to read. Aside from that, the truck was empty. I made it back to my car just as the dinner crowd thinned and Sylvus started loading up again.

For the next couple of hours Sylvus went out on calls into the hills where only ten years before there had been nothing but wild mustard and skunk weed. The houses all looked alike to me. Big houses jammed up next to each other with landscaped entryways and expensive lights. My students lived in them and I had been invited inside on occasion. They all had beveled glass doors. A chandelier centered in every room. Marble floors and fluted Greek columns in the foyers. Living rooms that looked like the showrooms at W.J. Sloan, as though only salespeople ever sat down in them.

Around midnight Sylvus wound up to the top of the Hill, where the mansions rose forbiddingly out of their miserly lots like giant elephants perched on stools, misplaced and too heavy to be moved. The biggest one resembled the Ark stranded on top of a rock after the waters had receded back into the bay. The delivery van stopped at a house that looked like the Taj Mahal and another that was Tara resurrected.

By now I had become adept at checking on the Chivas Regal. It was still in place when, sometime after midnight, he made the last delivery and coasted down to MacArthur. Instead of heading back to Coast Highway, he turned inland.

Somewhere on the interchange between the Costa Mesa and San Diego freeways I lost him. A steady stream of headlights came down the freeway from Riverside. The taillights extended in either direction as far as I could see. I took a chance and turned north. It still amazed me to see the traffic at this hour of the night, thousands of cars, all of them changing places. Just before I reached the Santa Ana turnoff I spotted him. The Beach Liquor van was in the center lane, going about seventy-five.

I stayed two cars behind and didn't let him out of my sight. He sailed under the I-5 and stayed in the fast lane all the way across and up into Orange. Smog that had accumulated during the day hung stubbornly over the flatlands. Beneath it, vast housing tracts spread away from the freeway as far as I could see. The dark, silent orchards, the scattered smudge pots, the faint smell of blossoms had all long since been plowed under. All that was left of the orange groves were the names of the families who had planted them: Bastanchury Road. Chapman Avenue. Collins Turnoff. Myford Road.

Sylvus followed the Riverside Freeway through the canyon and then, past Prado Dam, turned off at Corona. For the first time we were away from the lights and the stream of cars heading east and west. The road wound through dark canyons and across dry riverbeds. Occasionally we passed dirt roads leading off into sand quarries and brickworks. A black Porsche passed us at a speed of well over a hundred miles an hour. Otherwise we were alone on the road. My lights hit Sylvus' rearview mirror and glared back at me. I slowed and let him go ahead.

Lake San Malo lay like a great black sinkhole with the mountains behind it. The houses, prefabs and trailers, made a ring on the mudflats where the shrinking lakefront had once been. It was a mean little town, thrown up in hopes of a land boom that had never come. The lots were large, an acre or more.

Weeds and mud. It was dark as the inside of a mine shaft.

We followed the lake almost halfway around to the right. The park, with picnic tables and sparse trees, ran deserted and forlorn down to the water. The Elsinore Mountains rose straight up on our right and blotted out the sky. On the west side of the lake, past the Ortega Highway turnoff, Sylvus pulled up in front of a rusted iron gate and honked.

A dozen pit bulls came out of the blackness and threw themselves against the fence yelping and snarling. I passed the house, made a U turn and stopped about twenty yards down the road. After a minute or two a light came on. I could see the porch, set back about one hundred feet from the road, and a man standing underneath the light with a shotgun. He was tall and dark and bearded. He came out across the yard and opened the gate. The dogs escorted the van to the house. Sylvus stayed inside. He unlocked the door on the passenger side. The bearded man reached in for the Chivas Regal and transferred it to the porch. He handed a smaller parcel across the seat to Sylvus. When he was finished he called the dogs off. Sylvus turned and drove back out onto the road. The man shut the gate after him and then went back into the house. First the porch lights and then the lights inside went off. The pit bulls, cheated of a fight, snarled among themselves and finally settled down somewhere in the dark.

I waited for about ten minutes, but nothing happened. I had just reached for the ignition when I heard the click of the gate. They came out of the dark and hurled themselves against the car. There was just enough time to get my arm inside and roll up the window before teeth and muzzles exploded against the glass.

They must have been hungry. They attacked the tires, the hood, the doors. Bodies thumped sickeningly against metal. Skulls cracked against glass. The bearded man stood, silent, leaning against the gate, watching the attack.

The windshield cracked and held. Blood dripped down the glass. I put the car into reverse and then shifted into forward. The dogs hung on until I was nearly a mile down the road and then they dropped off one by one.

The windshield was covered with blood. I stopped in a gas station to wash it off so I could see to drive. I didn't stop shaking until I had caught up with Sylvus at a Jack in the Box on the outskirts of Costa Mesa. I waited while he finished up his hamburger and fries and then I followed him home.

I spent the night in the car, at the corner of Elden and Berry. No one came in or went out of Sylvus' house. The van sat there as isolated and lonely as a hearse. No one went near it. I got about two hours' sleep. A little after eight Sylvus lumbered out the door with a tackle box and climbed into the van. He hadn't changed his clothes or combed his hair. I followed him down Beach Boulevard onto the peninsula all the way down to the Pier. He parked in the public parking lot, bought a cup of coffee at the Orange Julius, and headed for the Pavilion. He bought a round-trip ticket to Catalina and boarded the boat with the rest of the passengers. The tackle box looked new and expensive. It was outfitted with a lock that was much too sturdy for a few rusted fish-hooks and a couple of sinkers. I made another in my long string of calls for help to the White's Bay Police Department from the pay phone in the Pavilion. Law-rence had not come in yet. No one was very interested in what I had to say. At the last minute I put down twenty bucks and got on the Catalina Ferry just be-fore they pulled up the gangway and got under way.

It was a thirty-mile trip. The sea was smooth as glass. The island was hidden, as it usually was, in the moisture that hung over the water and the smog creeping down from Los Angeles. Occasionally a fish jumped up out of the water and fell back in with a splash. A couple of huge tankers passed on the hori-zon en route from San Pedro to somewhere in the South Pacific. A steady stream of passengers went up and down to the lounge to buy Cokes and to go to the lavatory. Sylvus slept through the entire trip.

Two hours later we steamed into Avalon. The city shimmered in the sun and the haze the way it does in all the ads. The island rose, all brown hills and wild chaparral, around the town and stretched north out of sight for miles behind it. The passengers disem-barked. In a minute they were gone, dispersed along the waterfront and up into the town.

Sylvus headed for the nearest bar, a stale, dank place all fitted out like a Spanish galleon. I could see him through one of the small windows shaped like a porthole. He sat alone at the bar, back to the sea, and drank one beer after another. Occasionally he got up and went to the men's room. It was the first time I'd been to Catalina since Kate and I had come one per-fect spring day about a million years ago. We took a bed in an old hotel way up on the side of the hill and made love in a dusty sun-filled room until the boat went back to the mainland and the tourists were gone and we had the island to ourselves.

You can't go very far. The town is cordoned off from the rest of the island. It curves around the harbor and wanders back into the canyons. The thin strip along the beachfront is devoted to tourists. Behind that the island is the same as it has been since the thirties. Old houses cling to the hills. The Bird Park. The Holly House, Victorian, white-shingled, overlooks the town on one side, and the adobe of Zane Grey broods high atop the other. The rest of the island is dusty and barren, California the way it was before the water got piped down from the north and the land was changed forever. Buffalo and cattle, cactus, sunburned weeds, dusty hiking trails. And all around the sea, blue and green and clear as Kate's eyes.

I bought a cheap Instamatic camera and a roll of film and loaded it. I took a picture of the bar and the boat. About lunchtime Sylvus came out, blinking like a dormouse in the light, and ambled up the street to the Captain's Table, where he consumed two roast-beef sandwiches and another six-pack of beer. At about two o'clock he began looking at his watch and peering out into the harbor. It was the first time he'd shown any curiosity about his surroundings. I decided it was time to be more careful. I moved out of his line of sight and tried to figure out what it was he was looking for.

The harbor was a seething mass of yachts. There were hundreds of them, over for the weekend from White's Bay and Dana Point, down from Marina del Rey and Huntington Harbor. They fought over moorings in Avalon. You could practically cross the harbor on them. Boats rising and falling like huge bloated sleeping whales. Bronzed bodies lying supine on decks. Would-be jet-setters recovering from the night before, preparing for the big one to come.

I spotted the yacht the moment Sylvus did. It came around the point at the south side of the island, a big sportfisher that might have been fishing the beds off San Nicolas or San Clemente Island. It came into the harbor, its wake rippling through the boats, lifting them and setting them down again, and then disappeared into their midst.

Sylvus waited another twenty minutes and then rose, paid his bill and walked west along the waterfront to the Casino at the end. I followed him at a distance.

A young man was waiting for him by the Casino. He was lounging, arm thrown carelessly over the balustrade, as handsome as one of the Greek gods currently in vogue. He was tan, dark-haired, blue-eyed. Right out of *Town and Country*. He wore white ducks and Adidas. A sweater with a little emblem on the front fit as though it had been hand-loomed for him. He looked around lazily without seeming to notice Sylvus and took the tackle box the moment Sylvus set it down. It didn't take more than a second. The boy straightened up, took a long leisurely look out over the harbor, and then turned and walked back along the waterfront toward me. I pretended to focus on the water and then at the last moment turned the camera in his direction. He flung an arm over his face (it was an automatic gesture, not a sign of alarm) and hurried away before I could get the camera cocked again. He vanished into the Catalina Yacht Club. I tried to follow him but the guard at the gate politely refused to let me in.

I climbed the hill and sat on the edge of it under a grove of eucalyptus. From this vantage point I could see the entire harbor. A water taxi with a single passenger pulled out of the Yacht Club and disappeared into the forest of masts and hulls.

I waited there until the Catalina Ferry blew three long blasts on its horn. Sylvus reappeared out of another watering hole and lumbered back to the boat. The town emptied. The tourists scurried down the side streets and along the alleys to the docks like water emptying back into the sea. I heard the final blast of the horn as I climbed aboard the bus that would take me to the inland airport. I caught the commuter plane, a five-seater, to the county airport, picked up a taxi to the pier where I'd left my car and headed wearily for home.

The police raided the house at San Malo before dawn. They went in while it was still dark and surrounded the place. In the spotlights, egged on by the bullhorns, the pit bulls went into a frenzy. They turned into lethal muscular projectiles and launched themselves against the cops. They clamped on to the protective gear and the night sticks with steel jaws that had to be broken off. Five of the dogs were shot to death, and four others, found chained to the porch, were shot with tranquilizers so that the officers could get to the door.

The house was empty. The two men who had rented it had cleared out. The shed behind the house might have been used as a workshop where they cut and packaged the cocaine. The lab people came and took a lot of fingerprints and dust samples and stored them away with the roll of film I'd taken in Catalina.

Sylvus Bongaard was interviewed by Lawrence and two other investigators for over an hour. He said he had been at home from midnight until the cops woke him in the morning. His wife vouched for him. He didn't know anything about drugs. He had never been to San Malo and didn't even know where it was. He wanted to know who had made the report against him. Lawrence refused to tell him.

Lawrence came to Sven's house and examined the drawer under the sink. Then he asked if I would mind if he searched my apartment. I told him to go ahead. As far as I know he came up empty. He left tight-lipped and grim.

The boy came, reluctantly, into the house. Through the living room, pausing in the center, by Sven's old chair, listening to the silence, hearing the absence of clock ticking, the old man moving around, bumping into things, humming under his breath.

I called to him. Told him I was in the kitchen.

He didn't want to come. Obeyed anyway, feet dragging, white-lipped into Sven's kitchen. Stood in the middle of it as though he were afraid to touch anything. As though the house itself had died with the old man and left just the husk, the old man's outer skin, which might, at any minute disintegrate into dust. He stared at me across the table. Belligerent. Scared.

"What do you want?"

Friday afternoon. A year ago last spring. I had been alone then, as now, in the classroom, door closed against the noise. Basketballs thrown against lockers. Cars squealing out of the parking lot. Then, finally, silence. My papers spread over the desk. Deciphering scrawls on the exam I gave annually for those who wanted to take Advanced Placement English. Decoding the half-formed opinions. Trying to put some logical order into the feelings that had not yet hardened into thought. The boy knocked. Slipped through the door, books clasped to his chest. Tense. Shy as a deer.

I sighed. They came too often, these students of mine, despite my disclaimer that I was no priest, to confess. Told me about love affairs gone wrong. Demanding fathers. Drug addiction. Feelings of inferiority. Came to me because they'd got me mixed up with the books I taught. Attributed D.H. Lawrence's psychological insight to me. Endowed me with the humanity that belonged to Chekhov. The intellectual power of Donne. I am not the author, I told them every year in the beginning. I am nothing more than a fairly good English teacher. They came anyway, sure that I had the answers that eluded them. Now this strange pale boy stood in front of me. I was surprised. He did not look like the kind of boy who would make that mistake.

"I cheated," he said.

"Your name?"

"David McIan."

I nodded. Drew his test out of the others, held it out to him. He set his books down. Took the paper, eyes averted. Reached deep into the pocket of his jeans, thin legs pressing against cloth, drew out his ballpoint pen. Found the grade on the last page. Crossed out the A. Inscribed, very neatly, hand shaking, an F. Handed it back. Turned to go.

"Why?"

He turned to look at me. Eyes dark, wide, angry, as though it were a stupid question. As thought anyone would know the answer. Self-evident.

"I wanted to be in your class."

"You could have missed an answer. Several, in fact. The cutoff is eighty percent."

"I thought you'd notice me if I got it all right."

As a matter of fact, I had noticed him. The writing in the sample paragraphs was not remarkable, but there was a quality to it that was unusual. It wasn't all for show. There was an earnestness. A mind at war with itself. Inflexible. Daring to be challenged. Yearning to be pried open. Bound on getting at the truth of things.

"Do you cheat on a regular basis or just when you want to be noticed?" It came out more sarcastically than I had intended.

"No. I never cheat." It offended him, the suggestion. There was something complicated about him. Intriguing. Idealism? It was a long time since I had had one of those in my class. They came these days already formed, carrying briefcases, miniature business executives. Lockstepping to the pragmatic and amoral beat of their fathers.

Suddenly I wanted this boy, enigmatic, wide open, in my class. I wanted to fight with him and challenge him and hold him up to the others. To win and lose battles against him. Send him into the world armed against it.

I pretended to be reluctant.

"I accept you on condition," I said. "You can argue with me. Contradict. Challenge anything I say. You can get failing grades on occasion. But the first time you cheat, you're out. For good. No recourse. Is that understood?"

He nodded. Still angry. Walked to the door. Let himself out. I tore up the test. Hoped I'd not made a mistake.

"Sit down."

Now he looked at me, looked at the table where he'd sat with Sven all those hours, eating the sandwiches the old man had made for him, great hunks of corned beef on rolls, gobs of mayonnaise, lettuce, tomatoes. Refused to sit. Guilt in the line of his body. The restlessness in his eyes.

He was a good-looking boy. A little pale. Too much English in his background ever to get a decent tan. Someday he'd be like his grandfather Davidson. Ruddy-cheeked, little raisin scars where the skin cancers had been burned off. Now he was just pale. Dark-eyed. Too serious for a boy. Too sensitive. He reminded me of another boy who still, on occasion, stirred uneasily inside of me. It was a burden, sensitivity. To have to go through the world realizing *all* the possibilities, not just the one or two obvious ones. Reading meanings into words that sometimes weren't there at all. Noticing too many things so that they were not easily categorized, made sense of, stored away in neat packets in the brain. Throwing off slights that others did not even feel.

"I got your message. What do you want?"

I didn't want to scare him away. I smiled. "I thought we might talk. That you might have something you wanted to tell me."

He flinched, instinctive as a snail, antennae shrinking back into themselves at the first touch.

"Don't patronize me. If I'd wanted to tell you something I'd have come on my own." He stood defiantly. As though he hated me, hated himself.

"All right then." I tried to shock him. "Sven was murdered."

David didn't say anything. He looked down at his hands. They touched the table gingerly, ran lightly over the oilcloth like the fingertips of a blind man, feeling for something. Searching for the raised characters that would make all the meanings come clear.

"You knew that, didn't you?"

He didn't answer.

"Is that what you intended for your essay to tell me? That Sven was killed?"

"No."

"Were you there?"

"Of course not!" He rounded on me with fury. "If I'd been there it wouldn't have happened."

"What wouldn't?"

His eyes dropped. "I wouldn't have let them."

"Who?"

"I'd have saved him. I don't know who."

"What else do you know?"

"Nothing!" He looked me straight in the eyes. Defiant. Angry. "I don't know anything about it. Why should I?" His fists clenched. The slight frame shook, as though he were keeping himself from running away.

"I know that you know something. I saw the two of you sitting here at the table, plotting. That night in the kitchen. When I came in you slid a piece of paper under the table. What were you planning?"

"Nothing. We just talked. I was taking notes. I was going to write a book about the old man. I didn't want you to see. I thought you'd laugh."

"A book about Sven?"

He nodded dumbly, suddenly grief-stricken. He turned away from me toward the sink, eyes moving over the washboard to the refrigerator. Seeing the movements of the old man. The washrag he used to wipe up the crumbs. The wastebasket, cleaned out every night before he went to bed. The window where he stood watching for the boy to come.

For a moment we were bound together, close as only teacher and student can be when the chemistry's right. When one mind reaches across the chasm and touches the other. The two of us, mourning Sven.

"What happened, David? You saw something, didn't you? The two of you. Out there in the skiff, up the bay for a ride or fishing down near the breakwater. Saw something you shouldn't see. Crept home. Tried to hide it. Failed."

The boy shook his head. And then he began to talk. About Sven, about the stories. The old man's honesty. The hands like leather with grooves that the fishnets had worn across the palms. The wrinkles from all those years of working in the sun. The way he wiped the table clean. Knew everything there was to know about boats and the weather and the secret signs of the sea.

He talked almost without taking a breath. As though it kept him from thinking about something so terrible he could not bear to acknowledge it. A monstrous shadow looming in the background, kept at bay only by words, by a determined effort to speak of everything else, by a denial of its existence.

I tried to stop him. To tell him I would shield him if I could. Step between him and whatever threatened him. Tell him he didn't have to go it alone. It was too much for a boy not yet eighteen. But a teacher walks a fine line between responsibility and love, has the influence to do harm. I had never crossed that line. I couldn't do it, even now.

"What about the drugs, David?"

He stopped where he was, back to me. I could see his body stiffen and then relax. When he turned to face me, his eyes were clear again. He had stopped trembling. Relief stood out on his face. I waited for the rush of words that would come pouring out, purge him of the terrible burden.

"What about them?" he said.

"They were stashed there, under the sink. A million dollars' worth of cocaine."

David's eyes went to the drawer and then back to the table, over the oilcloth and the salt and pepper shakers sitting neatly in the center, the little plastic napkin holder with the cheap white paper standing inside. His eyes rested on the chair that stood between us as though he saw someone sitting there, indignant, silent, determined to get in on the discussion in what was, after all, his kitchen. David's eyes bored into the chair, asking the dead man what to say; what to reveal and what to hide.

I waited. Waited while the boy got his thoughts together, made his decision. Finally he answered me coolly. With finality.

"It was the week before he died. Night. We went up the bay. Sven was talking about how it was on the sea.

75

How when you were out there, on a boat, no matter how big it was, out there with nothing but the sea all around you, as far as you could look, the boat was nothing. A tiny island adrift. The sea was your enemy, he said. There wasn't anyone to help you. So you helped each other. It was the only way you could survive. If another boat came by and someone was sick or the ship was going to sink, or there weren't enough provisions, you did what you could for them. Shared everything. Because that was the rule. There wasn't anybody else. You couldn't turn them over to welfare or give them a number to call. You were, always, the last resort. And you did for them and trusted that someday, when you were in trouble, someone would come along and do the same for you."

I could almost hear the old man's voice coming through the boy's. It was Sven's credo. He repeated it to everyone who would listen. Hoping it would rub off. I remembered one night—gale winds blowing, and the trash cans banging behind the house. The old man was out in his pajamas, shivering, chasing them down the alley. Not his own, which were safe inside the garage, but his neighbors'. Fastening them down. Heaving them over the fences. Locking gates after them. Everyone else was inside, warm, safe, insulated.

"And that's when we saw the men transferring drugs from one boat to another. We didn't know what it was at first. But Sven was curious and we followed them up the bay and saw where they docked. We pulled the skiff in close under the bow and heard them talking."

"One of them was Sylvus. His son-in-law."

The boy stopped, considered. I could see the gears changing.

"Yes. Sven told me not to say anything. He said he would take care of it. Sven went back later, when there was no one out on the bay, and found the drugs stashed behind the bulkhead and brought them home. He put them in the drawer. The next night he was dead."

"Would you recognize the boat?"

"No. It was dark. Sven wrote down the name. I didn't see it. Is that what you want to know?"

I was about to answer but he didn't wait. I called to him to come back but he fled through the living room. The door slammed behind him. It echoed up the stairs and through the empty house.

The boy was lying. The lie was in the sudden stillness, the relief in his eyes. The drugs had taken him by surprise. He had never heard about them. Never seen them. The trip up the bay had been real but it was something else they'd seen. Something so much worse that even now, to save his own life, he could not name it.

I ran after him. I wasn't sure what I meant to do. Hold him. Tell him it was all right. Or shake him. Grab him by the shoulders. Force him to tell me the truth. Promise to keep him safe. Exorcise whatever demons had taken up residence in that beautiful, troubled mind of his. But he was gone by the time I got to the door.

The next day the registrar's office left a note in my box informing me that on the request of his father, David McIan had been transferred out of my class.

An earthquake, or what might pass for one, woke me long before I was ready to get up. The shock waves came up through the foundation and the sand below it and jolted the bed, nearly throwing the dog off. It was 6 A.M. I turned over and tried to go back to sleep. Heard through gritted teeth the high whine of an engine, gearing up, straining, and then the great crack and splinter of clapboard and joist giving way. Another old house, this one somewhere behind the alley, had met its appointment in Samarra.

It went on until almost noon. These old beach houses looked as though they'd been put up with spit and a ball of twine, but the wood in them, real two-by-fours in a day when the lumber yards hadn't started shaving off an extra half inch, had hardened over the years into something resembling concrete. It was practically impossible to drive a nail through them, much less break them in half.

About lunchtime the trucks started carting it all off. Chunks of foundation, splinters of wood, shingle, tile, all hurtled past on the way to the dump. A shower curtain went by, fluttering from where it still hung from the metal pipe. Bits of wallpaper stuck onto slabs of wallboard. A carpet nobody had bothered to remove still tacked to floorboards. By one o'clock everything was gone. Nothing left but a patch of sand. Nobody there to give the house its last rites.

I told myself I was getting out just in time. Growled resentfully at the eviction notice tacked beside the refrigerator, which gave me until noon on Tuesday to evacuate the premises. That was one hour after the will was to be opened and read and Sylvus took over.

It was conference day at school. My conferences had all been scheduled a week earlier and I was free. I spent the rest of the morning packing. Appalled that after all these years I had accumulated so little. A dozen cartons of books and two of clothes. A few pots and pans. A lot of files. Notes. Magazine articles. Manuscripts I'd written and then never had the courage either to send to the publisher or throw away.

After I'd left these walls, this window overlooking the alley, there'd be nothing left to remind me of the years with Kate. No mementos. I'd never kept any. Had always scorned anything inanimate to represent what was so clearly human and alive.

There were a lot of "For Rent" signs in the windows of the duplexes and garage apartments on the peninsula and the islands. All of them started at about $1200 a month. Unless, of course, I wanted to share one with about five eighteen-year-olds from UCI, male and female. I wasn't quite ready for that.

I finally found an apartment behind the Safeway in Costa Mesa. It was from month to month. They wouldn't take the dog. I made arrangements to leave him at the animal shelter. I drove down to Laguna and up the canyon to the dog pound. I got him out of the car and on the leash and up to the door and then, at the last minute, threw him back into the front seat, angrily, as though it were his fault, and went home again. I made a call to the manager of a one-room apartment in Santa Ana that advertised that it took animals and said I'd take it, sight unseen. No lease.

I packed everything in the car and left it in the garage. The dog and I spent our last miserable night at Sven's together on the floor.

Thurber's law office was in his home. It was on the beach, a big sprawling summer cottage with a couple of sand dunes for a front yard. The shingles had been whitewashed so many times they had finally given up and turned ash-gray. A deep veranda wrapped itself around three sides of the house which had been built in the thirties and glassed in about twenty years later. The window panes were encrusted with salt from the sea air, and the curtains had faded, nearly colorless, from the sun.

The inside looked like a warehouse for a used-book store. Books and files spilled out of the little dining room where Thurber holed up most of the time, into the hallway and parlor with its Victorian knickknacks and overstuffed furniture. The house had been furnished and decorated by Thurber's mother forty years before with cast-off furniture from their much larger permanent home in Pasadena. She was a charming and venerable woman, already in her sixties when I knew her. She had died while Thurber was still in law school and he had never found anyone to replace her. It was a veritable museum of antiques and bric-a-brac, if you could find them underneath all the books and briefs and yellow legal pads covered with Thurber's crabbed scrawl.

The reading of the will had been delayed at Erik's request and Sheila's reluctant agreement, until he returned from a charter to Mexico. Kate was there when I arrived. She and Thurber were thick as thieves. They were hunched over the pearl-inlaid table clipping editorials out of the local newspapers about the recall election and pasting them onto 8½-by-11 sheets of paper.

"Chandler!" Thurber bounded over to give me one of those tentative bear hugs with which he invariably greeted me whether we were in the supermarket with a couple of wire shopping carts between us or on the beach in flippers and diving masks. In the presence of strangers and most women, he was as shy as a maiden aunt and avoided public appearances with the single-minded determination of a monk which, in many ways, he resembled. He had a law degree from Harvard, which he kept in his bottom drawer, and he kept a low profile. He never appeared in court or sat on corporate boards. He spent twelve hours a day doing research and writing up the arguments for the fancy law offices on the hill. His spare time was devoted to Kate and her projects. He was modest in his dress and eating habits. He could have made a million dollars a year if he'd wanted to. But he didn't. He was a man with a mission. He was as happy as a clam.

The bell rang. I found a place to sit and watch the other legatees. Sheila and Sylvus did not seem overjoyed to see me. Sylvus gave me one of his contemptuous snarls. It wasn't any worse than the last time. I figured the hostility level never varied. Lawrence had kept his word. He hadn't told Sylvus who had followed him out to San Malo and turned him in.

The Bongaards had done themselves up in a new set of clothes. Sylvus clumped across the floor in a pair of alligator boots. He shot me a look of triumph that I pointedly ignored. Sheila twisted a fair-sized diamond ring self-consciously on her finger. Sven's son, Erik, dashed in late wearing white slacks and a T-shirt that showed his spectacular tan off to its best advantage.

Thurber fussed around us like an old woman, and as the guests arrived, he scurried between the parlor and the kitchen with coffee strong enough to set off an alarm, served in Haviland cups with Zee napkins. He switched piles of books from one chair to another and finally ended up setting them on the floor so that all of us could be seated.

He read the entire will. Not a whereas or wherefore was left unenunciated. I think legal language, to Thurber, was poetry. The five of us sat staring mutely at one another. Kate caught my eye and winked. Erik gazed boredly off into space. Sheila and Sylvus, perched uncomfortably on the dining-room chairs, which were authentic Chippendale, waited impatiently for the numerals and parentheses and footnotes to end and the document to begin. Sylvus' demeanor could only be described as expectant. Someone had inflated the value of Sven's modest legacy to him. He was going to be disappointed no matter which way it came out. Perhaps he had already spent what it had taken Old Sven a lifetime to accumulate. Maybe he hadn't yet figured out that he was going to have to divide it all with Erik.

"To Sheila Bongaard, the deed to the house at 2416 Berry Street, Costa Mesa, in which she resides with her husband Sylvus Bongaard.

"To Erik Svennson, the duplex in which he currently lives at 2115 Fifty-first Street, in White's Bay. All other moneys to be divided equally between my two children, Sheila Bongaard and Erik Svennson."

Thurber paused. Sheila whispered to Sylvus. He shook his head impatiently.

"Get on with it, you creep."

Thurber pretended he hadn't heard. His voice droned on for twenty minutes more before he came to the good part. I would have missed it except for the howl of dismay from Sheila and an unrepeatable word from her unspeakable husband.

"Maybe you'd better run that by me again," Erik said. Like me, he hadn't been listening very carefully. He leaned forward like someone who is only mildly curious about something that does not very closely concern him.

Thurber laid down his glasses and looked out at us, blinking like a lizard caught in the sun. Perhaps he had lost himself in the recitation of what was undoubtedly a beautiful document and had forgotten us entirely.

"Just cut the crap and tell us who gets what." Sylvus kicked a pile of books over onto the floor. Thurber watched the books slide in disarray across the parquet. He blinked again, astonished. He opened his mouth and then closed it. Put his glasses back on. Began to paraphrase. It went against the grain.

"The house on East Oceanfront and the lot directly adjacent to be placed under the joint ownership of Kate Llewelyn Jones and James Chandler Cairns. The only remaining property, which consists of Duck Island, also to be jointly owned by Kate Llewelyn Jones and James Chandler Cairns, formerly husband and wife."

Sylvus leapt to his feet. He came toward me, his big potbelly heaving with frustration and rage. Sheila took hold of his arm in a hopeless attempt to restrain him from choking me.

"We're gonna contest the will." Sylvus spit on the floor. The globule sat there on the Oriental rug while we all stared at it. "You can't do this. We already got a buyer lined up. The down payment is in the bank."

"Sorry." Thurber was noncommittal. "The house with the adjacent lot and the island belong to Cairns and Kate Llewelyn Jones."

Something seemed to amuse Erik. He started laughing. Maybe he hated his brother-in-law as much as his father had.

"Smart old bastard. Fucking smart old bastard. Owned Duck Island all that time." Erik grinned his admiration.

"Cairns is not even a relative. Her neither. We're gonna hire a lawyer. A real lawyer. Not a shithead like this one."

Thurber flinched. It was the epithet itself, not the reference to him, that offended.

Sylvus grabbed the will out of Thurber's hands and stared at it. Tried to read it. Realized the hopelessness of trying to decipher the legalese. Threw the first page back, trying to find what he wanted on the second. Finally slammed the whole thing down on the table. Took a step toward me.

"You forced the old man to do it. Didn't he, Sheila?" Sylvus grabbed her arm and made her rise to her feet, twisted it until you could see the pain. She nodded.

"The old man told us how you made him do it. He was afraid of you. Isn't that right, Sheila?" She nodded again. He gave her a poke.

"Yes." She spoke through clenched teeth. She stared at me with an expression of intense hurt. As though I were the one inflicting the pain instead of Sylvus. He let her arm go, tossed her away from him like some rag he had used and didn't need anymore.

Sylvus stuck his ugly face about two inches from mine, his mandible extended about as far as it could go without getting stuck in my windpipe. I moved back so I could look at him without being cross-eyed.

"He wasn't sane when he signed this will. You scared him into it. Sucked up to the old man. Told him to screw his family."

"Fucking old bastard." It was Erik. I gathered it was news to him as much as it was to me. Duck Island was nothing more than a sandspit in the middle of a nature preserve, worth nothing to anyone but the birds who inhabited it. Still, it was quite a surprise. "Fucking smart old bastard."

Sheila stood white-lipped behind Sylvus, like a child who has done something wrong. It wasn't going to be long before the blame for her failure to inherit would be directed at her.

"Sign it over, Cairns."

"May I remind you, Mr. Bongaard, that you are not a party to this will and have no rights whatsoever." Thurber's voice came across the room like a bucket of ice.

Sylvus swung at me and missed. He was big and slow and I had plenty of time to duck. I felt I was taking part in a farce. Sheila started to cry. She grabbed his arm and pulled him back. He shook her off and started to take another whack.

Thurber stepped between us.

It was such a goddamn brave thing to do that it startled even Sylvus. Thurber didn't even think twice about putting his remarkably unfit torso in the way of Sylvus' monstrous one. Sylvus could have killed him with a quick blow. But he didn't. He turned instead and slammed out the door. Sheila followed after him. Erik, at the first sign of trouble, had simply melted away.

I was numb. The dog was in the car. All my belongings. I could go back to my apartment over the garage. Unpack. I didn't know whether to feel grateful to the man who had foreseen that I would be summarily evicted from what had become my home, or troubled by the inconsistency of it. Kate and I avoided looking at each other. There was something so personal, intimate, embarrassingly so, about owning a house together.

Thurber seemed to think it was all a good show. He rummaged about in the Queen Anne sideboard. He was quite pleased with himself. He came up at last, triumphant, with a bottle of Chivas Regal, which he started to portion out into three little Waterford sherry glasses.

"When was the will made, Thurber?"

The bottle poised in midair, then was set back on the sideboard.

"The third of October." Thurber sighed.

Somehow that took all the fun out of it. It was the day Sven had died.

I was giving the dog a bath when the cream-colored Mercedes came down the alley and pulled onto the parking strip in front of the garage. Someone, I couldn't see who it was, worked for a while on the gate and opened it. She crossed the yard, all cream silk and high heels, and disappeared around the front of the house.

I rinsed the puppy off. With all the fur plastered against his collie ribs he looked about as scrawny and appetizing as a rat. I dried his head and chest with a towel, set him down on the floor and left him there to shake the rest of the water off by himself.

Ms. Trueblood was still standing on the front porch. She had stopped ringing the bell and was peering through the side window into the living room. She wore a different dress than two weeks earlier when she had rejected my rent application and suggested that I was not qualified to live in White's Bay, but the jewelry was still fourteen-karat gold, and the effect was the same. The shoes were a pale cream without a mark on them. I wondered if women like that bought a new pair every couple of days. I could see her sharp little hip bones through the silk.

"Hello."

"Oh!" She moved quickly away from the window, defying me to suggest she had been caught in the act of prying. "You startled me." It was not a confession. More like an accusation.

"I'm looking for the owner of the house. Mr. Chandler Cairns."

"I'm Cairns."

"Oh." It caught her by surprise. And then: "Have we met before?"

"I came into your office looking for a place to rent. You weren't very helpful."

"Ah." She seemed to remember. "Well, it seems you have come up in the world, Mr. Cairns."

"Did you want something in particular?"

"Could we go inside?" Her voice was suddenly all syrup and honey. She gestured toward the house.

"I left the key upstairs."

She waited for me to get it and when I didn't move, took another tack.

"Well, I don't suppose I need to see the house. I'm here, Mr. Cairns, on behalf of a client."

"Yes?"

"He is interested in buying your house."

"It's not for sale."

"Well, it's not exactly upscale, is it?" She looked up at Sven's bedroom window and the eave jutting out over it. "I suppose anyone who bought it would want to tear it down and start from scratch. It is a rather lovely lot, though, here on the sand. And, of course, with the lot next door . . . My client is looking for a place like this. On the beachfront. Not too expensive. Near the point."

"Perhaps you didn't hear me."

"Oh yes, I did, Mr. Cairns. Of course, people change their minds. You haven't been a homeowner very long. I don't suppose you have looked into the taxes on a place like this?"

"I'm really not interested in selling."

She whipped open a little notebook. It had a gold pencil attached to it on a gold chain. "Mr. Svennson paid taxes on the pre-1975 assessed value of the house. In 1978 and '79 the tax bill was $612. Of course when you inherited the house the assessment suddenly jumped to the real and current value of the house, which is in the neighborhood of $850,000. And the lot next door, of course. Another $800,000. So your taxes, as I figure it, are $20,000. Per year. Give or take a little." She smiled at me. A golden, happy smile. Like someone who has just lobbed a particularly effective serve across the net into a corner of the court where I could not hope to reach it. I didn't answer.

"I understand you're a teacher." This time she was radiant. She smiled again. Only a clerk at B. Dalton made less than I did. I wondered what it would be like to go to bed with this lady, all her gold chains clanking and the energy pouring out of that lean muscle. It would be, I guessed, like playing a game of singles with someone who played with nothing more in mind than winning.

"I'm sure your client can find another place."

"He is prepared to pay what it's worth. Perhaps a little more." She took a step and peered around the corner of the house at the four-foot easement between Sven's house and the next.

"There are plenty of little houses still left along the beach."

"Yes." Again the golden smile. "The people who own these old homes do tend to hang on to them. But—"

She stepped closer to me. I could smell the perfume. It smelled expensive. "You see," she shrugged as though it was something she simply couldn't help, foolish as it was, "he wants this one."

"Why Sven's house? Why this particular one?"

She shrugged again. Her beautiful shoulders, under the padded silk, rose up and down in a gesture that was almost poetic.

"Sentimental value?"

She laughed. She was good at it. I had the feeling she could make it come and go at will.

"I wouldn't say that, Mr. Cairns. But then, he didn't tell me. We don't inquire into our clients' motives."

"And who is this client?"

"Oh!" She seemed a little shocked. "That's confidential. You understand." Ms. Trueblood was not much more than twenty-seven or twenty eight. At that age Kate and those of my generation had still been trying to come to grips with the world. This young woman was already there. Had never had any doubts. But then her ambition was for far less complicated things than the ones we wanted. Hers only cost money.

"Tell him that if he wants to buy this house, to come see me himself."

She opened her mouth and then shut it again. She slipped the little Gucci notebook back into her understated cream leather bag and left. This time she went down the steps to the bit of sidewalk that fronted the beach. The tap-tap-tap of heels on cement came back self-assured, and financially motivated, all the way to the corner.

 "You know why Sven did it, don't you?"

Kate was angry. At Sven. At me. At herself. We had spent the last hour putting the house back in order after Sylvus' nocturnal search-and-seizure operation. The puppy trailed around after us, wagging his tail, sniffing at a trail that he innocently expected would lead him, eventually, to Sven.

Kate jammed a cushion back on the couch and gave it a vicious shove with her knee.

"Okay." I was trying to make peace. "It was to get us back together. Forgive him. He was an old man."

"Still." She bit her lip. "He might have had some consideration."

She was framed in the light. It came through the small-paned windows, blurring the edges of the copper curls, the expressive face, restless body. The sea outside was indistinct. Kate moved nervously out of the light, looked around her helplessly at Old Sven's possessions.

I tried not to look at her. She was dressed in cream and beige. No makeup. A sprinkle of powder, not enough to cover the freckles. There were faint lines that had not been there the last time I looked. They turned up around the corners of her mouth, at the edges of her eyes. She was still beautiful.

Suddenly she laughed. It sprang up out of her, unexpected. It reminded me of other days when I had looked for it, waited for the odd, frequently inappropriate outburst that, in less than a minute, changed the world.

"He had some gall! Matchmaker to the last! And do you know the old bastard propositioned me? Right here. In this very room."

I had a sudden vision of her as she had been twenty years before, sprawled across my bedspread, the soft copper hair, crown and triangle, highlighting her nakedness. She was all of one piece, my Kate, a blending of color and movement and sensation so that you could not simply make love to a part of her but must take everything else with it—the body, soft, lithe, charged with fire, electric to the touch; the lovely extension of the mind that turned and honed and burned within. And the words. They washed over us in waves, defining, recreating us. If someone were to ask what I longed for most in the long cold nights since then, the taste of her body or the sound of her voice, I would be unable to choose.

"Randy old bastard," I said. "At least he had taste."

Her eyes welled with tears.

"Thank you for that."

She sighed, ran her finger over the window seat, picked up a cushion, tossed it back. Already cobwebs were gathering in the corners of the glass panes and tiny gossamer-legged spiders were settling in for the winter.

"You take the front house. I'll stay where I am. We'll stay until the taxes eat up everything we have and then we'll sell. Split it in half."

"It's not honest." It was, I suspected, the real cause of her anger. "He meant us to live together. I suspect he had visions of the two of us bouncing around on that bed of his." She colored suddenly. The blush started at her neck and spread upward until, under the freckles, she was pink as a peony.

I pretended not to notice.

"It made him happy. He'll never know."

She moved away from the window. The white glare of the sand filtered through the glass, washing most of the color from the room.

"He never understood about us." She seemed almost wistful.

"Well, he was an old man. I don't think politics or

ideas or intellectual commitment meant anything to him. He could never see why we couldn't just coexist."

"It wasn't just that."

"I know."

"It was something more basic. I'm not sure it means as much to me now as it did then."

I couldn't even remember what our final quarrel had been about. It had been loud and terrible and hurtful and we had said things to each other that could never be taken back, so that when we looked at each other they stood between us. Thrown up like defensive shields. She accused me of being distant, cold. Ideas, she said, meant more to me than people. I said she was a hack artist, that she did not take her work seriously enough. It sounded rather tame now, but then it had seemed an insurmountable difference between us.

We had lived together for a few more weeks. Silent. Each wrapped in his own hurt so that we never touched in passing. Drawing apart. The ties that bound us unwinding, separating into individual spools.

After a while she had moved out and I had not tried to stop her. We remained friends, and after a year or so some kind of bond reestablished itself. We depended on each other in a crisis. Probably, not counting the sudden flare-ups of passion that came to the one or other of us from time to time for someone else, a passing flame, we loved each other more than any other single person. I still, on occasion, wept for her.

Kate went upstairs. I could hear her moving about in the bedrooms, straightening the beds, pushing the drawers back in, throwing old medicines into the wastebaskets. She sang to herself. It was almost imperceptible, a humming under her breath. But the pitch was true and clear and I wondered why I had ever let it get away from me.

The watercolor over the fireplace was hers. It was a wash of the bay and the fog and Sven's fishing boat, the *Anna Louise*, coming in from the jetty. She had painted it in about twenty-five minutes while I sat beside her criticizing. It was the boat I had objected to and the reason Sven had loved it. The painting was better than I remembered it. Everything was.

K ate moved in over the weekend. Already her little band of pilgrims were hard at work throughout the house. The staple brigade had set up shop upstairs in the guest bedroom. The newsletter paste-up was taking place in the kitchen. Out in the yard two old men, with a portable TV between them, were stuffing letters into envelopes and guffawing their way through the UCLA-Stanford game.

Kate was waiting for me at the foot of the stairs when I came down to put the trash out. She apologized for the commotion. I grinned back at her. Chaos surrounded Kate like a halo. I wasn't complaining.

She handed me a typewritten sheet.

"This is a letter to the *Times*. Would you look it over? Spelling errors. Grammar. Polish it up for me?"

I gave her a peck on the cheek and then, just so she'd remember how it used to be, kissed her square on the mouth.

The two old men looked up from the game and poked each other in the ribs in delight.

Kate turned away quickly. A becoming blush suffused the back of her neck and rose up around her ears. I glared at the men. They harrumphed and chortled and went back to stuffing envelopes.

They went home about dusk. By ten o'clock I finished correcting essays and started working on my class notes. I stood for a few minutes out on the balcony and then went down into the yard. October. The air was thick and soft. A hundred yards across the sand the waves were breaking against the beach. Not hard. Just big enough to let you know they were there. I could see Kate in Sven's kitchen. She was moving back and forth between the sink and the cupboard, the red hair tumbling, copper curls under the kitchen light. I was tempted to go in but instead I walked along the side of the house to the sidewalk that emptied onto the sand. The lights of the pier went out into the water, way up the beach. The reflections moved lazily in the swells that passed beneath it. Clustered around the pier was the fun zone—the theater, a few bars. The long stretch of beach between the pier and the end of the peninsula was dark. A string of houses sat far back from the beach. Most of the inhabitants had already gone to sleep. I waited until Kate had put the porch light out. Behind me I heard the lock turn in the front door, water running in the upstairs bath.

The unmistakable smell of beach town came across the night; the dampness of wood, iron corroding, cement and sand that never quite dries out, the taste of salt. The air was soft. A wave broke against the beach, paused and then slid back down the sand.

I walked out across the dunes to the edge of the beach and down along the tide line to the jetty. It stuck up out of the dark like the elongated spine of a whale. I climbed out to the end. There was just enough light reflected from the glare of cities up and down the coast to see the cracks between the chunks of granite. In the dark spaces below the rocks, the sea growled and gurgled and then fell silent.

It never occurred to me to look behind me. I had climbed out onto the jetty hundreds of times over the years. Run out to the light at the end and stood there, face into the wind, triumphant after my first day of teaching; dived off the end of it into the sea time after time, exulting in my love for Kate, not believing in my luck; sat alone, in the dark, making plans; crouched through the long nights coming to grips with the fact that I had lost her.

Tonight I stood on the farthest rock. Swells rose out of the dark, passed over my feet, swept behind me toward the beach. I didn't hear Sylvus until he was nearly to the end of the jetty. I turned and saw him, a bulky dark silhouette between the rocks. Even then I didn't realize who it was until I smelled the beer on his breath, felt the sharp metal of the shotgun as it knocked me over, saw the pasty-white face illumined with hatred. He was panting from the exertion. He could have shot me then but he paused to catch his breath.

I shouted for help. It was a waste of breath. The shout bounced off the water and was swallowed up in the hiss and slap of the sea. I grabbed the barrel of the gun and it went off, taking a chunk of my side with it. The pain was sharp and terrible. We grappled for the gun, the two of us slipping and sliding on the rocks in the gull shit and the blood that was pouring out of my side. I caught my foot between two of the rocks, felt it jam into the crevice and wedge tight. Sylvus thought he had me then. "Cocksucker," he said.

We held the gun between us. The muzzle was pointed at my chest. Sylvus clawed at the handle to get to the trigger and fired again.

I shot him. Or else he shot himself. The gun went off. It careened upward into his face and he went down on the rocks whining and crying and then finally silent. I heard the tide lapping against the rocks and the peaceful echo inside the jetty as the water flowed in beneath the two of us and out again. After that I lost consciousness.

A Vietnamese fisherman and his son found us sometime before dawn. They set their bucket and pole down on the end of the jetty and then discovered the two darker shapes against the rocks. They thought we were seals sleeping it off. The kid came close and took a poke with the toe of his shoe and went yelping back to his father. The older man jabbered at the boy and sent him back along the jetty to summon help. He squatted down about fifteen feet from us and watched, expressionless, until the harbor patrol arrived and the police helicopter was circling overhead.

The police took my story. Dr. Tingler took me down to a cubicle in the emergency room. He poured about a gallon of antiseptic into my side and did a lot of fancy stitching, which hurt like hell. Someone gave me a couple of aspirin. Kate took me home.

Kate put me to bed in Sven's room. She paid no

attention to my protests, plumped the pillows, cooked steaming bowls of Irish stew and soda bread, changed my dressing twice a day. She set her easel up by the window where she could keep me company.

The house was full of people at all hours of the day and into the night. I heard them in the yard and on the stairs, whispering in the corridor outside my room. The phone rang, was picked up, set down again. I heard the clack of typewriters. The sharp smack of stapler. Shrieks of laughter cut short. The hiss and slide of paper.

Kate came and went through it all. Clear-eyed. The lovely face. Hands smoothing and comforting. A detached smile. The watercolor was a delicate rendering of the dunes in front of Sven's house and the thin line of sea beyond, all of it framed by the second-story window. It had the look of paradise, out of reach, only vaguely remembered.

The puppy, feeling abandoned, learned to climb the stairs. In the middle of the night I heard the reluctant thump-thumping of the small body as he leapt from stair to stair and then the triumphant scratch of paws against the sheets. Kate padded barefoot into the room. Scooped the puppy up against the ghost white of her nightdress, cautioning him to silence, tiptoed out again.

She tore up the watercolor. Started a new one. Propped against the bolster and a mound of pillows against the old walnut bedstead, I watched her, lips pursed, eyes focused on neither the canvas nor the scene outside, but some inner vision. The hands moved swiftly, purposefully, like messengers. The real beauty lay in Kate. The intake of breath. The movements. The infinitely varied mind making choices. Laughing. Questioning. Impatient with the attempt at the impossible: capturing life. A sea gull flew past the window. I saw the shadow first, flitting over the easel, and then the white streak against the sea.

She caught me watching her. Smiled. Laid down her brush and then, undecided, took it up again.

The following Monday I was indicted for murder. Sheila, before she went into shock and had to be temporarily admitted to a hospital, told the police that I had called Sylvus the evening he was killed and lured him out to the end of the jetty with the promise of some kind of payoff. She didn't say what the payoff was for but the implication was clear. Sylvus had known something which could put me behind bars and I had killed him to keep him from talking.

A night watchman on one of the dredging barges came in to the police station to report that I had been in the boat with Sven on the night of October 3 when Sven rowed up the back bay to his death. The man's name was Gifford. He said the little skiff had come too close to the mooring and he had turned the spotlight on the two of us just for an instant until he saw that it was just harmless Old Sven. It had slipped Gifford's memory until he saw my face staring out of the morning paper in connection with Sylvus' death. It was me, all right, he said. No doubt about it. I had come back alone, about an hour later, on a paddleboard which I must have hidden earlier in the day, somewhere in the reeds. The police found the paddleboard in the garage and took it away.

It was flimsy evidence but Thurber said that technically the D.A. could indict someone as long as he believed there was enough evidence to convict in a court of law. It was a judgment call. Thurber thought the D.A. must be responding to pressure from somewhere in the city. Neither of us could figure out who it was or why they were after me.

The police put me in a lineup. I was the only one with my arm in a sling and Gifford pointed me out without a moment's hesitation. The police booked me carefully and with a precision that was chilling. I spent the night in a steel-and-cement cage. In the morning Thurber put up bail and got me out. He promised that I would not leave the country.

The principal of White's Bay High School was on the phone by 6 A.M. the next day to inform me that I had been suspended from all duties. He hoped I would understand. A teacher under suspicion of murder was not allowed in the classroom. Rosenberg, the man who would take over my classes, would come by to discuss lesson plans with me later in the week. The school board demanded my assurance that I would not attempt to enter the school premises. I told him to go to hell and slammed down the phone.

"You're going to need a lawyer." Thurber's voice was grave over the phone.

"I thought you'd defend me."

There was a deep sigh. It was aimed, I supposed, at

my ignorance. "I'm not a trial lawyer, Chandler. I write arguments. I find the sticklers in the law. I'll do everything I can, but swaying juries is an art form. I'm not an actor. You're going to need the best there is."

"How much will it cost?"

He paused.

"Everything you've got."

"What do you want, Cairns?" After refusing several calls, Lawrence had finally condescended to speak with me. "I haven't got all day."

"You've got the wrong man."

"Cairns," Lawrence's voice took on the hardness of a steel drill. "You're as guilty as hell. I thought so from the first hour after we found the body. The guilt stood out on you like a goddamn spotlight."

"You're wrong."

"Prove it." He hung up on me.

McIan refused to take my call. A few minutes later the phone rang.

"Don't you dare call me again, Cairns." The voice was edged with dislike. It came over the phone like a charged wire.

"The boy knows nothing that will save you. If you

think you can save your ass by burning his, you're even stupider than I thought."

I started to protest. His words drove right over me.

"The boy is off limits. Anyone who hurts him will answer to me. Got that, schoolteacher?"

The phone went dead.

Sheila answered the door and tried to shut it in my face when she saw who it was. Her face was chalk-white. She was still in her dressing gown. Her hair had not been combed. The face, staring out at me through the slit between the door and its frame, was indecisive and scared.

"Go away. I'll call the police."

"Why did you tell the cops I had killed Old Sven?"

"It's true. Sylvus saw you."

"You're lying, Sheila."

"Go away. The cops said you'd come. I don't have to talk to you." The pale pasty face quivered and then the door shut in my face. Behind me a patrol car came slowly down the street and pulled up behind mine.

"You Cairns?" The cop who got out was someone I had never seen before. "You're not allowed to bother a witness." He jerked his thumb in the direction of the street.

"Get moving or I take you in."

Hank Gifford was a lousy night watchman. I had to yell half a dozen times into the dark before he appeared, grumbling, half asleep, and peered down over the edge of the barge at me.

My skiff was in the shadow of the barge. A huge crane thrust, black and ugly, up into the sky like the neck of a dinosaur stuck in a tar pit. Gifford fired up a spotlight and turned it in my direction.

"Can I come aboard? I want to talk to you."

It took him a minute to figure out who I was and when he did he pulled a gun out of his belt and pointed it in my direction. The big bulky body swayed against the sky. His voice, when it came, was slow and his words were slurred.

"Get away from the barge. This here's private property."

"I want to know why you lied to the cops, told them you saw me with Svennson when you didn't."

"It was you."

"Maybe you were mistaken. What was I wearing?"

"Same thing you're wearing now. Now get out of here. And I mean right now." He bent down and picked an empty bottle up off the deck and heaved it in my direction. It was a pretty good shot for a man who had been drinking. It hit the prow of the skiff and exploded into a hundred sharp pieces. Gifford leaned down to pick up another one.

I backed the skiff away from the barge and rowed back into the safety of the bay. The spotlight followed me all the way across the water until I had rounded Bay Island and I couldn't see it anymore.

Somebody fed my name into a computer and it spit out every bill I owed and some I didn't. They started coming in the mail at the rate of three a day. My VISA card was revoked. My automobile insurance had to be paid in full by Friday or it would be canceled. The county informed me that they were holding up transferring the deed of title for Sven's house until after the outcome of the trial. Even the home in Pasadena suddenly found it necessary to raise the monthly fee for my mother, effective immediately.

I emptied the savings account and started digging into my retirement.

Ms. Trueblood took this auspicious moment to renew her client's offer for the house. I caught her trying to badger Kate into signing over her half of the estate. The two of them were together in the kitchen circling each other like polecats. The enmity in the air was thick enough to smell.

They were a study in contrasts. Kate stood, her back to the sink, holding two earthenware mugs out in front of her, full of steaming hot coffee. She looked as if she was getting ready to throw one of them at the cool, self-possessed young woman in her kitchen. Kate's slacks were worn. The bulky gray sweatshirt had American Field Service written across the front of it. A smudge of blue paint shone on her cheek where she had rubbed it with her forearm. The copper hair was pulled back with a rubber band to keep it out of her eyes.

Ms. Trueblood, on the other hand, ten years younger, perfection itself, sat forward in the chair, in the cream-colored suit with the beige silk blouse and the bow at the neck. A nylon-encased, Gucci-shod foot moved impatiently against the leg of the table. She tapped her little gold pencil on the oilcloth, coolly imposing control.

"Ah, Mr. Cairns. Your friend has taken offense at my client's offer."

I raised an eyebrow in Kate's direction. She was flushed and angry.

"He wants Duck Island."

I laughed out loud.

"It's all or nothing. The house and the lot with the island thrown in. But it's the island he wants."

Ms. Trueblood stood up, teetering ever so slightly on the immaculate soft leather heels, and walked over to where I stood in the doorway. I could smell the perfume. Not too much. Just right. She reached up to slip the little engraved card into the pocket of my shirt. The perfectly manicured nails lingered a moment longer than necessary against my chest.

The smile was brittle, expensive, promising. She was every upscale investment banker's dream. A girl to match the bevel-edged door, the walnut-stained coffee table in a house where everything still bore the price tag. She thought she was the cat's meow. All packaged and deodorized. She didn't stand a chance against the real thing: Kate. That thinking, feeling, paint-smudged person leaning against the sink.

I told Ms. Trueblood I would think about the offer and showed her out.

Thurber gave me the names of a couple of lawyers he said were good solid defense attorneys. I made a few tentative calls and gave up in despair when I calculated that even if I was acquitted I would have lost everything defending myself and probably be in debt for the rest of my life. I sat around the house moping like a two-year-old until Kate got me busy proofreading and editing the newsletter they were going to distribute citywide.

After a while I got interested in it. At least it kept my mind off more immediate problems. Most of it was an attempt to awaken the citizens of the town to the fact that someone (their best guess was that it was an outsider or someone new to the area) was attempting to buy their city. For thirty years no one had paid much attention to the city council members. We had elected, time after time, eccentric old guys, retired, who wanted a forum to gas off about their pet peeves. A few reformers. Well-intentioned. They were nice people and the city ran just fine. No one took them very seriously, least of all the city council members themselves. The town still had a sense of humor then. They got a couple of dollars for showing up at the council meetings once a month and pondering on the problems of dog ordinances and cracks in the sidewalks, and were given a spaghetti dinner once a year. It didn't much matter who was mayor. Life went on the same. The tides came in and out and the teenagers blew in for Easter week and blew out again.

And then one morning the sandspits on which we all

lived were as valuable as if there were oil underneath. Suddenly the city council was the arbiter of fortunes. The power was unimaginable. Zoning laws made millions for developers or took them away. Building permits were worth pure gold. Perhaps the single most powerful man in the city was the planning commissioner, who was appointed by the mayor. Whoever owned him, owned the town. You couldn't get away with it in LA, where there were hundreds of different interest groups all watching each other and the city council. But the little town was still small enough to be bought. Ripe for the pickings. A million dollars had been spent on electing the four rather nondescript city councilmen whom no one could remember having heard of before. Kate was sure that the four photogenic, bland young men had been shoehorned into office for the single purpose of rezoning the city for the men who had put them there. It was these four men who were the target of the recall election.

Most of the old-timers, who had the most to lose, walked blissfully along the beach, unaware, or forgot to vote altogether, while steadily but surely the developers closed in an ever-narrowing circle around them.

I changed a few words around, gave the leads a little more punch, and took them off to the printer.

Rosenberg finally came by the apartment to collect the syllabus and materials for the second quarter, which had started on the day I had been relieved of my job. He was embarrassed and apologetic about taking my place and looked about as happy as though he had been dragged in to be witness to an unseemly death. I gave him the pile of Meditations which I had corrected and my notes on *Portrait of the Artist as a Young Man*. We went over the syllabus quickly. Rosenberg was too nervous to concentrate but I knew he was a good teacher and that he would do his best for the students.

After he left I took a long walk on the beach. I wondered how long it would be before I stopped calculating my life not by a calendar but by my class schedule. Wondered if I'd ever again meet another student like David.

He'd been sitting on my steps one afternoon during the summer when I'd returned from a swim. I had assigned all of the students who'd applied for AP English a book to read before they came to class in September. This year the book was *Heart of Darkness*. David wanted to talk to me about it. He had read it in one long evening. It had been for the boy, unsettling, a journey back into the far reaches of a man's soul, into evil, and he wanted help in making sense of it. We had wrestled over the theme of the book like fledgling contestants in a ring. When he left I gave him the *Trial of the Catonsville Nine* to take home and then, when he returned again, *Antigone* and *The Plague*. It had been an exciting time for me. We challenged each other. The thing the boy was grappling with was something greater than conscience. The question we seemed to return to over and over again was the degree to which a man is personally responsible to his society and what kind of moral commitment is required of him.

It was during this time that David got to know Sven. What possible connection did that accident of friendship, so innocuous and gentle, have to do with all the events that followed?

By the following Monday I was getting restless. Kate was putting in some time at the studio on Old Heights Road where she ran a gallery. Thurber had taken the phone off the hook. Even the dog had lost interest in me. He ran halfheartedly behind the ball when I tossed it across the grass, gave it a sniff, and went to lie down on the kitchen stoop to wait for Kate.

I made an appointment with Tingler. He took the stitches out of my side and told me I was as good as new. I sure as hell didn't feel like it. I drove up to the high school and parked across the street like some love-struck kid and watched the students passing from Nutrition to third period. It was at that moment that it hit me that the worst could happen. That I might never again stride into the classroom, throw my books down on the desk and challenge a dozen uninterested faces to think about something more difficult than a TV sitcom. Never again shake some silly teenage girl by the scruff of her metaphorical neck and pitch her headlong into a world where ideas matter and intelligence gives life its edge.

It was the one thing I was good at. I could not imagine a world in which I did not wake up each morning with a sense of anticipation for the fight ahead of me. I loved the challenge. The excitement when synapse and word took flight. The spark igniting behind glazed eyes. Even, in some elemental way, I loved the kids. Being a teacher, a goddamn Advanced Placement English teacher in a high school for a bunch of snotty, spoiled, potentially interesting kids, was the only thing I wanted to do.

I'd be damned if I was just going to sit on my ass and let them take it all away from me. The cops had stopped looking for Sven's killer. I felt silly as hell playing detective but it looked like no one else was going to do it for me.

I put the car in gear and headed back to the beach.

Either the tides were getting higher every year, or the island was sinking. I got the last ferry over to the island before the water started pouring over the ramp and the fire department arrived with sandbags to stop it.

Davidson was out in front of his house trying to plug up the holes in the sea wall. The bay was coming in through the seams, a tiny gushing stream, about a teaspoonful at a time. The sidewalk was already six inches deep in water. Davidson was barefoot, pants rolled up around his old man's pale white legs, trying to stick roofing tar into the cracks.

"Hold this." He handed me the bucket of tar. I held it out of the water while he stuck a paint stirrer in the goop and smeared it down the seam between the two sections of sea wall. It held for a minute and then gave way. The two of us watched the bubble forming, swelling until it burst. The stream of water seemed larger than before.

"Dammit!" Davidson jabbed the stick back into the bucket, smeared another gob of tar over the hole and held the stick against it for support.

You wouldn't guess to look at him that Ernie Davidson, ruddy-faced, white-haired, feisty as hell, was worth about twenty million dollars. Davidson was a fixture on the island. Old breed of developer. McIan was right. He was more construction chief than businessman. He still lived in the same old two-story gray-shingled house with the deep front porch he'd built sixty years ago for his family. It sat on the curve of the island across from the Pavilion. A eucalyptus tree, about sixty years old, leaned over the roof. The roots buckled the sidewalk, and he and the city were in a constant battle about cutting it down. While all the other bay-front houses had been remodeled, turned into let's-pretend town houses, he alone still lived with ancient plumbing and a boat stored under the front steps. Lived frugally. Did his own gardening. Took his "constitutional" around the island before breakfast and again after dinner. Knew everybody. Nodded a perfunctory greeting to the island regulars. Touched his hat in a rather touching old-fashioned mark of respect to the female members of his generation. Noticed everything. Called the city about every leaky faucet, every dog without a leash, every errant skateboarder. Grumbled and carped at the influx of tourists and the change of the island from beach town to status symbol.

"I'm Jim Cairns."

He glared at me. "I know who you are."

I suppose he still blamed me for Old Sven's funeral. Maybe he actually thought I had killed him.

"I came to ask if you saw Sven the night he died."

Davidson motioned to me to bring the bucket of tar closer. We watched the bubble forming again, the water breaking through in a thin, cheerful trickle. He slapped another gob of tar over the hole.

"That last night. In the dark. On his way up the

110

bay, he must have come by here, past the buoy out there. Maybe even stopped by to get you to go with him."

Davidson turned his cold blue eyes on me. It was easy to see he'd been good-looking in his youth. Still was. Rugged. Well-built. Sensitive. Probably grew up trying to overcome the sensitivity, a fault to be ashamed of, hidden away. He was part of that generation of Californians that the hordes of yuppies pouring into Orange County had replaced. The old aristocracy with its own set of rules. Wealth carefully understated. Shunning publicity. Competitive as hell but civil about it. Played by the rules on the tennis court and in the boardrooms. Protective of family. Loyal to friends. Thought it was important that a man wear white on the courts and that his children practice good sportsmanship.

"I go to bed every night at ten. Wouldn't have seen him even if he did come."

The Catalina Ferry passed down the bay in front of us. A long wave in its wake slid up over the wall and gushed down onto the walk. Debris from the estuary and the inland gutters pressed up against the wall and caught in great ugly piles under the docks. Davidson's sailboat, a beautiful vintage thing with spruce mast and teak deck, rose and fell as the wave washed over the dock.

"There was a stash of cocaine squirreled away under his sink."

That got his attention. He looked up sharply. Unbelieving. The salt water was flowing over into the small garden now. Earthworms wriggled up out of the grass and floated out over the sidewalk. Davidson waded back to the house, found a rag in the boathouse and tried to stuff it into the hole.

111

"Sven was crazy. Peculiar. Stubborn as hell. It's the Norwegian blood in him."

"I thought he was from Sweden."

"Nope. Little island between Alesund and Bergen. Peculiar. But not that crazy. Course I haven't talked to him in a long time."

"How long?"

"Twenty years, maybe more."

"How come?"

The ferry moved out from the dock into the middle of the channel and just sat there. Across the bay the water had flowed over the embankment and flooded the fun zone. The Ferris wheel stood like an island in a pond. A city truck moved in to pump the water out of the video-games arcade.

"I thought you were friends."

Davidson shrugged. "We had an argument. Sven took it harder than I did."

"I suppose it was over money."

He nodded. "It was. Sven loaned me about five thousand dollars. That was just after the war. Lots of soldiers stationed out here at the Fairgrounds were going home. Back to their families in Ohio and New Jersey and Minnesota and Kansas. But they'd got spoiled. Liked the climate. The slow, easy way of life. So they came back. California was friendly then. Like Sven. We were all more or less like that. It was a matter of pride to Californians. Give you the shirt off his back, Sven would. Invite you into his home. When you came back after the war, with the wife and the kids, he helped you move in. Brought you dinner your first night there. Generous. Neighbors helping neighbors. Everybody welcome. Help yourself. Thought there was enough land for everybody. Hah! And that was just the beginning. Never thought there'd be more of them than there was of us—"

Davidson jabbed viciously at the wall with the stick. The water continued to flow through. If the wall broke, just a foot or two, the whole bay would pour through and flood the island. Five, ten minutes, and fifteen hundred homes would be standing in salt water.

"Well, right off they needed housing. I had the land but no cash to build the houses. But Sven, he had some stashed away. Pretty canny old guy. Course he wasn't old then. Asked him to loan me some money to get started. He didn't want to do it. I put up some property for collateral. Pushed him into it. Built the first development and made a pile. Every home sold out within a week."

"What was the collateral?"

He scooped up a gob of tar, stuck it back in the hole. Answered reluctantly. "Duck Island."

"What happened to Sven's money?"

"He wanted it back. I kept it. Plowed it into the next tract. Bought more land in Costa Mesa. Up behind the Heights."

"So you screwed him."

Davidson didn't answer. The tide had risen another quarter of an inch. Another seam had broken open and another trickle of water was bubbling down the wall. Some of it was disappearing into a crack in the sidewalk.

"You made millions and Sven got nothing."

A couple of joggers came around the north end of the island and stopped at the edge of the growing pool of water. They were breathing hard. Clad in matching pink Dior sweatsuits and Reeboks. Davidson looked up. They passed by without speaking. They jogged along the top of the wall—young, healthy, full of themselves—and passed out of sight.

Davidson scowled. "We didn't speak for twenty

years. Don't blame him really. Just once. I offered to buy it back from him a few years ago. Offered him the accumulated interest. He refused." He worked for a moment in silence, then: "Why did you think I might have seen Sven?"

"Your grandson knows something."

Davidson froze. His hands stopped moving.

"He wrote an essay. It was as though he were there when Sven died. His father took him out of my class."

Bitterness crept into the old man's face.

"Bastard!"

The enmity between Davidson and his son-in-law was legendary. No one blamed the old man. McIan had taken his daughter and her percentage of the company. Forced the old man out.

"Tide peaks in fifteen minutes." Davidson took up a bucket and tried bailing water off the grass. As soon as a bucketful was gone it was replaced with another from the bay.

"Used to be quiet here at night. Bay so still you could hear the waves breaking way out at the end of the peninsula. And in the winter you could hear the rain coming before it got here, hear the squall hit the docks, one by one, all the way up along the sea wall from the lower end until it got here. Now all you hear is radios and charter boats chugging up and down and people getting drunk and shouting at each other. And the cars. All night the cars going past on the highway. Engines racing up Jamboree. They're the ones who killed Sven."

For a moment I was confused and then I realized he meant all the new people, the ones who grew up in cities and couldn't live without them and who had brought the noise and the smog along with them.

"You know what I mind most?" Davidson turned and looked at me. His eyes were bleak, an old man's eyes.

114

He gestured across the bay at the fancy shops, the designer houses, the row on row of expensive yachts. "The honesty of the place is gone."

I didn't ask him what he meant. I guess in a way I knew. He took the can of tar from me and set it on the top of the wall. I left him there to plug up the holes, battling old age and the crumbling sea wall and the bay leaking in, bit by bit, threatening to deluge the island and the old man and an entire way of life.

Erik Svennson was between charters. He was aboard the *Flyaway*, hosing down the deck, when I finally caught up with him. It was a sailboat, a sixty-footer, shiny and white, all the lines coiled in the right direction. Not a scratch on it. Erik saw me coming and moved onto the other side of the cabin. I had to call twice to get his attention. He crimped the hose in his hand to shut off the flow and came to see what I wanted.

He reminded me of Sven. Lots of blond hair. Blue eyes. The aquiline nose. A kind of Scandinavian cast to him. The same lean bony structure. But Erik was taller. Easygoing, where Sven was not, restless. Took the easy way out. According to Sven, Erik had no other ambition than to do what he was doing: crewing on someone else's boat. Bedding the ladies.

He smiled lazily. A shy, disarming smile. Swished a pile of water off the deck into the bay with one of his bare feet. The slacks, clean white, were rolled up around his ankles, his shirt open at the neck. His skin was gold, evenly tanned. A kind of Viking god except that there didn't seem to be any harm to him.

"Can I buy you a drink?"

"Sure. Why not?"

We found a table on the dock where Erik could keep an eye on the boat. The charter companies and yacht brokers occupied most of the offices on the boardwalk behind us. Tied up at our feet were the yachts for sale, about a hundred million dollars' worth of fiberglass and stainless steel, bumper to bumper in the water. Beyond that, the turning basin flowed between the mainland and Harbor Isle. It was almost noon. In the absence of a sea breeze, the smog had seeped down the riverbed from LA and lay over the water in a blood-tinged haze.

"I suppose you've heard I'm under indictment for killing Sven?"

Erik shrugged as though it were a matter of indifference to him. Or perhaps he just wanted me to know he didn't hold it against me.

"Did you?" He spoke casually, a question of form rather than curiosity.

"What?"

"Kill my old man."

"No. Of course not."

"Well, it doesn't make much difference now, does it? Who killed him, I mean."

"I think it makes a hell of a lot of difference." It was a mistake to get angry. He looked at me curiously.

"He was a good father. I can't complain. Always on me about something or other. Finish school. Get a job. Find a nice wife. Settle down. Wanted me to get ahead. Talked my ear off about saving for the future. But he didn't interfere. Always came through when I needed something. You couldn't dislike him. Nobody did."

"When was the last time you saw him?"

Erik smiled blandly. "July, maybe. August."

116

"I thought he talked to you the week before he died."

"No. I was away the whole month of September. Took a party down to Puerto Vallarta. One of these yuppie couples." He grinned.

He was lying. Sven had waylaid me in the alley when I came home from school the last week in September and started in about his son. How he'd just been to see him. Found him on the *Flyaway* having a party with three girls in the middle of the afternoon. It was the laziness that bothered Sven, not the girls. He was hot as a bantam cock. He'd found a boat for sale. Checked it out. Offered to put a down payment on it for the boy. Erik refused. Said he didn't want to run his own charter. It was too much work. He liked what he did. "Irresponsible!" The old man had shaken his fist at me and repeated the word until, in self-defense, I had agreed. Sven had followed me up the stairs to my apartment, clucking and shaking his head. Yapped on while I made rude noises about having a lot of work to do. Finally left. Talked himself into going back to the *Flyaway*. Making the offer again. Pointing out to the boy the advantages. I told him it was a good idea. Practically shoved him out the door. Heard him get the old Chevy sedan out of the garage and go battling down the peninsula. Next day, in a moment of aberration, I'd asked the old man what had happened. He'd been strangely subdued. Said the boy turned him down a second time. Never mentioned it again.

The waitress brought our drinks. She was young and healthy, one of the sprightly army of college students who manned the restaurants when they weren't busy lying out in the sun studying for exams in econ or engineering. She had on a sailor outfit, cut low on top and nothing but legs underneath. She stood a lit-

117

tle closer to Erik than was absolutely necessary, leaned over his shoulder to set the drinks on the table. He gave her a long lazy smile that intimated something more to come later.

"Skoal!" Erik threw his head back and lifted his glass against the sunshine. I was caught off-guard. For an instant Sven came back to life. There was the same lift of the chin, the tongue curled sharply around the Scandinavian word. The clear eyes. The same good humor. Then, just as quickly, the old man vanished into the boats and the haze of the turning basin and only the kid was left.

"I understood Sven had his eye on a boat for you. Offered to put the down payment on it."

"Oh, that." The boy waved it off. He lied as easily as he smiled. "That was last summer. Middle of August. I forget just when. I should have taken it. At least I could have sold it. Gotten the money back out of it."

I watched the boy over the rim of my glass. I wondered what harm it would have done to admit he'd seen Sven the week before he died, talked with him. Fathers and sons did meet on occasion. It was not grounds for murder. Unless, of course, he was the one who had killed Old Sven.

"Sven had about a million dollars' worth of cocaine in a drawer under the kitchen sink."

Erik's eyes remained clear and blue. There was not a hint of surprise anywhere in his face.

"Doesn't that shock you?"

"Not particularly." He shrugged. "Everybody else is into drugs. No reason the old man shouldn't be too."

"What do you mean, 'everybody'?"

He saw that it would have been wiser to have pretended to be shocked. But it was too late now. He waved his hand out toward the boats, the glare of the water.

"Cocaine flows in and out of this harbor like sand."

"I don't believe you." I was the one who bicycled to school, crossed the ferry every morning at seven, walked around the island at night, swam in the bay, ran along the beach. I saw it the same way I'd experienced it as a kid when I slept in the bunk room on Collins for two weeks every summer and thought I was in heaven.

Erik was amused. He'd grown up here. Didn't see the bay through nostalgic eyes. He'd changed with it. Liked it the way it was.

"You're behind the times, Cairns. Southern California is the market, and White's Bay is *the* place to be. All that money just floating around. Yuppies with wads of it sticking out of their Gucci wallets. Who notices another million? Nobody asks where they got it. As long as they wear a coat and tie and buy their shirts at Nordstrom's."

I looked out across the turning basin. It looked as calm and indolent as the backwater town that had once existed beside it.

"How does it work?"

"Oh . . ." His voice trailed off. He shrugged as though the subject wasn't worth talking about. I bent across the table toward him.

"I want to know. I want to find out about Sven."

Erik leaned back in his chair. He was as at home in this world as though it had been created expressly for him. He was charming. Friendly. He reminded me of the pup waiting for me in Sven's yard.

"Well," he smiled benignly. I suppose he decided it would do me no harm to know the facts. "It comes up from Colombia, Peru, Mexico. On fishing trawlers. They stay way out in international waters. It's safer there. The other side of Catalina. San Nicolas. San Clemente. Down Baja way. Mr. White's Bay, lately of

119

Cleveland or Buffalo or Denver, gets on his beautiful new yacht and goes over to Avalon for the weekend. Sets his pals and the girls ashore for dinner and takes a run out to one of the islands or the other side of the isthmus. Comes up alongside the trawler and makes the transfer. It's usually pure. A million dollars' street value. It fits inside a cardboard carton. He goes back to Avalon and parties until Sunday afternoon, when he comes home, in through the channel with a couple of hundred other boats. The weekend's over. Everybody's tired. The Harbor Patrol doesn't stop them. Why should they? Customs can't sit out there at the end of the jetty and check every boat that comes in. It's easy as rolling out of bed."

I didn't ask him how he knew the routine but he knew what I was thinking. It seemed to amuse him. I suppose he thought I was as naive as his old man had been.

I showed him the photo I'd taken in Catalina. It was the one of the boy with his arm flung across his face. Erik glanced at it, pushed it back across the table.

"Where'd you get that?"

But I wasn't going to tell him. Suddenly Erik got a vague look in his handsome face. It had something to do with fear. His eyes shifted uneasily from the picture to the line of boats rocking back and forth in the smog. He pushed his chair back and stood up. Said he had to get back to the boat. He thanked me for the drink.

I watched him lope back down the gangway and along the floating dock to the *Flyaway*, blond hair shining in the light, as graceful and fair as Sven must have been one day when he was young and the world was still ahead of him.

I called Pacific Charters from a pay phone on the dock. I said I was mad as hell at the captain of one of their boats who'd stolen my mooring from me. It happened on the morning of September 28 in Puerta Vallarta. The name of the boat was the *Flyaway*. I wanted to know what they were going to do about it.

It took about three minutes for the sales agent to check the charter schedule and inform me, with unconcealed contempt, that the *Flyaway* had not been near Puerto Vallarta that month. On that particular day it had arrived in White's Bay from a trip to Ensenada and remained here until the following Wednesday.

I said I was sorry to have made a mistake and hung up before he got around to asking who the hell I was.

The boy is out there, on the edge of my life, circling, out of reach, moving closer. I see him nearly every day. He is on the opposite ferry when I make the crossing to the island in the morning. We pass each other, fifty feet across the water. He sits with his back to me, ramrod-straight, as though he does not notice me. His bicycle is chained next to mine when I come out of the market. I see him walk down the beach several times a day. He glances toward the house and then away. Today he walked past without looking in my direction. I bicycle down the alley to the wedge. I am waiting for him when he gets there.

David scowls when he sees me. Pretends he is watching the surfers.

The waves are breaking from the west today. They strike the end of the jetty and roll in toward the beach, squeezed by the triangle of rocks and sand into twelve-foot waves. One by one they build into a mountain of water, tower over the beach and then fall, tons upon tons of water, hard and clear as glass. Half a dozen surfers paddle out, tumble down the face of it, recover, paddle out again.

David tries to look me in the eye and fails.

"I've been indicted for the murder of Sven."

"I know."

He shrugs. Pretends indifference. His lips tremble. I would like to ruffle the boy's hair. Give him a bear hug. Tell him that it is all right. That I hold nothing against him. But he is too old for hugs. And, even on furlough, I am a teacher. So, instead, we stand, slightly apart, on guard against each other. For the first time I admit to myself that what I feel for the boy is deep and futile. That he is the son I would like to have as my own.

We watch intently as a wave rises along the jetty, catches three of the surfers up. The sun comes through the wall of water, silhouettes the surfers as they slide down the translucent green. One of them dives for deep water. His board jets high into the air against the sun and falls heavily back into the sea.

David brushes past me. I catch his arm. He jerks away but doesn't leave.

"Who killed Sven?"

He is so close I can feel him trembling. He moves away from me.

"David!" It stops him. The authority of teacher over student reasserts itself.

"For God's sake, tell me what you know."

He can't answer. Tears stand out in his eyes. A wave breaks below us. The foam sweeps up the sand and over our feet. He thrusts a sheet of paper into my hands and then turns and runs away from me. I watch until he is only a small black dot moving along the tide line.

The paper is a list, a copy of a computer printout. It contains eleven names, all male, none of which I recognize, and their addresses. There is no title or search request to tell me what they mean. But I know it is important. I fold it carefully and slip it into the pocket of my jacket.

Thanksgiving week seemed endless. The temperature of the sea plunged to 55 degrees. A series of weather fronts drifted off course and the rainstorms blew in, one after another, from the North Pacific. Kate and I were isolated, she in her house, I in my flat over the garage. The rain beat down in the yard between us. All the accumulated trash in the gutters washed down into the bay where it lodged against the docks and floated out into the channel with the tide.

I made the trip out across Orange County to the foothills and then west to Pasadena to eat dinner with my mother. The turkey was pressed, sliced so thin you could see through it. The cranberry sauce came in a little paper cup with all the taste removed and the gravy came out of a can. I took along a tape of Richard Burton reading *Under Milkwood* and played it for her. The two of us listened to it during the long afternoon while the rain slid down the windows and the sound of patients' families came and went in the halls. Mother's eyelids fluttered as though she were trying to remember something, and once, at the appropriate moment, she laughed out loud.

Afterward I recounted the story of Tintern Abbey and the day the two of us had spent there. I had been only twelve. It couldn't have meant much to me then, but it had been her favorite; the best, she said, in her whole life, and she'd told me about it so often that I knew it by heart. A day in Wales. Coming down the road from Monmouth, stopping by the road for a picnic. The two of us had wandered off, downstream, through the fields, had come unexpectedly upon the abbey abandoned in the meadow. More beautiful than all the cathedrals in Europe, she said. Roof open to the sky. Arched stone framing the sunlight. Daisies growing out of the walls, spread across the green velvet English grass carpeting the floor. I had run ahead of her, she said, shouted to her to come and see, peered into the monks' quarters, climbed before her up the stairs leading to the sky. Happy as lovers, she said. Close as twins. A perfect day. Just the two of us. Mother and son. I thought of Ellen McIan, David's mother, and wondered if she had shared an hour with her son which she would treasure for thirty years, until her brain was gone and she could no longer remember anything.

The old face was slack. The eyes closed. I sat by her for another hour while she slept and then drove back through the rain to my home on the beach.

E lizabeth Chandler Cairns died sometime during the night. The morning nurse found her and called me. The doctor confirmed that she had died peacefully, probably without knowing it, late Thanksgiving or early the next day. I gave them the name of a mortuary and then drove up to collect her things. There wasn't much. A plain gold wedding band. A necklace I had brought to her from college. A few bars of soap.

I don't remember the next few days. I walked along the beach and stood out on the end of the jetty in the rain. I sat in my apartment with a book open on my lap for hours without reading a page. I brought the dog in from the yard and cradled it in my arms and cried, yelping and whining as he had cried for Sven.

I left a note on the door for Kate, who was in Oxnard for the weekend. She returned sometime Sunday night. I heard the resolute tread on the stairway, the key in the lock, and then she was beside me in the dark, holding me in her strong fine arms through all the long dark hours while I cried it all out. When I woke in the morning she was gone.

By Tuesday the worst part was over. I woke as though I were going to school, shaved and dressed, ate a big breakfast. I called the nursing home and asked the amount of the charges I owed them, wrote a check and put it in the mail. I got out a map and charted the addresses on David's list. I started with the nearest one.

*   *   *

Ocean Boulevard stretches like a single artery down the long finger of the peninsula. Running across it are about fifty streets. They run from the bay for two short blocks to dead-end at the sea. The only way off, except to turn around and go back again, is by boat. About a quarter of the way from the end of the peninsula the pier juts out into the ocean on one side and the ferry takes passengers to the island on the other.

From June 15 to September 15, the peninsula is wall-to-wall people. It is something you get used to, like the return of the swallows, or the invasion of jellyfish, once a year, into the bay. The summer cottages look like a scene from *Animal House*. People hang out of windows or crowd, feet up, on the railings of the old-fashioned porches, watching the parade of traffic, bumper to bumper, move at a snail's pace down to the end of the peninsula looking for a place to park, then inch back up again. Bodies fill the beaches like ants at a picnic, brown, bikini-clad, on the move. Ghetto-blasters, all tuned to different stations, give the place the feel of a carnival. Surfers wax their boards and wait for the perfect wave.

On September 15 the mass exodus begins. The last of the tourists—families, dogs, vacationers from Iowa and Manitoba and Garden Grove—squeeze into cars packed with all the detritus of the summer and leave the peninsula. The beach town reverts once again to its regular inhabitants. Along Ocean Boulevard there are places to park. The beaches are empty. Ice-cream stands close down. Students from UCI, splitting the rent four ways, unpack their belongings and settle in for the winter.

The house I was looking for was on Tenth Street, just off the main drag. It looked like all the other old houses. The years of weekly rentals had taken its toll and given it a seedy, typical beach-town look. The shingles were split and the coats of white paint flaked off like dandruff. A couple of VWs and a Toyota sat at the curb. The summer porch had been glassed in. Two of its residents, still in pajamas at 10 A.M., were slumped on a wicker couch. I asked for Todd Van Damm. They pointed inside the house. "Upstairs. First room on your left."

The door was open. The kid sat at a computer, punching in numbers and watching them flash on the screen. He was about twenty, blond, soft brown eyes. There was something wrong about him. Unfinished. He was beautiful in the way boys are beautiful before a beard begins to show and everything inside them begins to toughen up.

In contrast to the rest of the house, the room was neat and orderly. Books lined up on the shelf. The bed made. All the equipment in the room was state of the art. TV and VCR. Compact-disc player. Computer by Apple. Printer and screen by Epson. The kind of things it takes a lot of money to buy.

There was a sterile quality to everything. Except for the paintings. They hung over almost every square inch of wall space. Oils done by the same artist. Thick gobs of paint drooled down the canvas. Harsh blacks. Vivid crimson. Orange. Vortices and spirals. Whirling masses of lava. One of them looked vaguely like a funeral pyre.

I knocked.

Van Damm turned away from the computer and blushed as though he had been caught doing something dirty.

I told him I was taking a survey for the city and asked if he would mind answering a few questions.

He hesitated. He had the kind of face that shows everything, as though he didn't have quite enough skin to cover it all. The nerves and muscles were so close to the surface you could almost see them.

127

"We won't use your name. This is just a sampling of peninsula residents. Just to get an idea of what kind of businesses would do well here."

"All right." He didn't want to do it but he was too polite to say no. I uncapped my pen and held the clipboard in front of me.

"Age?"

"Twenty-one."

"Occupation?"

"I'm a student. A junior at UCI."

"Major?"

"Engineering."

I pointed to the paintings on the wall. "Are these yours, then?"

Van Damm nodded and blushed again. "It's just a hobby." He seemed nervous about them. Maybe he thought they revealed something about him he didn't want me to know. He needn't have worried. They were just blobs to me.

"Do you have a job?"

"No." He hesitated and then, when I looked at him expectantly, pen poised officiously: "My parents pay for everything."

"Do they live here in Southern California?"

"No." I waited. Then, reluctantly, almost painfully, "I'm from Montana."

I made a mark on my clipboard and looked up.

"Do you ever use the harbor facilities?"

"No. Not much. I walk on the beach sometimes."

"Boats?"

"No. I get seasick easily."

I decided I was wasting my time. I asked him a couple more questions. I showed him a photo of Sven and Erik and another of David McIan. He didn't recognize any of them. I watched the sensitive face carefully. I was certain he was telling the truth. He seemed intelligent. Lonely. I wondered what Kate would make of him.

"I have a friend who has an art gallery."

"Oh, yes?" He brightened.

"Up in the Heights: Kate's Gallery. She'd be glad to take a look at your work. Tell her Chandler sent you."

For the first time the boy seemed animated. He stood up. Behind him the computer flashed green lights at the ceiling.

I told him how to get there and left.

Huynh Nguyen was not at home. The little Vietnamese woman who answered the door spoke no English. She was a tiny, frail little thing. She looked as though, if I breathed especially hard, she would simply blow away, like some kind of dried-up maple leaf. She scurried away into the dark interior of the house. After a few minutes her daughter came to the door.

"Huynh not at home." She was a plain-faced girl in her twenties. She wore jeans and a T-shirt. Her hair was pulled back from her neck in a ponytail.

"Do you know where I can find him?"

She grinned at me. It was an impish, likable grin. Her mother peeked around the corner of the hallway. The grin vanished as though she had slipped it away in a drawer.

"No. Huynh go out looking for a job, I think."

The house was one of the thousands of tract houses that had sprung up one winter in the strawberry and asparagus fields on the flats of Costa Mesa. The shades were pulled. A new Honda Civic sat on the drive. The girl inside looked as fresh as though she had come in off the farm.

"You from the government?"

"No. I'm a teacher. You speak English very well."

She giggled. "Not so good."

"Is Huynh your brother?"

She nodded.

"How long have you been here?"

"Ten year. Maybe more. We boat people. I was only a schoolgirl. Huynh and I very happy here. Not so much venerable parents. They miss the old ways. Don't learn the language. Very hard for them. You understand?"

A sudden torrent of words flowed from the old lady's lips. Like a steam tap being turned on and then off again. The girl answered her in Vietnamese.

"Mother afraid you are a government welfare person. Checking up. I tell her you are a teacher. She wants to know what you want with Huynh."

"Someone gave me his name. As a translator."

The girl laughed. It was infectious. She seemed as American to me as though she'd been born in Ohio.

"Huynh's English no better than mine. Wrong Huynh, perhaps?" The sound of the words amused her.

"David McIan mentioned his name."

"Oh." She said it politely. "Maybe knows Huynh from employment board."

"Thorvald Svennson?"

She tried to repeat the name. The consonants defeated her. She laughed again.

"Maybe you want my sister, Thu. Her English very good. Study physics at UCI. How much you pay?"

I tried to remember the going rate for translation. I think it was twenty-five dollars a page. I told her five.

"You leave your number. I tell Thu when she get home."

I scrawled my number on a piece of paper and gave it to her. Inside the house a baby started crying. The old lady started scolding the girl. She gave me another grin and waved good-bye.

"You from the welfare service?"

The voice spoke to me from behind a row of rose-bushes. I spotted her through the thorns. She was middle-aged. Plump. The pale smooth skin of someone who stays out of the sun.

I nodded noncommittally. "I was looking for Huynh."

She snorted. "I suppose they told you he is out looking for work."

I nodded again.

"Well, I can tell you he isn't looking for a job. Has two jobs. Works at McDonald's all day. Is cashier at U Totem at night. All of 'em work. Even the old man. Works in a factory where they put little toys together. The old lady, too. Collect welfare on top of that. There are eleven of them in that house. Smells like onions all the time." She sniffed. All I could smell was roses and the faint odor of toilet water.

She came out from behind the rosebush just far enough so that I got a glimpse of her apron. It wrapped around her like a butcher's uniform.

"See that house on the corner?"

It looked like all the rest of them. Probably went for sixty thousand several years ago. Was worth three times that now.

"They own that, too. Rent it out. I hope they catch them. You tell them welfare people. Isn't fair. Cheating the taxpayer is what they are doing. You know why they keep the shades down all the time, don't you? So you won't see all the gold lying around the house."

I got in the car and slammed the door. The rabbity face disappeared behind the roses.

N ed Burroughs lived in a barrio on the outskirts of Santa Ana. It was instant culture shock, like crossing the border into Mexico. The prim white batten-board houses, built in the forties by refugees from Iowa, each with its front porch, the little bit of wood filigree under the peak of the roof, two sash windows, one on each side of the door, had relaxed and settled into poverty. The yards were bare. Massive old pepper trees drooped untidily over the drives and made cracks in the sidewalk. Mud streaked the sides of the houses. The once neat picket fences leaned or were gone altogether. Those few houses with anything worth protecting were surrounded by chain-link fences. The houses bulged with recently arrived illegal aliens. The wetbacks, mostly young men, slept ten to a room, gathered on the porches, spilled out onto the streets, squatted together on street corners to pass the time of day, joined in the constant parade of dark Indian faces that congregated on the sidewalks. The talk was guarded. The language was of Sonora and Tijuana and Yucatán.

I pulled to a curb in front of the address I had for Burroughs. The air smelled of Mexico, of tortillas frying and frijoles spiced with chili. A radio, tuned to a Spanish language station, played through an open door. A kid rode down the street on his bicycle to get a closer look at me and shouted, *"La migra."* Instantly the street was deserted. Yards and porches emptied. Only an old man who might have been deaf shuffled slowly down the sidewalk pushing an ice-cream wagon in front of him.

The woman who answered the door was hardly more than a child. She held one baby in her arms. Another clung to her ankles. She was very beautiful. Her skin was a lovely translucent brown. The dark hair hung, shiny and luxuriant, to her waist. Her dress was clean. She was barefooted. Through the door in the dark house behind her I could see an old woman sitting on the couch watching me.

The girl seemed bewildered rather than frightened. She looked at me through the screen door. A flimsy hook latched it to the frame.

"Do you speak English?"

The older child stared at me with wide dark eyes, as solemn as a priest. The baby did not look Mexican. His skin was pale, almost white.

"No hablo inglés."

I had not spoken Spanish for twenty years. Still, it was worth a try.

I asked her if she was the wife of Ned Burroughs. She didn't understand. I gestured to my ring finger. She pointed to her own and the cheap gold band on it. *"Está Vd. la Señora Burroughs?"*

"Sí." She looked bleak as she said it as though she did not like to be reminded.

I used the only vocabulary words I could remember. There were about ten of them. The tenses were wrong. Sometimes I had to repeat my question. But finally she seemed to catch the idea that I was looking for her husband.

Is the Señor Burroughs here?

"No."

Would he be in later?

"No."

Tonight?

"No."

Tomorrow?

"No."

Would she tell me where I could find him?

This produced a great rush of Spanish that I could not follow. There were many words and much gesturing. I caught the idea that he had been gone a long time. That she was left without any money. He had promised to send her *dinero* for the children and for her mother but he had not. She would not have married him if she had known what would happen. There was no way to find him. He was in a place called Carsel. It was far away.

The baby started to cry. The child with the sober expression tugged at her skirt. I could feel a dozen hostile eyes watching my back from behind dark windows up and down the street.

Is your husband Caucasian?

"*No entiendo.*"

A *gringo*?

"*Sí.*" She said it without any enthusiasm. A little distaste.

"*Cuantos años tiene su esposo?*"

She was not sure. He was forty, maybe fifty years old. I had a vision of a middle-aged loser, one of those sexual incompetents who had to come to the barrio to find someone young enough and hungry enough not to reject his advances.

I had reached the limit of my second-year Spanish. I managed to say *gracias* and *adiós* and left her.

I drove around the block, and then, in case she had been lying to me and Burroughs had come out of hiding, drove past the house again. The wetbacks, those who had not found a job for the day, had drifted back onto the street. They lolled on the porches, congregated in good-natured ribaldry around the ice-cream vendor. Their faces were dark, no *gringo* in sight. One of them watched me drive by. Our eyes locked for no more than an instant before he turned away. It was the look of a man who senses danger everywhere. Camouflage. The instinctive response of the illegal who has crossed the river at night and watched his compadres drown, or cut through a barbed-wire fence and been robbed by bandidos from both countries. Paid a year's wages to be smuggled through disease-laden sewers that converge under the border and been thrown back the next day. Sneaked through not once but many times. Was this man Ned Burroughs?

But the baby had been light-haired. I drove down Harbor Boulevard. There were still a few of the men left out of the hundreds who congregated every morning before sunrise in the parking lot of the 7-Eleven or Albertson's Drugs. I looked for a white face. It was too easy. To cruise by at six in the morning, look over all the dark, expressionless faces, settle on Burroughs. Jerk rudely for him to hop in the back of the pickup. Take him off somewhere for a day's work at minimum wage or less. See to it that he did not come back.

I bought a Coke and sat in the car and watched them. Even in the comparative safety of the parking lot they hung back in the corners, kept to the shadows. Escape routes always at their backs. An army of them was dropped off in the beach towns and the developments around Pacific Plaza every morning at seven. They loaded bricks. Dug trenches for foundations. Hung scaffolding. Shinnied up trees. Pulled weeds. Hauled trash. They worked without stopping, quietly, anonymously, on construction jobs and in the gardens, and then, just as mysteriously as they had come, they vanished when the sun went down.

No one asked their names. Javier Morales and Jorge Chavez and Jesús Gonzales came and went in the rich cities along the coast without even being noticed. The citizens of Huntington and White's Bay and Rancho Pacifica took them for granted, if they thought of them at all. While inside the barrios they gradually became acclimated, lost that frightened look, mingled with the growing population of middle-class Americans of Mexican descent, married, produced beautiful dark-skinned children who went to school, learned to read, eventually passed over into the middle class themselves. More wetbacks crossed the border to take their places.

The gangs roamed the barrios preying on them, took quick forays into Costa Mesa and Garden Grove. One of these days they would penetrate as far as the coastal communities. But until they did, investment brokers with their picture-perfect families would take tea at the Four Seasons and the bird watchers and the Friends of the Bay would walk the beaches and conduct their little wars in the city-council chambers, blissfully unaware of this alien culture massing outside the city limits and which would, someday, by its sheer burgeoning numbers, burst out of the barrios and the middle-class Hispanic communities and supplant the yuppie culture with its own.

It rained all the way out to Riverside. I passed one Christmas-tree lot after another. Figures in yellow slickers slogged through the mud, hauling the rain-heavy firs down from the trucks, nailing a stand to the bottom of each trunk. There wasn't a customer in sight.

I found Tim Baker in a trailer on the outskirts of town. It was standing on four cement pilings in the middle of about an acre of weeds and rusted cars that had been abandoned there and never hauled away. The woman at the house on the front of the lot refused to open the door. She pointed around the back of the house to the trailer. It was one of the old silver models, made in the days when trailers were still small enough to haul. Rust ran with the rain down the sides. A TV antenna leaned precariously from the top.

I had to pound on the door for several minutes before he answered it. A pile of beer cans stood about five feet from the apple box that served as a doorstep. It was just about the distance a man, sitting inside the trailer, could throw one without getting up. He had on a pair of pants with suspenders. A dirty white T-shirt. He hadn't shaved for about a week. His eyes were red. The trailer smelled of bacon grease.

I told him I was selling life insurance.

He gave a kind of sardonic half-laugh and said I'd come to the wrong place. His life wasn't worth a damn to anybody, including himself.

I told him I was taking a survey for the insurance company and I'd pay him five bucks for answering the questions. I don't think he believed me. He just stood there until I fished out a bill and handed it to him. He stuck it in his pocket and let me in.

The trailer was about seven feet wide and twelve feet in length. It was loaded with old clothes, paper bags, dirty plates. Nothing had ever been put away. There was hardly room for the two of us to stand.

Everything was old, worn, used. The television was a black-and-white model he must have picked up at the dump. The pipe under the sink was rusted through and patched with a piece of hose that emp-

137

tied onto the ground outside. I whipped out a note-book and started firing questions at him.

"Age?"

"Sixty-two."

"Occupation?"

"Retired."

I had a feeling that he meant that he was unemployed.

"What did you do before you retired?"

"Trucker." He liked saying the word. Maybe it brought back memories of happier days. Self-respect. "I used to haul machine parts, cotton, practically any damn thing between Mesa, Arizona, and Tucson. Sometimes over to LA."

"Why did you retire?"

The red eyes shifted uneasily. He reached in his pocket for the bill. I was afraid he was going to give it back.

"I lost my license."

"Drunk driving?"

"Something like that." He rummaged automatically in the heap of clothes beside the sink for a bottle and came up empty. Either he'd misplaced it or it was already out there on the heap with the rest of the empties.

I asked him if he'd ever been to White's Bay.

He had to think a minute.

"Sure. I was there a couple of times. During the war. Me and a friend. We went dancing there. The Rendezvous Ballroom. Stan Kenton. Then I moved to Arizona. Always meant to go back there. Haven't got around to it yet. Is the old Rendezvous Ballroom still there?"

"It burned to the ground sometime in the sixties."

He sank back inside himself. One more thing gone wrong.

"How long have you lived in Riverside?"

"Six years. Seven." He hesitated; then: "Off and on."

It was the "off and on" that sent the alarm bells ringing. Teachers either develop a sixth sense or get out of the business. It's a fine-caliber vibration that starts when a student begins to prevaricate about why he didn't do his homework or finish his paper, or stayed home from school. For some reason this poor, tired, middle-aged man in a trailer in the middle of nowhere had something to hide.

I didn't give him a chance to think about it.

"Where did you live when you weren't here?"

He didn't want to tell me. His hand reached into the pile of clothes and came up empty again. I took another five-dollar bill out of my pocket and held it up. He sighed.

"Ventura County."

"I need you to be more specific."

He looked at the five-dollar bill. Mumbled something.

"I didn't hear you."

"Camarillo."

I gave him the five dollars. It was wasted money. Camarillo is where they put the mentally disturbed. Drug addicts. I suppose they have a place for alcoholics.

I made one more attempt to connect him with Sven's death, the cocaine, David. I showed him the photos. He studied them carefully. He had trouble focusing his eyes. He held them out and then brought them closer.

"What the hell would I be doing knowing people like that?"

I believed him. I almost told him his name was on a

list that David had obtained somewhere and that had to do with a murder but it seemed better not to.

I said thank you and left. I trudged back across the field. The weeds brushed against my pants and worked their way into my socks. By the time I got back to the car I was soaked. I took a last look back. Baker had closed the door. The trailer stood forlornly in the field, tied to the world by nothing more than a single black string of wire that someone had run to the house for electricity. Beads of rain gathered on it, weighting it down. I suppose it was as good a place as any to sit alone and drink yourself to death.

Somewhere in the canyon somebody spun out on the rain-slick pavement and the Riverside Freeway came to a full stop. We sat there, twenty thousand of us, in the dark, like turtles, hunched, one to a car, while the rain sloshed around us and some poor devil lay out there, bleeding away into the roadbed.

As far as I could see I had come to a dead end. David's list had netted me a college kid whose addictions ran to painting rather than drugs, an entrepreneurial Vietnamese refugee who was working two jobs and screwing the welfare bureau, and one of the world's many losers sitting in his trailer, drinking to pass the time until he could die. None of them were apt candidates for drug couriers or middlemen. I couldn't picture any of them as someone you hired to put a bullet through Sven's head. If there was a pattern, I couldn't see it.

The ambulance picked its way along the shoulder, lights flashing against the rain, siren yowling into the dark. About twenty minutes after that the traffic got moving again. It was stop and go all the way to the beach.

Kate was mad enough to kill. She saw me opening the gate and came out onto the porch gunning for me. The smell of garlic and fresh-cut onion came out into the rain after her. Experience told me that all that Celtic wrath and indignation was about to be unleashed on me. I didn't have time to ask why. She let me have it as I walked into the yard.

"It isn't bad enough that I've had your real estate lady friend on the phone a dozen times today or that the city attorney has ordered the gallery closed until all the electrical wiring has been replaced. You choose today to send lousy artists around so that I can have the distinctly unpleasant duty of informing them that they are not and never will be a Van Gogh or a Dali, or even, God forbid, another Charles Bragg."

I just stood there, rain dripping down my face in front of this vision of wrath, and couldn't think of anything to say in my defense except to mumble feebly that I had meant to warn her before he showed up.

"I mean, Chandler, thanks a lot. That was just what I needed today. The Friends of the Bay are being sued for two million dollars. The court has ordered all publications to be recalled until they can decide whether or not they are defamatory."

"I'm sorry, Kate."

"Couldn't you see that his work was just awful? I mean, my God, it was terrible."

"I've seen worse. Your pal the art collector has an eight-hundred-thousand-dollar Coke bottle that takes up the whole wall of his dining room. That is not exactly what I would have called awe-inspiring."

"At least you can tell it's a Coke bottle."

"And what is Van Damm's stuff?"

"It's a wet dream, for God's sake." Suddenly she laughed. I was aware that she was laughing at me. Still it was welcome. Rich and full. Like chords running up and down a cello. I tried to look as dignified as it is possible for a man standing forlornly in the rain. Mud on my shoes. Pants soaked up to the knees. The old Irish tweed hat she had given me a thousand years ago drooping down around my ears. Rain falling in a circle around me so that I looked like a comic caught unexpectedly in a sad play.

"Chandler, you look like a man who has lost his last friend. Come in. I'll give you some New Mexican enchiladas."

She opened the door, stood back, let me into the kitchen. I followed her in without protest. The proverbial pooch scolded, forgiven, and let back into heaven.

The salsa was boiling over on the stove. Kate turned down the fire and gave it a stir. A stack of corn tortillas sat on the sinkboard. She handed me a grater and a brick of Jack cheese.

I took off my coat and hat. Washed my hands. Grated the cheese into a bowl.

"What happened?"

"It was pretty awful. The kid came bursting in, just after noon, with an armload of those horrible oils and his car packed with more of them and asked me to take a look. The city inspector was there and I was trying to convince him the place had been safe for fifty years and ought to be good for a week more.

"The kid was pathetic, really. I asked him about one of the paintings, a lot of squiggly lines, like tiny licks

142

of flame, and he explained it was a symbol of religious converts speaking in tongues which, it seems, his father used to do, dragging the kid all over the Plains States with him and preaching on street corners and in revival tents. He shivered when he spoke of it."

I told her about the list, about Burroughs and Huynh and the alcoholic sitting alone in his trailer.

"What about Van Damm? Do you think he could have been part of a drug-smuggling operation?"

"Never." Kate shook her head vigorously. "He's too nervous. It's the kind of sensitivity that you can't trust. He got very upset when I told him, as gently as I could, that I couldn't take his paintings on. His skin got all spotted. It's the blood vessels contracting. Even his hand had all these purple splotches on them. He just stared at me. Utterly without expression. Not a word. Nothing. Then he picked up his paintings and left."

Kate plopped a tortilla into the bacon grease. It gave a sizzle and started to go limp.

"I'm sorry."

Kate turned the tortilla over with a fork, waited for about ten seconds, and then slid it onto a plate and handed it to me. I piled on a handful of cheese and sprinkled some onions on top of that. Smothered the whole thing in salsa and then started piling on a second layer.

"Why drugs, Chandler? Why does it have to be drugs?"

"What else could it be?" I recounted my visit with Sven's son, Erik. "He said cocaine flowed in and out of the harbor like sand."

Kate turned and looked out into the dark, into the rain falling over the dunes, as Sven had peered out in the last hours before he took his skiff up the bay and never came back.

143

"There is something else, Chandler."

"What's that?"

Kate waved into the night. Toward the sand and the waves beyond. All I could see was darkness and the rain falling.

"The sand itself. That's the real gold, Chandler. That's where the money is. Like oil. Only it never runs out. Keeps producing. Rent. Leasehold. Percentage of profits. Year after year."

I touched her soft hair with my fingertips. Held a curl, all copper and burnished gold, in the palm of my hand and then I let it go again. Nothing trivial about my Kate. Wanted to believe Sven had died for something more important than a handful of white powder.

"We can't blame the developers for everything."

She laughed. Smiled ruefully. Agreed with me.

We ate the enchiladas. Shared a pitcher of beer in the warm little kitchen under a circle of light that came as much from Kate as it did from the fixture overhead. I helped her wash the dishes and finally, when I'd run out of excuses to stay, let myself out into the rain for the quick run across the yard to my own room and another in the long procession of cold and comfortless nights without her.

I don't think I had a moment's doubt that Sylvus had killed Sven, just as he had tried to kill me. It must have been Sylvus who had followed Sven out into the estuary and then shot him because he couldn't wait for the inheritance that, after all, had escaped him. Or maybe it had been because Sven had discovered Sylvus was dealing in drugs and threatened to turn him in. Either way I was certain it was Sylvus who had pulled the trigger.

The puzzle was simple enough for a child to figure out. The only piece that didn't fit in nice and neat was

144

David. If he had witnessed the murder, why hadn't he said so? He owed nothing to Sylvus. As far as I knew they had never met until the day of Sven's funeral. And Sylvus was dead now. He couldn't hurt anyone.

So why not tell the police? What else was there to know? What did the list mean?

For about the thousandth time I wished the old man were back, rattling around in his garden, wanting to talk. Folding the hose. Shouting up to me. Launching into one of his interminable stories. This time I would ask more questions. Listen when he gave the answers. Keep him company on his last lonely vigil in the estuary. Save him. Save myself.

Forgive me, Sven.

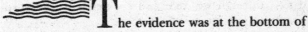he evidence was at the bottom of the bag of puppy chow.

By the end of the first week, the collie pup had forgotten Sven and fallen in love with Kate. The moment I let him out in the morning he was at Kate's door, scratching and whining until she came out in her bathrobe and scooped him up. It made me jealous to see them. The puppy nuzzling against her, the sturdy little tail thump-thumping against the door jamb in ecstasy. She fed him scraps from her hand, let him into the house where he followed at her heels until she left for the studio. Only then did he return, disconsolate and down at the mouth, to me. And to whatever was left of the puppy chow. The two of us toughed it out together for the rest of the day.

The key was in an envelope, taped shut. The envelope had been used before. Old Sven never threw anything away. So thrifty he drove me crazy. Kept every shopping bag and scrap of paper. Cut open the toothpaste tube to get at the last bit. Resoled his shoes until they fell apart. This time I didn't mind.

The envelope had come from David. Across the back of it he had scrawled:

Sven—
Meet me tonight. Duck Island. 12 P.M.

David

The date on it was October third.

I dug out the Orange County section of the *Los Angeles Times* for the fifth of October. Sven's murder was the lead story, along with the photo that David had thrown down the classroom table at me with such unexpected belligerence. In it the estuary was still shrouded in fog and the little skiff was eternally being drawn through the tule and the reeds to the small group waiting for it on the shore.

The photo of the McIans was there on the first page of the Society Section. It was a study in the relationship of a family. David and his father were handing a check for a hundred thousand dollars to the chairman of the Music Center. The bond between them, a kind of shared energy and affection, was obvious even in a black-and-white news photo. Ellen McIan, wife and mother, a pretty, pale creature, stood beside and slightly behind them. She stared out at the camera as though she, too, was aware of being left out.

McIan had sworn that David was with him all night but, of course, even the Moscow Classical Ballet eventually ends. McIan and I both knew that. Still, it was an alibi of a sort. The note made everything different.

146

I picked up the phone and called Lawrence. The note wasn't conclusive but it was evidence enough to cast doubt on the theory that I had been the last person to see Sven alive. On the strength of it they could question the boy, maybe pry out of him the information that I had failed to get. It would be enough to clear me. No one would believe that David had killed Sven. Or would they? Was that what McIan was afraid of?

The desk clerk patched me through. Lawrence answered. I jammed the phone back down on the hook.

McIan's fierce loyalty had unnerved me. I had wondered about just how far he would go to protect his son. Now I wondered the same thing about myself.

David was not at school. The attendance office confirmed that his name was on the absence list. The woman who answered the phone at the McIan residence refused to let me talk with any member of the family. She said she would leave a message in a tone that told me she would not. A wall had been erected around the boy that only the rich can afford. It was as solid and impregnable as the Berlin wall.

McIan's office was on the top of the new McIan Tower in Pacific Plaza. I took the elevator up. The lobby took up almost the whole floor. It was all smoked glass and black marble. The color scheme was teal blue and warm pewter. It had a silk carpet thick enough to sleep in. Expensive couches arranged informally around coffee tables. Leather accent pieces.

Antique tables. A few objets d'art placed with studied carelessness. *Country Life. Gourmet* magazine. A bowl of candy. The walls were hung with tapestries of wild-flowers. Gulls and pelicans swooped down over a white background.

For a moment I thought I was alone. Windows on three sides looked out over the bay. The black glass cut the glare. Below the tower the parking lots of Pacific Plaza spread out around the department stores like soiled skirts, doming the hill, half empty this time of morning. White's Bay lay beyond that. I could see the steeple of the high school across the estuary. The students in my third period would be anguishing over D.H. Lawrence and the destructive influence of mothers on sons. The bay was placid. The ferry plowed between the island and the peninsula. A thin strip of sand ran down the outer edge of the mainland to the wedge. The dredging barges were moving slowly up the channel between the jetties.

I had the envelope with the note from David to Sven in my pocket. I walked over to the door at the far end, which seemed to be the only one around. A small brass plate, understated, expensive, was engraved "William P. McIan, President."

"May I help you, sir?"

She had an English accent and a face that might have come off a piece of Wedgwood. Translucent skin. Dark hair. She was dressed in what the fashion editors call dove gray. An Italian silk blouse with long sleeves, a high neck. Tiny pearl earrings. Everything about her said class. She sat at a W. and J. Sloan replica of a Louis XIV desk in the lobby behind me. There was nothing on it but a bouquet of fresh flowers: Peruvian lily, azalea, and what looked like a sprinkling of Queen Anne's lace and wild roses. And a little gold-and-white telephone.

"I'd like to see McIan."

She had a high, tinkly laugh, like bells ringing. She ran it lightly up and down the scale for me. "I'm sorry, sir. Mr. McIan is in conference and will not be available for the rest of the day. May I take your name. . . ?" She opened a drawer and pulled out a small pad of paper and a gold-encased pencil. It paused for a moment over the paper. She turned her lovely lavender eyes up toward my face.

"Cairns. Chandler Cairns."

The pad disappeared inside the drawer under the table. It slid shut soundlessly.

"Cairns," I repeated and spelled it for her. She smiled. Her hands remained folded in her lap.

"You couldn't tell me how I can get in touch with his son, could you?"

She laughed again. This time the sound trilled upward like bells moving up a hill and then tumbling down the other side.

I laughed with her. Her lovely hand slid along the desk and rested on the phone. The elevator door glided open and waited for me. We laughed some more.

A guard materialized out of nowhere. He stood behind and to the side of the lovely English secretary. She smiled sweetly, her eyes following me until the doors had closed over me and the elevator expelled me swiftly and silently out of the building.

I went back to see Davidson. It was ten o'clock in the morning and already the temperature was in the eighties. There were sandbags all over the sidewalk and against the sea wall. It looked as if he were barricading himself for a war that was about to be launched against him from the Pacific.

"Looks like another Santa Ana." Davidson didn't take his eyes from the railing along the pier which he had been sanding. He ran his hand along the wood to see how smooth it was.

I agreed with him.

"There's always one during the first days of December. Tomorrow's the first. Sven and I had a Christmas-tree lot up on Newport for a couple of years. After three years we gave up. Every time we got the trees up, the goddamn Santa Ana blew down from the foothills. Blew 'em all down. Dried 'em up. They turned brown. The last time we lost our shirts. Sold 'em to a fellow who sprayed 'em all with white junk. He made a killing."

The smog lay in a thin ridge out over the ocean. The water had a red cast to it, like copper plate. The wind blew in gusts down across the mesa and out to sea. The planes from the airport had reversed direction. They came in over the channel, lining themselves up with the cliffs, and followed the estuary back to the runway. A plume of smoke rose from somewhere down the coast, in the empty stretch between Mesa del Mar and Laguna.

Davidson straightened, looked at the smoke, shook his head. He gestured toward the peninsula. "A Santa Ana blows up, someday there's going to be a fire out there. All these tourists riding up and down the peninsula, the fire trucks won't be able to get there in time. Whole damned peninsula will burn down."

The old man was in his doomsday mood again. I tried to talk him out of it.

"Well, not today. The tourists have gone home for the winter."

"Maybe." He squinted across the bay to the peninsula. The long line of houses was low, practically touching. Many of them were the original single-wall wood frame, shingled, let out for rent.

"I'm looking for David."

"Oh?" That seemed to interest him.

"I need to talk to him. He was with Sven the night he died."

Davidson gave me a sharp look, then bent back over his work. The sander had a long orange cord that snaked along the pier and across the sidewalk to an outlet on his porch. He turned it on, switched it off again.

"What makes you think that?"

I took the envelope out of my pocket and showed it to him. He had to find his glasses, dust them off, put them on.

His lips pursed and moved over the message, an old man's way of reading. He took the note from me, jammed it deep into his own pocket. I let him do it. Knew myself for a fool. Decided to show him the list.

"Recognize any of the names?"

"Nope." He shut his lips firmly, as though he wasn't going to say any more. And then: "Where did you get it?"

"David. I haven't gone to the police yet. I need to talk to him first. Do you have any idea where he might be?"

Instead of answering, Davidson switched on the sander and bent down to run it along the underside of the rail. A cloud of white dust rose around it and skated off in a gust of wind.

I waited around for a while. Finally Davidson switched the sander off. I thought he was going to say something but then he changed his mind. He yanked the orange cord another six feet. Set the sander down on the rail and switched it on. The noise rose around

151

us like a hive of angry bees. A cloud of fine white powder rose up between us. In the distance the plume of smoke widened and blew out toward the horizon.

I waited until nearly midnight and then took Sven's skiff down to the beach and out into the bay. The wind had shifted. It came down over the hills, dry, smelling of the city.

The bay was deep and black. The houses loomed dark on the islands and along the peninsula. Here and there a night light glowed faintly through plate-glass windows. The wood oars felt solid in my grip, worn smooth by the old man's huge hands.

I pulled over into the shadows of Harbor Island and sat there watching the long shoreline of the Bay Club. The terrace was empty. The windows of the dining room were dark. Flood lights shone down on the docks. McIan's boat was tethered below the parking lot. It was dark like the others. The top deck was protected from the damp by tight-fitting canvas covers.

I stayed there until the Bay Club guard came down from the main gate to make the rounds of the dock and then returned back up into the club rooms. I rowed over into the shadow of the *Mach 10* and pulled myself aboard.

Someone had left the companionway unlocked. I knew that it was foolish to go inside but I did so anyway. The boat was empty. I felt my way through the saloon and the staterooms using the flashlight sparingly in quick stabs into the dark corners and down into the engine room. I called David's name softly into the dark. There was no answer.

I heard McIan come down the dock laughing in that arrogant masculine way and the faint echoing tinkle of Miss Silver Bells. I could see him through the windows that ran around the cabin. He had a magnum of champagne in one hand and the other was having fun inside her silk Italian blouse. They stopped for a moment while he performed an arpeggio on her earlobe. It gave me just enough time to exit out the front and then slip down over the side into the water. I waited in the dark while they made rude noises and locked themselves inside. I heard them fumble their way into the stateroom with the big double bed. I untied the skiff and pushed it out from under the boat and swam with it down to the Sea Scout Base. Then I hauled my soggy self aboard and rowed home.

Delilah Hendershott guarded the city files as though they contained plans for the allied invasion. She pursed her lips and drummed impatiently with long nervous fingers while I made my request, and then sent me across the street to the Planning Commission.

The Planning Commission was about as helpful as the Pentagon during a stage-one nuclear alert. By the time I'd repeated my request three times I was ready to forget the whole thing. That's when the door to the inner sanctum opened and, wonder of all wonders, its occupant emerged. If he wasn't the planning director he was a good imitation.

"Jonathan Kramer, here." He extended a hand attached to the far end of an elongated arm. He was a tall, bald specimen, not unlike a caricature of a pelican. A fifty-year-old veteran of planning wars, humorless, seedy-looking, with black horn-rimmed glasses and a foul, ulcer-producing breath that blew over me like the back bay at low tide.

"Duck Island, is it?" He pulled his lips back with the same jerking motion with which a stagehand yanks open the curtain in a run-down theater, and with much the same effect. The smile was gaping and empty. One of his teeth had a metal band around it.

He turned officiously to the secretary hovering near the door. "Find the latest survey map of bay and estuary, will you?"

There was a whole file of them. Kramer leafed through them, drew one out and spread it across his desk.

A map can be a work of art. This one had been done lovingly by someone in the U.S. Coast and Geodetic Survey. Contour lines followed the coast, wave after wave along the ocean floor, and then marched up onto the land. The markings were delicate, a soft marine blue on parchment. Accurate to within a foot.

The bay was about five miles long and nearly a mile wide. All the water in the bay came in and went out through the narrow channel between the cliffs of Mesa del Mar at one end and the long tip of the peninsula which enclosed the bay. The bay flowed inland, parallel to the coast and the cliffs that rose steeply behind it. Islands took up about half the area. Halfway up the harbor, between the entrance channel at one end and the turning basin at the other, the bay crossed under Coast Highway and flowed inland through a break in the cliffs. Here, beyond the sound and sight of the sea, the water spread out into a large shallow basin that flooded and emptied with the tides. A few half-formed sandspits dotted the water just above the high-water mark. The small whale-shaped one at the north end of the estuary was labeled Lot 201.

"That," said Kramer self-importantly, jabbing his long bony finger down on the map, "is Duck Island."

It looked perfectly harmless to me. I tried to remember what McIan had told me about why Rancho Pacifica, which owned everything else, didn't have title to the islands and the peninsula. I asked.

"Because . . ." Kramer's eyes gleamed. You could tell he loved telling the story. "When the Spanish land grant was made in 1810 that later became Rancho Pacifica, and the royal cartographers made a map of it, the harbor wasn't here. The peninsula, the islands didn't exist. The waves broke right along the cliffs here, where Coast Highway is now. And then one day the Santa Ana River shifted. The sand came pouring down out of the canyons and across the flood plain. The river brought it all down and dumped it here." He jabbed his thumb on the end of the peninsula and drew it up to the place where it joined the land. "And here." He pointed to Harbor Isle. "And here." He rested a bulbous knuckle on the big island.

"So who owned it then?"

"Nobody. Not a damn soul. It was called swamp and overflow land and became part of the state holdings. If Rancho Pacifica had thought of it, they could have bought it all up for a song. A dollar an acre. But of course they weren't interested. They owned all this vast tract of land, mostly unoccupied, down the coast and inland for miles. It never occurred to them that the sandspits and the marshes might someday be worth spit.

"Leland White bought the big island and went broke trying to develop it. When the bottom dropped out in 1915, Davidson's father bought up a lot of the peninsula lots for twenty-five dollars apiece. Mostly down here on the lower end, where it was cheaper." He pointed to the area stretching from Sven's house across to the bay and up toward the pier.

"What about Duck Island?"

"The state owns the estuary now. All along the water and the marshes. Except—" he paused and looked at me accusingly, as though I'd been caught fiddling with the accounts—"Duck Island."

"So what's it worth?"

"Nothing. Not a penny. Taxes on it are a little over a hundred dollars a year. You can't build on it. Can't even put in a boat landing or erect a sign without the state's permission. And they'll never give it. Environment people got it locked up tight." I thought of Kate. She'd been part of the crusade to save the back bay from development by Rancho Pacifica. It might have been one of the things we had fought over.

"So why would anyone want to buy it?"

"They wouldn't." He didn't even hesitate.

"Someone has offered one point five million for Sven's house on condition that the adjacent lot and the island go with it." I showed him where Sven's house was on the map and the vacant lot next door. "But that's just to sweeten the deal and keep us from looking too far into it. My best guess is that Duck Island is what they really want."

"You got the deed?"

"No. It's been temporarily mislaid. The county has sent it over to the tax office and hasn't got it back.

The original is probably locked away tight in a safe-deposit box we haven't found yet."

Kramer frowned. It was that suspicious, bells going off kind of alarm when a supervisor finds out something is happening in his district that no one told him about.

He ran his fingers over the map, feeling the contours of it, like a blind man caressing a Braille manuscript. He was familiar with every ridge and curve of the bay. The little squares with lot numbers were just marks to me. To him they were houses and permits and names. Vacant lots with "For Sale" signs. Grocery stores. Right-of-way easements. I had a feeling he was mentally taking an aerial flight over the city, like one of those goddamn police helicopters, looking for something, circling, circling, spotting his target, running tighter circles, coming down for a look, zeroing in.

He found it.

The hands stopped moving across the map, withdrew. He straightened. The glasses had slipped further down on his nose. He took them off and wiped them with a voluminous white handkerchief that had been stuck in his pocket. He tried to hide his excitement. It came out on his forehead in little beads of sweat.

"What did you find?"

"Worthless," he said. "Your island's worthless. I'd advise you to take the money and run." He rolled the map up carefully and slid it into a cardboard cylinder.

I knew there was a question I should ask but I didn't know what it was.

He didn't put the map away but placed it alongside his blotter. As I left the office his hand was resting on it. I didn't know if he was guarding it against being stolen or if he was caressing it. Like something that was going to bring him a lot of luck.

T his time I pulled Sven's outboard motorboat in from its moorings and motored up the bay toward the estuary. It was almost dawn. The islands floated low in the water, dark as tombs. The incoming tide lapped the sea walls. The ferries were mere shadows lashed to the docks. Two dredging barges sat like stones in the turning basin. Above the huge ugly shells a man stood guard. I saw the red tip of his cigarette lift and fall. Lift again.

Past the bridge, under Coast Highway, I cut the motor and let the boat drift while the sky turned gray. The bluffs rose a hundred feet on all sides, so that within a space of minutes I was completely cut off from the rest of the world. The mist moved in patches over the water. Islands appeared and disappeared beneath it as in a conjurer's trick. Tule and brown reeds stuck up out of it like fine brush strokes in a Japanese watercolor. A flock of herring gulls rose out of the mist as though dawn had released them. They floated upward, silently, spread out, turned and disappeared in the direction of the sea.

I tried to think of nothing at all. I let the boat drift up through the mudflats with the current. Everything seemed unreal. I could feel Sven, or whatever was left of him, in the boat with me. Lost. Out of focus. Reflections of the reed islands wavered in the water around me, blurred, unfamiliar. I felt a momentary panic as I lost my bearings, a man adrift in a strange world with only a ghost for companion.

A family of mudhens paddled into the current behind me. Somewhere in the reeds a heron stirred, was silent again. I felt disoriented. Islands sank and floated again as the mists shifted. The colors changed definition. Gray blended into brown. Ocher into burnt sienna. In the condominiums far off on top of the bluffs somewhere, a woman screamed. The echo hung over the estuary like a question mark and then was swallowed up in the silence.

Duck Island rose out of the north end of the estuary, long and flat. I pulled the boat up onto the sand and just sat there ahead of the tide. I found what was left of Old Sven's duck blind. A few pieces of rotting wood. Some shells, rusted, in the sand. A railroad tie that had floated there and taken up residence.

What did someone want with Duck Island, this barren little spit of land? It was part of a nature preserve. Inviolate. And what did it have to do with Sven's death? I tried to imagine the scene. The darkness. Just the faint swish of water against the prow as the little skiff made its way up through the reeds. Pulled up here where I was, on the island.

What face had hidden here in the duck blind? David? His sensitive eyes hardened against what he was about to do? The gun sighting along the railroad tie? Or Sylvus? Half drunk. Finger eager on the trigger. No sleep lost, no doubt to disturb his brain. Or was it one of the men on the list that David had left for me? The student who painted lurid pictures and played with his computer? The loser, drinking away his life in the trailer on the edge of Riverside? The Vietnamese immigrant? The *gringo* husband of a pretty Mexican alien? Was it Davidson who wanted his lot back? Or Sven's own son, hoping to inherit?

For a minute I saw Old Sven, the white hair rising

in tufts around the thin face, hand raised in greeting, pulling his skiff in beside mine, already talking a mile a minute. Telling me about the mackerel. The sharks. His beautiful wife. The boat he had built with his own hands. And then the streak of fire out of the reeds, the old face thrown backward. Silenced forever. The gallant old heart thumping away, pumping the life out of him into the sand and the reeds and the floor of the skiff. For a moment the answer came to me and then I lost it.

I picked up a handful of sand. It was soft and cold. It ran through my fingers like a fine sifting of silk. "The sand itself. That's the real gold. That's where the money is." Duck Island? Was that why Sven had died? Or was it something else, something that hadn't happened yet? Something so terrible that David had risked everything to tell me, wanting me to find out and stop it?

The form of Old Sven, slumped in the boat, tried to rise, pull itself up, tell me something. And then it was gone. I heard the splash of a mudhen diving to the bottom and then silence.

Behind me the tide lapped at the edges of the island. It lifted the boat, set it free. Across the water, mirrored against it, a siege of herons, long-necked, elegant, emerged from the reeds and stood motionless, watching me. When I looked again they were gone. The tide flooded in under cover of the mist, in over the reeds and the tule, the long flat sandspits and the mud. It covered the feeding grounds and the long, winding channels so that there was nothing left to hint of their existence. Only one gray unbroken expanse of water. It stretched across the estuary all the way to the bluffs and all its secrets were carefully concealed beneath it.

Kate's studio was a 1400-square-foot shack that she rented for four hundred dollars a month along Old Heights Road. The front opened onto a patch of gravel. A sign over the door, in gold leaf with a bright red poppy, advertised "Kate's Gallery." Most of the work was hers. It hung over every square inch of wall space. Mostly wildflowers and marsh grass and herons in flight, but some of them were stock scenes of the bay: the Pavilion, sea gulls along the jetty, children playing on the beach. The oils were rich-textured, with spots of color in unexpected places. The watercolors were subtle washes of the sea, soft blues and grays, light coming through the fog. She practically gave them away. It was the postcards that paid the rent, and the commissions from some of the better-known artists that stood on easels around the room.

The Edison Company was just leaving as I pulled up. A condemnation warning was tacked to the door. Kate was sitting at her worktable repairing an oil that had been damaged by the rain. She had taken it out of the frame and was rubbing the oxidized paint with quick deft strokes. The light from the window fell across her arms. She kept her face away from me. It was the only sign that she had been crying.

"What's the condemnation notice for?"

She glanced up at me and then back to her work.

"Oh, that . . ." She tried to sound light-hearted, as though it were all a joke. "The city in its infinite wisdom has decided suddenly that the gallery is unfit for a commercial establishment. Someone complained."

"Who?"

"Oh, it's nothing really. Just a little harassment. Marilyn McIver had her water cut off because the bill was three days overdue. Mr. Saba was ticketed for doing twenty-six in a twenty-five-mile zone. The hit squad hasn't gone into action yet."

"Rancho Pacifica?"

"No. It's someone else. Someone a hell of a lot rougher." Kate gave a vindictive jab to the can she was using, knocking it over. The alcohol spilled over the newspapers and onto the edge of the canvas. I grabbed the can and righted it, pulled the painting out of the way. Kate looked up, stricken. Tears pooled in her eyes. I gathered up the newspapers and tossed them into the trash can in the back room. I found a dry rag and wiped up the rest of it. When I had the whole mess under control I kissed the tears off the still summer-gold cheeks and sat down again.

"I need some help," I said.

Kate drew a picture of the face as I described it. After three hours and dozens of wasted sheets of paper, we got it as close as it would come to the original, hidden under the up-flung arm, the one that had come toward me from the Casino on Catalina Island, swinging the tackle box alongside him. It fit almost a quarter of all the sons of stockbrokers and company executives who lived in the big houses on the hill. I had already been through the high school yearbooks for the past six years. There were dozens just like him.

I spent the afternoon making the rounds of the yacht clubs. Most of the gates were manned with graduates from the high school. All of them knew Old

Sven. They tried to be helpful. They sent me out on a dozen well-meaning wild-goose chases. Invariably the young man, who was a deckhand on one yacht or another, looked enough like my sketch to have posed for it. With one slight difference: It wasn't the right guy. By ten o'clock the next morning I had covered every club on the bay and was starting in on the week-end charters.

And that's when I got lucky.

He was driving down Coast Highway, coming straight at me, in a turquoise Mustang with the top down and the radio blasting out in all directions. The face seemed tanner, the hair even more blond, if that was possible. He looked like an ad for J. W. Robinson or Ralph Lauren. I made a U-turn and got in the line of traffic behind him.

Maybe he saw me. At any rate he took the long way around: left on Dover, up the hill and along the bluffs and the curve of the estuary. At the corner of Jamboree and Bristol one of the McIan construction trucks, hauling dirt from the site for seven hundred new condominiums, hurtled across the road without looking either way. The Mustang shot ahead of it. I jammed on the brakes and spun out to avoid being mangled under a ton of dirt.

I caught up with him at the entrance to Pacific Plaza. He circled the department stores and the parking lots to the ring of buildings that housed the financial center, the proliferating medical community, the corporate offices of Rancho Pacifica. They were arranged in a circle like a modern-day Stonehenge, a dozen monoliths growing out of what had once been a mustard-covered hill. Kate called them the Black Hole. "You watch," she had said, "everything gets sucked into them, the brown fields, the estuary, the islands, a nice little beach town, and then gets spewed out again in the form of asphalt and glass, bank transfers, and a vast sea of condominiums."

The turquoise Mustang pulled into a slot reserved for employees of McIan Tower. The kid leapt out over the side of the car without opening the door. It was an island of color in all that sea of pearl-gray Mercedes and jet-black Sevilles and the omnipresent BMWs. I plucked a ticket out of the slot and parked my little green MG, circa 1960, in between a black Ferrari and a silver Rolls.

He made a beeline for the new building and took the elevator to the top floor. I went with him. I stood inside the elevator and held the door open just long enough to see the kid bound across the blue carpet, give a sharp rap and slip inside McIan's office. Miss Silver Bells rose from behind her desk as though to bar the way to her boss's office. I punched the door button and descended to the lobby. I felt slightly sick. And scared.

I called the police department, left a message for Lieutenant Lawrence, and then waited around for several hours for the phone to ring. When I hadn't heard from him by three o'clock, I drove up to the station. Lawrence was just leaving his office when I got there. I followed him across the parking lot to his car.

"Jesus, Cairns, you don't give up easy, do you?"

"I found the kid who was on Catalina with Sylvus."

"It's not my case anymore."

He stuck the key in the door and opened it. "Go find somebody else to bug."

"He works for McIan."

For a minute he hesitated. Then he took the key out of the door and closed it.

"What makes you think so?"

"I followed him up to the McIan Tower. He went into McIan's office. The sanctum sanctorum. An English dragon lady made of Dresden and steel stopped me at the gate."

The parking lot was at the edge of the bluffs. The tide was out. The mudflats of the estuary looked like the slick underbelly of a toad. Duck Island was out there somewhere.

"Maybe you were mistaken."

"I'm not. It was the same kid. He drives a classic turquoise Mustang. He walked into McIan's office like the prodigal son come home."

Lawrence swung around to look at the tall black tower on the hill. His gaze was thoughtful. He flicked an imaginary piece of dust off the cuff of his suit jacket. He noticed me watching.

"I've graduated to plain clothes."

"Congratulations."

"You're sure?"

I nodded.

"All right, Cairns. I'll follow it up. It will probably come to nothing. Maybe he's just a friend of the family. A delivery boy. Could be one of a hundred different connections. I don't suppose you've told anyone else?"

"Not yet—"

"Don't."

"Not even my lawyer?"

"Especially your lawyer. McIan has a lot of power in this town. He won't take it kindly when he hears that you are going around accusing him of being mixed up in drugs. If it turns out to be wrong, he's got an entire firm of lawyers, forty of them, working for him who will be on you like a pack of wolves. You understand?"

I said that I did.

"Good."

He took the car keys out of his pocket and tossed them in the air, caught them neatly. His face was smooth-shaven. His hair had been done by a stylist with slight waves at the front. His cuff links were brushed gold, expensive, understated. It crossed my mind that he and Ms. Trueblood might make a good pair of bookends. I put the thought out of my mind as being unworthy. Maybe I was just jealous.

"I'll handle this, Cairns. Don't go near McIan or the kid. I'll let you know what I find out."

He slipped behind the wheel of the unmarked white Pontiac and shut the door. He turned on the air-conditioning. I hadn't noticed that the air was particularly hot.

"I'll get back to you, Cairns." He made a smart three-point turn and headed up the hill in the direction of Pacific Plaza.

he body of the boy was found floating in the San Diego Harbor the following day. The turquoise Mustang had been abandoned somewhere in El Cajon. By the time it was picked up it had been stripped. All that was left was the paint job.

Lawrence had taken a leave of absence. His replacement took my story and passed me on to someone else who said he'd forward it to San Diego. The murder was out of their jurisdiction and there was nothing they could do about it. Lawrence was on indefinite leave. The connection between McIan and the handsome young man now laid out in the morgue was now severed for good.

I tried to get hold of Thurber. I found a note pinned to his mailbox that he had gone off to Washington, D.C. He would be back at the end of the week. Kate was preparing to confront a planning commission meeting, trying to save the city from some known or unknown fate. I was on my own.

====

Miss Silver Bells was at her post when I arrived in the lobby of McIan Construction. She rose from her desk, alarmed, and moved into my path to bar, with her own porcelain frame, the sanctuary of her boss.

"I want to see McIan."

I brushed past her and strode to his office. I didn't bother to knock. The door was open and I went in.

The office was empty. The desk was bare, the leather chair vacant. Miss Silver Bells, distraught, rushed in behind me and started jabbing at a buzzer under the desk with a long rose-tipped finger.

"Where is he?"

"Mr. McIan is out for the day."

"My name is Cairns. I want to talk to him."

"That will be impossible." She was white. I took a quick look at the executive bathroom while she jabbed another couple of times at the button on the under-side of McIan's desk.

The four men materialized out of nowhere. They looked like ex-football players turned bankers in their dark suits, ties knotted around beefy necks. They surrounded me like the defensive ends of the Green Bay Packers and hustled me out of McIan's office and across the lobby to a Windsor bench behind a potted palm. We sat there against the wall while Miss Silver Bells tried to find someone on the phone who could tell them what to do with me.

The elevator door opened. I wouldn't have been surprised if the Swat Team had arrived. Instead, a middle-aged woman, dressed in a little Gucci tennis outfit, stepped into the lobby and stood there, diamonds clinking impatiently on her thin fingers, waiting for someone to come to attention. Miss Silver Bells was making frantic punches on the phone. She murmured into the mouthpiece and finally looked up.

"Oh! Mrs. McIan!" She made little deferential noises to her boss's wife. It didn't fool me. I wondered what effect it might have on the lady herself.

"Bill asked me to meet him here."

I tried to get a good look at her through the palm fronds. I couldn't decide whether she looked more like McIan's wife or Davidson's daughter. She was a slight, nervous woman in her late forties. Blond hair. Tan. Fashionably thin. Deep-set eyes carefully made up to make the face seem even thinner than it was. The legs beneath the short tennis skirt were like sticks. The tennis shoes had tiny little blue fuzz balls at the ends of the laces.

The two of them stood there a moment as though bound together. "We're trying to locate your husband now. May I get you a cup of tea?" Miss Silver Bells smiled, demure, sweet as a baby. Her face was fresh, the skin pliant, moist, loveliness all wrapped up in one body. Perfection itself. Ellen McIan turned away impatiently and strode over to the far end of the lobby, tossed her purse and keys onto the couch. The little tennis skirt hung limply over her hips. An expensive Italian scent followed her. The young woman's eyes watched her. I wondered what she was thinking. Was she wondering if McIan had ever enjoyed making love to all those bones in search of a little flesh? Ellen McIan picked up a magazine, put it down, picked up another one.

I started to get up but one of the gentleman bullies leaned over a little and kept me in my place. The elevator hummed a little and Lawrence, formerly Lieutenant Lawrence, emerged into the lobby. The suit was about a hundred dollars more expensive than the one he'd worn a couple of days before and he'd turned in the onyx ring for a yellow diamond. Otherwise he was the same nice, deceitful fellow he'd always been. He took a quick glance over at the potted palm into the corner where the five of us sat pressed together like books on a shelf and walked into McIan's office to see, I suppose, if they'd overlooked an accomplice.

The phone rang. It tinkled like a set of door chimes. Miss Silver Bells answered. Her voice was neutral. Sweet as honeysuckle.

"Good morning, Mr. McIan. We've been trying to locate you." She raised her voice just enough to send the silver trill across the lobby. McIan's wife turned away from the window to listen. Her thin face had the alertness of a fox. The lovely secretary gazed steadily back at her while the phone whispered into her ear. For a moment there was an absolute stillness in the room. Only the two of them existed.

Ellen McIan broke the spell. She moved away from

the windows and crossed the lobby toward the desk. She passed within a few feet without a glance in our direction. Without the backlight to soften the outline I could see the fine wrinkling around her throat, the upper arms. Up close she no longer looked young or even beautiful, but merely chic. There was a hard surface to her, like the lacquer the Japanese bake onto their lovely art ware. I wondered, if you chipped it all off, if there would be anything underneath.

She took the phone and spoke into it briefly, then handed it back to Miss Silver Bells, who replaced it for her. "We're having lunch together." She sounded triumphant and weary at the same time.

Lawrence executed some kind of body movement I didn't even see and the four horsemen stood up, freeing me. Lawrence punched the elevator button and I got into it. He pushed another button and we hurtled downward. I tried not to look sick.

"I thought you worked for the city, Lawrence."

"It amounts to the same thing."

He watched the little numbers just like everybody else who hasn't got anything to say. When we hit bottom he walked me through the lobby and out onto the parking lot.

"Stay away from here, Cairns. One little phone call and your bail will be revoked so fast you won't have time to take a pee before they throw you back in jail."

I stood there for a moment looking at Lawrence and wondering how it was possible for a man to change sides with such ease. He was young and personable. He had all the right things: intelligence, looks, ambition. What was missing was any kind of basic values, even the simple ones like right and wrong. He reminded me of a sleek, well-designed sailboat whose architect had neglected to build in a rudder.

He waited for me to get in the car and flip on the motor before he turned and went back into the building. I sat there in the parking lot, watching the door in the rearview mirror. I still wanted to see McIan. If Miss Silver Bells wouldn't lead me to her boss, then Ellen McIan would.

I t didn't take a professional detective to follow Ellen McIan. She drove a Silver Cloud Rolls-Royce. The license plate, if you could take your eyes off the soft silvery grays and satin cream of the interior, was embossed with the initials of the pale-blond lady inside: EDM.

She drove sedately, even cautiously, as though the car, if dented, might be taken away from her. It slid out of the parking lot and down the hill to the Coast Tennis Club. She parked under the porte cochere. One valet opened the door for her. The other drove the Rolls to a shady spot under a tree.

No one challenged me. I walked up along the greens of the golf course to a spot where I had a good view of the tennis courts. Ellen emerged from the locker room almost immediately with a tennis pro and two other women, chatting animatedly. They were younger than she was by a few years but catching up fast. Same outfits. Same hard, skinny bodies. Ellen had the biggest diamonds. They were big as headlights when the sun caught them and reflected back over the court. I don't know how she held the racket on top of all that weight.

The pro took Ellen's side. He kept score and made

suggestions, crouched protectively behind her, laughed at her comments as though she were the most amusing and desirable woman in the world.

There was a strange, almost surreal quality to their play, a kind of commedia dell'arte, staged and over-acted. The women were as animated as puppets. There were two competitions going on. The tennis game was the least of them. The ball was batted back and forth over the net with a kind of manic frenzy in which the object was not to win but to wear them-selves out. Stretch the muscles. Make them cry out. The other, keener battle was entirely psychological. They volleyed observations back and forth to see who was the gayest, the wittiest, the leader of the pack. It made me tired to look at them.

Ellen whacked the ball a little desperately, as though she were afraid of it. It wasn't her game. She pushed herself to do it, engaged, I supposed, in a continual war against age and the subtle infighting against loss of status. The frontlines were here on the tennis court.

They played for exactly an hour. Afterward they sat at a table under an umbrella and drank tea served in a silver pot. A continual parade of women trooped by Ellen's table, stopped to exchange comments and hard little outbursts of laughter. I kept waiting for McIan to appear. At twelve on the dot the Rolls was whisked to the front of the club. Ellen bounded out a moment later, her sweater tossed around her thin shoulders, although she was still perspiring, slipped inside the Rolls, which provided another layer of pro-tective covering, and left.

I followed her up the hill to the section at the top. It was the newest and most expensive of the develop-ments on Rancho Pacifica, whose chief assets were its two-and-a-half-million-dollar-per-lot price tags (land only), and the 360-degree view. Today the usual blanket of smog had come down the river from Los Angeles and obliterated the coastline. The sea shimmered faintly beneath it, red-tinged and ugly. The bay was a smudge across the city. Visibility was about five miles.

Trees were not allowed on the Hill. The Rolls purred along the curving streets, avoiding the cul-de-sacs with which the entire Hill was booby-trapped, and pulled up to the door of an elephantine, honest-to-god Southern antebellum house, with Doric columns shining in the sun, a giant carriage light swinging under the portico, and a little black iron figure waiting on the drive to take your horse. It was as big as a hotel. It didn't look like Ellen to me. I couldn't imagine the girl who had grown up on the bay, cut her teeth on the small white-sailed boats, the Snowbirds, dived off the rickety dock in front of that old, comfortable shingled house, dreaming up this monstrosity. I'd have bet this was McIan's idea of grandeur, not hers. The house swallowed her up. No security guard came out to chase me away.

The street was a cul-de-sac called St. Cloud. I had plenty of time to look at it. There were five houses. Each lot was not quite a quarter of an acre, entirely covered by a gargantuan structure, way out of proportion to the size of the lot. Only a few feet separated McIan's imitation Tara from its neighbor, a simulated mosque. Brilliant blue-and-gold tiles flashed from the walls and from the minaret that rose from the center. The pile of bricks across the street was supposed to look like a manse out of *Lorna Doone*. Two lots remained vacant. Two-million-dollar views witnessed only by an occasional jackrabbit and a few clumps of milkweed. The whole thing looked like a set for a Hollywood movie or the backlot on a Universal Studios tour.

I sat there for an hour. No one came up the street or left. There was not a sound from any of the houses—no human voice, no radio. If there were people inside they did not open the windows, let the dog out, rattle the trash, or call the children in from play.

When she finally emerged, Ellen was dressed to match the Rolls. Her outfit had probably cost several thousand dollars. It was made of silk, all beige and cream, with touches of silver and a broad-brimmed hat to match. The blond hair was combed smooth. A pair of expensive dark glasses hid her eyes. She looked elegant and chic. If I hadn't known how old she was, I might have guessed her to be in her early thirties. She pulled out of the drive and drove down the hill.

Los Coyotes Country Club was perched on the rim of a great big sinkhole that had been converted by clever promoters into one of the poshest enclaves in the city. The canyon, cut off from a view of the sea by Pacific Plaza, which rose behind it, had been carpeted with a golf course and rimmed by million-dollar homes. The sign on the door said "Members Only." I gave the man at the desk my name and said I was meeting William C. Thurber the Third. He nodded and told me I could wait in the bar.

From the lobby I could see over the bar into the dining room. A group of dowagers, old-timers, was planted around an octagonal leather-topped table, engrossed in a game of bridge. From the size of the

Scotch glasses, the pile of cigarette butts in the ash-tray, and the absence of small talk, I supposed that they were more or less permanent fixtures in the club. Age-spotted arms, laden down with bracelets, clanked dangerously every time they picked up a card or laid one down.

The tables in the dining room were filled. No junior executives here. The accumulated wealth of the occupants, if used in concert, could have raised or lowered the Wall Street Index by several points. I recognized the president of Ward Multinational Chemicals, the owner of Coast Publications, who was responsible for the rise of big-league Republicans in California, the retired admiral who sat on the board of several defense-industry firms. The women were arrayed throughout the room like exotic birds. They perched on the massive armchairs and chittered and chattered while they picked at their quail salads and sipped their Chablis. A sixty-year-old developer-turned-politician walked through the lobby with a sweet young thing half his age. His ex-wife sat at a table by the window, a chain-smoking, bitter old lady who'd been tossed out the day their fourth and final child graduated from USC. The last ten years of her life had been singlemindedly devoted to lawyers and court appointments in an attempt to wrest something from the thirty-five years she had invested in her husband's ambitions. Through all this Ellen McIan walked to her table, elegant and fragile and very careful, as though she were navigating a minefield.

McIan never showed. Ellen ordered a spinach-and-mushroom salad and ate alone. For the hour and a half that she sat there, she was on display, back erect, face composed and alert. Everyone who walked in or out stopped to pay a courtesy call, which she accepted spiritedly. I felt sorry for her. She was a cipher. I wondered if she didn't sometimes long for the security of being Davidson's daughter that she had exchanged for the struggle to keep up as McIan's wife.

By two-thirty the room was emptying. Ellen took a single bite out of her raspberry tart and pushed it aside, wiped her lips delicately with a gold napkin, and nodded to the waiter to bring her the discreet leather-encased check to sign.

I left the club before she did. On the way to my car I passed the Rolls. A thick sheaf of architectural plans lay across the back seat. I tried both doors but they were locked. The parking attendant gave me a suspicious look. I pretended I'd made a mistake and went on to my own car.

I stayed on Ellen's trail for the rest of the afternoon. She belonged to a world completely alien to the quiet unpretentious little beach town in which she had grown up. She and her friends flitted from one boutique to another in search of the perfect handbag, the most stylish pair of shoes, the most expensive belt. I sat outside Le Chic for two hours while tall, angular females with French accents served Ellen champagne in her private showroom and brought one item after another for her inspection in the quest for the perfect little dress.

It started to rain at about five-thirty. Shoppers and salesgirls scurried from all directions across the dampening parking lots in search of their cars. The manager of Le Chic, a pale, anxious-looking man, escorted Ellen to the Rolls, holding a silk parasol over her head.

Ellen's last appointment was with her hairdresser. I could see her through the great plate-glass windows in the second-story studio of Jean Louis. I sat below them in the parking lot. The hill dropped away to the coast. A steady stream of traffic moved up and down Pacific Coast Highway and threaded its way inland along Jamboree and MacArthur. It was almost dark. The salon made an island of light in the darkening landscape. Ellen was the only client. Jean Louis fluttered around the shop like a dancer, telling jokes, giving instructions to the three assistants, passing a tray of canapés, while Ellen sipped champagne and chattered back at him. He ran his fingers through Ellen's hair, held her chin up, examining her as seriously as he would a work of fine art for flaws, pointed to a curl that needed snipping. Occasionally he came to the window and looked out at the parking lot and the rain, the black sea swallowing up the edge of the world.

For the first time that day Ellen seemed to be having fun. I could see her tension drop away. It was as though, for this hour, she had been released from the need to be on guard against the world. Jean Louis was charming, animated, non-threatening. The camaraderie between them was obvious and real. They giggled and chortled and traded secrets while the girls chipped away at her hair. The two of them formed a conspiracy, plotting together to outwit the world of one-upmanship that lay outside the warm, light-filled loft.

A little before six, a BMW so new it still had the price sticker on the window purred into the parking lot and stopped next to the Rolls. The door opened and Lawrence, McIan's new winged Mercury, emerged in a London Fog raincoat. The key to the Rolls was on his key ring. He reached in and took the architectural plan off the back seat. He relocked the Rolls, careful not to let the rain in on the leather seat, got back in his own car, and purred off down the hill.

In the loft above, Ellen took her last sip of champagne, stood up from the chair renewed and resplendent, said good night and came out to the parking lot. Jean Louis watched her from the window until she was safe inside the Rolls, doors locked. He blew her a kiss and turned away to close up for the night. Ellen turned the headlights on and drove off to the glittering battleground of her husband's world. I went back to mine.

They looked like little girls playing dress-up, all of them, for some reason, in black, festooned with sequins and ostrich feathers, they stepped out of chauffeur-driven limousines like long-necked birds, stalking on heels too high for their thin legs and trotted in pairs, mated, presumably, for life, in and out of the Founders' Club. Ears dripping diamonds, hair sleek as boys' hair, they moved in flocks beneath the glittering Lippold *Firebird*, fluttered chirping and cooing to their seats in the newly built Arts Pavilion. Orange County society imitating New York, having not yet quite got the hang of it. Full-length fur coats transplanted into the middle of an orange grove.

McIan and his wife came late. David stuck close behind them. They strode past Henry Moore's *Reclining Figure* to the second-story entrance and disappeared into the Patron's Lounge. Kate and I made our way upstairs to the balcony. McIan had his own box. Ellen played hostess. They weren't yet up there with the owners of Rancho Pacifica, but they were getting there. Maybe that's why McIan had picked this place where everything was still so new. You could still buy your way to the top. No one asked for credentials, bloodlines, education. It made for a lot of laughs. Maybe it was more democratic that way.

David saw me. Even across the theater I could see him turn pale. I waited for him to nudge his father, point me out, but instead he rose and moved to a seat in the back of the box where I could no longer see him.

The orchestra performed Beethoven's Fifth Symphony. There was a lot of clapping between movements and bravos thrown in places where tradition called for awed silence. I gave them brownie points for eagerness. You never knew. Maybe some of it would take. The place glittered like a palace. For some reason I kept thinking of the sea wall down at the end of the Island where it was dark and the bay made lonely slapping noises against the rock.

I waited for McIan outside his box. He came out at intermission. He saw me and brushed past, surrounded by his guests. A bodyguard blocked my way at the head of the stairs. I watched them sweep down the rose-carpeted stairway, under the Lippold bird toward which McIan had donated half a million dollars. Light refracted from the great sheets of glass and the chandeliers and the diamonds that passed underneath, as hard and precise as the laughter that accompanied them.

The door opened magically. The limo was waiting. By the time Kate and I had disentangled ourselves from the security guard in the tuxedo and run down after them, McIan was gone. Palms rose out of the cement into the night sky. Miami or Palm Springs erected on the ghosts of asparagus farms and lima-bean fields. I stood for a moment under the red stone arch and gazed down the hill to the blackness that hid the sea. A faint breeze came up from the bay and ruffled the palms. For a brief instant, before the exhaust of the cars came up and overwhelmed it, I caught the faint, sad, salt taste of the sea. Or maybe I just imagined I did.

"Twenty thousand bucks by noon tomorrow or the team of lawyers up on the Hill will cease to represent you."

Thurber didn't like playing messenger. He sounded harassed. "I can loan it to you, Cairns, but you've got to stop fooling around playing detective and get serious.

"I know you're innocent and *you* know you're innocent. But that is not going to keep you from spending the next thirty years in a six-by-ten-foot cell which, providing you are a good boy and survive, will make you about seventy when they open the doors and let you out."

"Twenty thousand?"

"That's just for starters."

*   *   *

The mail turned up a tax bill for Sven's house. It was about half of what I earned in a year. The first quarter payment was due by February 15. The contractor arrived at the house with his estimate for bringing Kate's gallery up to code. The two of us practically choked to death laughing. If someone was trying to force us into selling the property Sven had left us, he was pulling all the right strings.

Ms. Trueblood had traded in the cream silk and fourteen-karat gold for Italian paisley and sterling silver jewelry. A wreath from Del Mar Gardens with a red velvet ribbon and half a dozen brown partridges obscured the window in the door. A fire twinkled from a gas log in the fireplace that was built into the corner of the office.

The contract was sitting on the French provincial desk. With a fingernail, long and tapered, painted pewter to match the earrings, she tapped the place where my signature would go. Typed in above it was the description of the property. It contained Sven's address and the numbers of the three lots.

"It's a very handsome offer, Mr. Cairns. I would say you were a very lucky man."

"What does your client want with Duck Island?"

"I wouldn't know, I'm sure."

"Suppose we won't sell it. Only the house."

"Then the deal's off." Her mouth snapped shut. I wanted to stuff the piece of paper down through her

181

porcelain teeth. Only the lawyer bills—utterly incomprehensible to a teacher—stopped me.

"I'll take the contract home. Think about it. Talk it over with Kate."

"This is the only copy I have." Ms. Trueblood whisked the contract from the desk. "I do urge you to sign it at your earliest convenience." She pulled open the drawer in the cabinet behind her desk and flipped through the files. Officiously, she slipped the contract into its proper folder. She realized her mistake the moment she made it and slammed the drawer shut. But she'd been a quarter of a second too late. The name on the divider gave her client away. McIan was the one who wanted to buy Sven's property. Surprise, surprise.

The voice had a heavy accent. He said his name was Jorgensen. He was a member of the Scandinavian Club.

"I have some information you might like to have about Sven."

Last Thursday of the month. For thirty years the Scandinavian Club had met at the Elks Lodge in Costa Mesa. It was Sven's night out. He hadn't missed one for as long as I had lived with him. It was a ritual.

Sven would leave the house about nine. The 1969 Chevy was in the garage, directly beneath my bed. Sven had the idea you had to prime the engine in order to get it going. Something like cranking up the old-time buggies or pumping up a woman to get her in the mood. Foot down on the gas pedal, full speed, he sat there in the garage for a full five minutes, pumping away, engine roaring like he was doing sixty, bucking and heaving like a team of Clydesdales. Finally, when he figured he'd juiced it up enough, he'd stick it in gear and the car would shoot, back end first, out of the garage and screech to a halt about two inches from the fence on the other side of the alley. Usually he got one of the trash cans. Then the car would have to sit there whining like a jet while he picked up the trash, banged the garage door down, pumped the gas a couple of more times for good luck, and then went racketing up the peninsula in his one good shirt and tie to court the old ladies of the Scandinavian Club.

I went with him once. The meeting never started until it was pitch dark and all the kids were tucked in bed and the dinner dishes done. They'd been doing it as long as I could remember. I suppose it reminded them of the long winters of their childhood when they didn't get a glimpse of the sun for weeks at a time and got together in warm, light-filled houses to thumb their noses at the dark outside.

I was exhausted just watching them. All these old-timers with names like Krudson and Boldt and Gjuldenstern and Dykstra, having a lovely time jerking each other around the floor doing polkas and waltzes as if it were 1932 and they were back in the Old Country. Sven was the star of the show. A bevy of old widows, and some of them not so old, swarmed around him like bees around the honey pot. He ate it up. Took them out on the floor for a spin, one by one. He'd feel them up a little, drop them off when they were exhausted, pick up the next. Those bandy little legs kicked out beneath him and he hopped from one foot to the other like a goddamn Norwegian troll, pulling the ladies along with those strong fisherman's arms of his and the great big hands clutching their waists. He was randy, too. You couldn't miss it. The women loved it. Made them feel young again. Wanted. About one or two in the morning they broke up. Two-thirty on the dot the car would roar down the alley like the Spruce Goose coming in for a landing. The garage door banged up against the floor under my bed so that the whole apartment vibrated as if it had been hit by a tank. Sometimes he brought one of the old ladies home with him and I could hear them giggling and whispering as they crossed the yard and then the sound of that old bedstead banging against the wall for half the night. Tonight I'd have given anything I owned to hear the car start to heave and buck and see old Sven riding it down the street like a jockey on a horse. But the car sat silent and cold in the garage beneath me.

In its place was this strange voice inviting me to come to his office. The Scandinavian-American Bank in Costa Mesa.

He gave me the address and said 10 A.M. would be fine.

He was a big man with oversized hands and feet, and ears hanging away from his face like windflaps. He wore a banker's suit, a couple of years old and not quite in style. I remembered him now that I saw him. Sven and I had helped him move his piano one Saturday morning. According to Sven he was tightfisted but honest and he owned enough stock to buy half the city.

The bank, of which, it seemed, he was president, was about the only old building left standing near the intersection of Ocean and Harbor boulevards, just inland from the beach. It had cement curlicues over the door and windows. Dark wood paneling. Marble floor. Someone had tried to modernize it with a carpet and a couple of light-colored couches, but it still looked like a bank. There was no automatic teller in front. There were still some people, I guessed, who liked to feel their money was locked away all safe and sound in a vault.

He sat behind his desk and motioned me to sit across from him.

"Sven was my friend." It came out of Jorgensen like a confession of guilt. He had a dour face. It wasn't given to making rash statements.

He moved his big hands nervously over his thighs, finally settled them on his knees. After forty years in this country he still spoke with a heavy accent. I had to listen carefully, and even then I had to guess at one or two of the words.

"Sven and I argued all the time. For forty years. Politics. Women. Money. He didn't believe in banks. A person was a fool to trust them after what happened in the Depression, he said. Wouldn't open up an account. Wouldn't invest. Called me a pennypincher. But when my son got thrown out of the high school and then even continuation school wouldn't keep him, Sven took him on as a fisherman, put him to work, taught him a trade. Saved his life."

Jorgensen pulled a handkerchief out of his pocket and unfolded it. It was enormous. He blew his nose on it. Wiped his eyes. Put it away.

"Sent the Hufbauer girl to Harvard."

I blinked.

"You didn't know that, did you? Came here and

185

borrowed the money. Paid it back, every cent. Imagine. Didn't graduate from high school. Sent a girl to Harvard."

"Sven talked about you all the time. Bragged about how you were so smart. An English teacher. Stanford graduate. Loved you like you were his son."

Jorgensen's desk was covered with neat piles of documents, pencils lined up, an old-fashioned pen set. A bookcase held a few reference books, interest tables, a telephone directory. A computer, state of the art, sat at a typewriter table in one corner of the room.

"Sven wasn't at the September meeting of the Scandinavian Club. It would have been the last one before—" He paused, changed his mind. "While he was still alive."

I suppose I looked startled. Sven hadn't missed a meeting in all the years I'd lived with him. I tried to think back to the last Thursday in September. It seemed like a year ago. School had been in session for three weeks. We'd been reading John Updike's "Pigeon Feathers." It was about a boy trying to make order out of a disordered universe. The students were struggling with it and I was upstairs in my apartment redoing my lesson plans so that we could spend another day examining the story. I'd seen Sven in the kitchen, his hair all wet down, tie knotted around his neck. Exactly like all those other Thursday nights except that this time, now that I thought about it, he hadn't asked me to come with him. He went out at the usual time. Came back sometime before two in the morning. Banged the garage door up against the floor just as Kate floated toward me in a dream. I'd wakened with a jerk and a sudden sense of despair. Sven had put the car away and gone into the house alone.

Jorgensen stood up and walked to the window. The

186

street outside was jammed with traffic. A new construction project was going up on the corner.

"I was coming up Coast Highway toward Dover on my way to the Elks Club. I was late. Sven turned in front of me and went up the hill toward Pacific Plaza. I thought maybe he was going to pick up Clara. Maybe you heard Sven talk about her?"

I remembered Clara. She was the lovely old lady in the wheelchair. Hair white as snow. Fine-lipped. Startling blue eyes. Sven had visited her in the hospital every day for six months. Put on his tie and a clean shirt and drove all the way to Orange to sit by her bed for an hour. Bought flowers for her from a little stand by the freeway. Tulips. Freesia. Iris. Just as if he were courting. Gave her something to live for. Brought her home when she was well enough to come.

"Clara lives in a condominium behind Los Coyotes. But she was not feeling well that night. She had already called me and I thought I could save Sven the trip. I honked and waved but you know Old Sven. He was driving like he was in a steeplechase and he didn't see me.

"I followed him up to the financial center on the hill. The place was deserted. Parking lots empty. Kind of eerie, all those buildings, dark offices, and Sven just circling around and around them.

"By then, of course, I'd figured out that he wasn't going to pick up Clara. It wasn't like Sven. So I watched to see what he was going to do. Finally he parked. It was under a row of eucalyptus behind the theater. I saw him get out and walk back up the hill toward the McIan Tower like he was going to meet someone. I knew it was none of my business, so I left and went on to the meeting. Afterward, when he never came, I was curious, so on my way home I drove back up to the center. Sven's car was still there.

All alone in that huge center. I waited there for a while, maybe fifteen minutes, and when he didn't come back to the car, I went home."

"Did he ever tell you what he was doing there?"

"I didn't want to ask. I was a little worried. I called him the next day. From the office here. I said I'd missed him at the meeting the night before."

"What did he tell you?"

"He said he had a touch of the flu. He thought maybe it was food poisoning. He had decided to stay at home."

Jorgensen shrugged. "It's possible. Maybe I made a mistake. Maybe it wasn't Sven I saw. It looked like him. Like his car. But maybe, in the dark, I was wrong."

He plucked his glasses off the bridge of his nose, held them up to the light, put them back on again. He looked at me. It was my turn.

"Sven didn't have the flu. He told me he was going to the Scandinavian Club meeting and went out."

Jorgensen had hoped for a different answer. He sighed.

"Well, Sven was about as honest as they come. If he lied to me he must have had a very good reason. I told the police. They didn't seem very interested."

I stood up and walked to the door. He followed me.

"Maybe if you can find out what he was doing up there, it will help you. I wouldn't want to think you killed Sven. Sven wasn't the smartest man I ever knew. But he wasn't usually wrong about people.

"Find out who killed him. Sven had a lot of friends. He never did harm to anyone." And then softly, "Good luck."

Davidson hung up on me.

I called him back three times before he'd talk to me.

"You're crazy as a loon, Cairns."

"Sven was inside the McIan Tower. He found something. A few days later he was dead."

Davidson exploded in mirth.

"You should be certified, Cairns. Locked up in Pacific View."

"David is the one who took him in."

That stopped him. The old man loved his grandson. Child of his only daughter.

"Sven came by your place, didn't he? Asked you to go with him? Get him into the tower? And you refused."

"Goddamn right I did. Wanted to know what McIan was up to. How the hell am I supposed to know what that candy-assed bastard is doing? Whatever it is, it's no good. Nothing I can do to stop him."

"So David took Sven up there one night. Who else could do it? They were great pals, Old Sven and your grandson. David probably thought it was a lark. Taking Sven's side against the power and might of his father's company. Battling windmills on behalf of a crusty old fisherman."

"Hmph!" The old man couldn't make up his mind whether to be scornful or proud. "The kid would never go against his father. Thinks the sun rises and sets on that bastard."

"This time he did."

Davidson started humming the "Battle Hymn of the

Republic." I guess it was his way of informing me that he had stopped listening.

"Maybe your son-in-law killed Sven."

The grapes of trampling wrath ended in a growl. "Bastard! I wouldn't put it past him."

"Take me inside."

"No."

"You owe it to Sven."

He didn't say anything. I could almost hear him waiting.

"It's your chance to get even."

I had him then. The old man circled the hook, looked at it from all sides. Deliberated. Made up his mind. He hemmed and hawed for a couple of more minutes. In the end he agreed.

"Maybe he'll kill you, too, Cairns." The idea didn't seem to upset him. One the contrary, he thought it was as funny as hell and chortled away as though he'd just farted at a fraternity brawl. I laughed with him. Even in my own ears it sounded as thin and fake as a piece of tin.

We set the time for 11 P.M.

The moon came up late. It floated up behind Saddleback and came to a full stop over Pacific Plaza. It hovered there like a spotlight. Beneath it the McIan Tower stretched into the sky as cold and empty as the outline of a metal trap.

Davidson was already there. I parked behind the theater and walked across to where he waited in the parking lot. We covered the distance between the car and the door to the tower in silence. It seemed taller than I remembered. Heavier. Stanley Kubrick's Monolith transported to the California coast for some mysterious purpose. Not a light showed in the building unless you counted the faint glow from the lobby and the tiny red light on the roof to warn airplanes away.

It took a couple of minutes for the guard to leave his post and come across the lobby to let us in. He was about Davidson's age, or a little younger, leather-cheeked, hard-jawed, the wreck of a once handsome man. His paunch strained against the clean beige uniform. He peered out at us and then, recognizing Davidson, let us in.

"Son of a gun! You still alive?"

Davidson peered over his glasses at the face, squinted at the name tag, growled when he finally placed him.

"Working for the enemy, I see."

The guard grinned like a kid.

"Ranch land's all gone, in case you didn't notice. Sold off the last of the cows last year. Tore down the feed store and put in a Chucky Cheese. Rancho Pacifica let me go. McIan took me on as part-time security guard. You'd think they had enough Chucky Cheeses, wouldn't you?"

Davidson growled again.

They reminisced for a few minutes while I looked around the lobby. Tried to spot the cameras. The alarm bells. Beside me the two of them cackled away like old women recounting the days when they were kids and went to school in a one-room affair on the beach. Before one of them had gone to work for Rancho Pacifica as a ranch hand and the other had developed a couple of lots and become rich.

I listened with half an ear. Envying the old coots.

Nights they sneaked out to camp in the cave at Pirate's Cove and swam naked across to the peninsula. Built a campfire just about here where Pacific Plaza now stood and set the whole hill ablaze. Fished and shot ducks and chased rabbits across the miles and miles of marsh and ranchland. Before the developers moved in and paved it all. Built shopping centers. Set up row upon row of condominiums. Before cowhands had been forced to hire out as security guards.

Davidson was enjoying himself. He started into a long harangue about Rancho Pacifica but I stopped him. Touched him lightly on the shoulder.

"Well," he said. "Good to see you again, Ennison. Us old guys got to stick together."

He started across the black-and-white marble foyer toward the elevator.

"I'm sorry, Ernie. I can't let you go up there."

Davidson stopped. Turned around. Ennison stood his ground nervously. The camaraderie vanished. The age-old imperative of rank took its place.

"What do you mean, I can't go up there? You want my driver's license? Master Charge? I'm Ernie Davidson. I own this place."

Ennison was trembling. I suppose it was on the tip of his tongue to tell the old man that he didn't own it anymore. He had to make a choice. The old power or the new. He ran his finger down the list of names fastened to his clipboard.

Ennison shook his head apologetically. "We've got a new security man, Ernie. No one is allowed upstairs without authorization. Your name isn't on the list."

I thought Davidson was going to explode.

"Give me that list." He stuck his hand out imperiously. I felt sorry for Ennison.

The guard hesitated. Gave the clipboard to Davidson.

The list was typed. Triple-spaced. I supposed that Miss Silver Bells might have done it when she wasn't too busy looking pretty in the outer office or playing hostess aboard the *Mach 10*. Davidson scrawled his name at the bottom of the list. Added a period for good measure. Jammed the clipboard back into Ennison's chest.

"Now, then, do you see my name on that list?"

"Yes, sir."

"Well, then, I am going to go up to the twentieth floor. My friend will accompany me. We are going to look out the window and see the lights in White's Bay, much of which is still registered in my name. And whatever else we do is none of your goddamn business."

The elevator door was open. Davidson stormed across the lobby and into the black-mirrored cubicle. He jabbed at the buttons. Behind us his old pal picked up the security phone. The elevator bore us swiftly up through the cold shafts of steel into the black silence of the tower.

A single night light glowed by the elevator door. Beyond it the lobby was dense and black. All the blues blurred together like ink spilling down a well. Davidson figured we had six minutes before someone came to throw us out of the office. I told him to go back down. Argue with Ennison. See if he could delay them another minute or two. I heard the elevator descend, stop somewhere below, continue down.

I moved away from the reassuring glow by the elevator into the darkness. The silence of the place was overwhelming. I listened for the little hums and whirs that usually made up an office. The click of machines turning on and off. Recording devices slowly unwinding. There were none. Every sound was buried deep in the carpeting and behind locked doors.

The only light came from outside. The smoked glass at the far end of the lobby kept most of it out but a small portion got through. Lights from the city reflected back from the moisture in the air. The bay was silver under the moon. Two shadows stood out at the entrance to the estuary. I couldn't make out what they were.

I felt my way along the bank of doors until I got to McIan's office. The key slipped into the lock and turned. The door opened and I went inside. Felt along the wall for the light switch and flicked it on.

The place was about as big and empty as the lobby. There was a fireplace made of black marble and a bookcase full of leather-bound books that looked unreadable. An enormous desk with nothing on it but a great big sheet of glass and a phone. I went through the drawers. They were as neat and uninteresting as the top of the desk. No bills, no letters, no contracts. Except for the set of plans. I didn't stop to look at them. The copier was in the next room. I got the first five or six pages done before I heard the faint far-off vibration in the elevator shaft. I replaced the plans and ran across the lobby toward the elevator, which was moving slowly upward. It stopped on the floor below. Footsteps converged in the stairwells. It sounded like a small army positioning itself for an assault.

I slipped a credit card out of my pocket and poked it into the crack between the two elevator doors, sliding it up and down until I broke the beam. The door opened an inch, just enough for my hand to get inside and force it back. The top of the elevator sat there, about two feet below the edge of the lobby floor. Just as it purred into action, I stepped out on it, crouched, and lay spread-eagled across the top.

It stopped just under the roof. I heard the troops clatter out of the elevator and burst up the stairwell into the lobby. Heard a voice that sounded ominously like Lawrence shouting orders. Guards positioning themselves around the lobby. Doors opening and closing. Rooms being searched one by one.

It took them about ten minutes. After that they began working their way downward, floor by floor, while I lay in the dark, vibrating shaft that ran through the center of the building. The steel cords dangled and looped and held taut by turn. Below me the elevator filled with guards and emptied, filled again and moved down. One of the guards remained in it for the duration of the search. I could hear him moving nervously, butting his gun up against the doorway beneath me.

By midnight they had gone through the whole building and started up again, floor by floor. The elevator trembled and lifted, trembled and lifted. Sometimes it sped upward for twenty floors and then dropped back down to the basement while I lay there in the dark, willing myself not to be sick. Finally it anchored somewhere between. By then I had lost track of where I was. Things seemed to quiet down for the night.

The cold came up through the shaft and the great mass of the building pressed in on me. I must have drifted off to sleep because I woke suddenly, sweating, with the certainty that the building, like a black hole, was trying to absorb me into it.

I waited until the morning staff came to work. Until the typewriters started tapping and the phones ringing. Waited for the appraisers and the brokers and the admen to begin their dapper parade in and out of the building before I worked the escape plate loose on the top of the elevator and slipped down inside. I got out on the thirteenth floor and made my way to the stairwell. It led down to the basement, and finally, out into the light of day.

"Cairns?" It was Davidson. He was mad as hell. I was afraid he was going to have a heart attack over the phone.

"What the hell happened to you last night? You left me hanging high and dry."

"I spent the night in the elevator shaft."

"Goddammit. You should have come out with me."

"And get myself shot?"

"I told them you were my nephew."

"Have you got a nephew?"

"Dozens." He said the word bitterly. Rich men accumulate them like flies. "No one would ever know the difference."

I didn't bother to tell him Lawrence would. I waited for him to get to the point.

He took a long breath, steeling himself to do something he didn't want to do. I had a good idea what it would be.

"What did you find, Cairns?"

"Nothing."

"Run that by me again." He sounded unbelieving.

"Not a goddamn thing. The office was as clean as a silicon lab."

"You mean I spent the night talking to a bunch of goons for damn all nothing? It was a wild-goose chase?"

"If it's any consolation to you, I found out what the key was for."

"What's that supposed to mean?"

"It means that Sven had the key to McIan's office." I waited. He said nothing. "Someone gave it to him, and if you didn't, then it must have been your grandson."

I waited until that sank home. There was a long silence.

"There must have been something, Cairns. They were scared as hell."

"Nothing."

"You're sure?"

"I'm sure."

I could feel the relief over the phone.

"Well, if you get any more hairbrained schemes like maybe breaking into the White House or storming the Kremlin, be sure to count me out."

He banged the phone down so hard it bounced against my ear. The soft click came a second later and then the dial tone.

We published the plan. Thurber advised us that it was probably illegal and that we were setting ourselves up for more lawsuits. We did it anyway. Kate and I wrote the preface. We had the first fifteen thousand back from the printer by noon on Tuesday. By late afternoon several thousand of them were in the mail and Kate's volunteers were distributing them to markets and libraries.

The plan puzzled all of us. We spread out the architectural drawings on the floor and pored over them, the three of us. It was nothing less than the reconstruction of the entire last third of the peninsula. All of the houses, except for a few of the large ones on the bay side, were gone. In their place was a line of high-rise hotels and apartments down the center like a spine. The dunes beyond Sven's house were gone. On both sides, down to the water, were a golf course, teahouses, tennis courts, and restaurants. A gate cut the peninsula off from the mainland. From the peninsula point, just north of the jetty, a four-lane bridge arched up over the bay and ended on Bayside Drive below Mesa del Mar.

It reminded me of the Costa del Sol. My father, a professor at Pomona College, had spent one of his sabbaticals in Spain and we had lived in a tiny house down on the beach near the little village of Torremolinas. In front of the house there was nothing but miles of sand and the waves breaking in off the Mediterranean and at night the little lights of the fishermen's boats winking across the dark. When we returned a few years later a wall of hotels cut off the view of the sea. Bodies packed the sands. The water was too polluted to swim in. The little house and the woman who had cooked our fish and the husband who had caught it had all disappeared.

"He can't do it. First of all, the dunes. That's public land. And then what about zoning laws?" I shook my head. "This place is inviolate. Can't even put up an apartment house along here, much less a hotel." I suppose I sounded indignant.

Kate nearly laughed herself to death over that one. "You're so naive, Chandler."

I raised an eyebrow.

"What do you think this whole recall election is about? Zoning laws are changed all the time. Planning permits are issued by the city. The city council can vote to make exceptions to zoning laws or change

198

them altogether. They've already done it six times this year. That's why we're trying to get rid of them. Before they do something really big. Like this." She brushed her hand impatiently across the plan.

"McIan is pouring money into the election to fight us. Three quarters of a million dollars already."

"Maybe he's just being patriotic."

That got a good laugh.

"My guess is that he's already got those four city councilmen in his pocket and he doesn't want to lose them. With them he can call all the shots. He can be, without stepping inside city hall, the power behind the city. Sit up there in the tower and pick up the phone. Point his finger. Nod his head and someone else makes the move for him."

"Has he done it?"

Kate shook her head. "No. That's the funny thing. He hasn't asked for a thing. I think he's just biding his time. Waiting for his big opening."

"What's all this got to do with Sven? No one would murder an old man over a city council race or a couple of lots on the beach."

Kate threw up her hands in exasperation. It was the years of harassment as she and her little band walked the streets and sat in front of post offices; had the sprinklers turned on them as they approached a house; the biting contempt of the local newspapers.

Thurber growled from his corner. "Money, Cairns. People murder for a safeful of diamonds. Strangle old couples in their beds for a fifty-thousand-dollar inheritance. Kill guards as easily as they swat flies so that they can break into a bank and get away with half a million. That's peanuts, Cairns. Do you have any idea what kind of money a project like this will generate?"

I shook my head.

"Hundreds of millions. Billions. A renewable resource. Not just once but every year. Year after year. One roll of the dice and the money starts flowing in. All you've got to do from then on is hire a roomful of accountants to keep track of it all. *I* sure as hell wouldn't want to be the one person who stood between McIan and all that money."

"Well, there is another little matter," I volunteered smugly, in an attempt to get my own back. "McIan doesn't own the land."

That stumped them. Rancho Pacifica, McIan's rival, was rich because it owned the land. Bought it for practically nothing. Miles and miles of it. Better than oil. Better than gold. It was like starting out to build a hot-dog stand with a billion dollars, all clear, sitting in the bank just collecting interest, waiting to be spent. McIan didn't have that advantage. I didn't know how much it would cost to buy up all those lots near the end of the peninsula, but I didn't think even Rancho Pacifica would want to make that investment. And, of course, most of us wouldn't sell. And nobody owned the dunes.

"McIan's father-in-law owns all this." Thurber moved his hand across the center strip of the peninsula. "But it is leased land. The contracts still have fifteen years and more to go. Nothing in hell is going to make the lessees pack up and go. Davidson owns the land but the residents own the houses. Even if Davidson died and left it all to Ellen, McIan couldn't do a thing with them until about the year two thousand. And then, of course, more than half the lots are privately owned. Like Sven's."

We mulled that over for a while. Thurber got out his calculator and began to add up the price of the real estate. Kate tried to help him. They finally gave it up.

"But what about Duck Island? Why does McIan want that? It isn't even in the plan."

"He doesn't." Kate was very sure about that. "That was just to throw us off the track. A little bit of sleight of hand. It's Sven's lots he wants. But why?"

"That's crazy. It's just a little ocean-front lot. Two of them side by side. Worth about half of what he's offered for them." We sat there staring at the map for a few minutes.

Thurber caught it first. It was the same thing the planning director, searching his city map, had discovered, zeroed in on, kept for his own lucrative secret.

The lot number in Sven's will didn't match the one on the lot next door to his house. According to the plan that lot belonged to a man named Whitley who lived in Gambier, Ohio.

"Well, where the hell is it? According to the will the lot is adjacent."

"What's the number again?"

"One-one-eight-four-oh-two."

It took us a while to find the right lot, and when we did we simply sat and stared at each other, unbelieving.

Old Sven owned the entire end of the peninsula. All the dunes between the bay and the oceanfront, running down to the wedge. No one had ever built on it. Everyone assumed it was just part of the public beach. It had never even been subdivided into lots. Someone had bought it whole. Old Sven owned the whole thing.

For the first time we were stunned into silence.

I picked up the phone and dialed Davidson. He was livid. He had just gone down to the market and found the copies of the plan sitting next to the cash register.

"Davidson. This is Cairns. Who owns the dunes?"

Davidson growled like a grizzly with an acute case of appendicitis. "You do."

"How did Sven get it?"

It was a sore point with Davidson. He didn't want to tell me. I threatened to come over and steal his sandbags.

"The dunes were mine. I gave them to him."

"Gave?"

"Well, it amounted to the same thing." He drummed impatiently on the receiver. It sounded like he was hammering on his teeth.

"I had the chance to put up another housing tract in Costa Mesa. But I needed the money to get it off the ground quick. A couple of thousand. I talked Sven into loaning it to me."

"And in exchange you put the whole end of the peninsula up for collateral. Just like Duck Island."

"Damned fool thing to do."

"Why didn't you redeem it? I suppose when Sven wanted his money back you kept putting him off."

"Sore as hell he was, too. Didn't want the property. Never forgave me. I offered to buy it back about ten years ago. Wouldn't sell. Said if I built on the dunes it would block his view of the ocean. I said he could have the best lot. He nearly blew my head off. Told me his neighbors thought they owned beachfront property. Nobody had told them the dunes didn't belong to the city. Said a new development would spoil the peninsula. Went on about the birds and the kids who played there and the young couples who hid in the dunes and made love at night. Goddamn fool. He could have been a rich man."

"He *was* a rich man."

Davidson started to hang up.

"Davidson!" I stopped him.

"What's McIan planning to do? How can he get his hands on the rest of the peninsula?"

"He can't. I own those lots. Even if I die and Ellen gets them, he'll have to wait another fifteen years before most of the leases come up for renewal." Davidson was nobody's fool. He'd had time to examine all the possibilities. I took his word for it. He banged the phone down.

I turned to the others and grinned.

"He can't."

That's where all of us were wrong.

 "David's gone!!"

It took me a minute to wake up and then another to recognize the voice. There was no Miss Silver Bells to make the call for him and ask me to hold the line. I looked at the clock. It wasn't quite six in the morning.

"What's the matter, McIan?"

"David's been missing for two days. He left for school on Wednesday and never got there. Where is he? Have you got him?" It was more threat than question.

I tried to peer through the window. It was still dark outside.

"I haven't seen him since a week ago last Monday night at the Arts Pavilion. He was with you. Why would I know where he is?"

"We had a fight. It was about you and the goddamn trick you pulled with the plans. He took your side."

The bitterness crept like corrosive acid over the phone lines between us. The voice was controlled, deadly. "I'm warning you, Cairns. I want the boy back."

"Don't be ridiculous, McIan. David isn't here. He

hasn't left one father to come to another. He's probably making his own kind of protest."

"Is that what you teach them in AP English?" I recognized a new quality in his voice. The contempt was gone. It had been replaced by hatred. Neither of us was going to win this conversation.

"I don't know where David is. I'll let you know if I hear." I hung up on him.

I saw the envelope as soon as I put down the phone. It must have been stuck under the door sometime during the night. There was no return address, and it was addressed by hand. The handwriting, which he had not attempted to conceal, belonged to David. Inside, folded in thirds, was the original deed to Duck Island and another to Sven's house. Stapled to them was the deed to the dunes.

All of them had been signed over to Sven by Ernie Davidson. Tucked inside with them was the weather forecast from the *Los Angeles Times*. It didn't tell me anything I didn't already know.

I hadn't finished shaving before the phone rang again.

"Where's David?"

It was Davidson. The old man sounded as if he'd been running in a marathon and was about to collapse.

"How the hell should I know?"

"Ellen called me. She thinks he might be with you."

"For Christ's sake. I'm not the boy's keeper. He's just a kid I had in a class. I don't even teach there anymore."

"She thought you might have heard from him."

The envelope with David's handwriting stared at me from the nightstand. I didn't say anything.

"She wants to see you."

"I'm busy."

The old man growled. It sounded like a police dog just before he goes for your jugular.

"This is my grandson, goddammit. He isn't to blame for the war between you and McIan."

I almost hung up on him but before I could get the receiver away from my ear he said the magic word.

"Please." He would have gotten down on his knees if it would help his grandson.

"I'll try."

Davidson clicked off.

The Bay Club was a beehive of activity. Every boat in its more than forty slips was being provisioned for the boat parade that started that night. Delivery vans pulled in and out of the parking lot. An army of workers unloaded cases of liquor, canapés, baked goods, flowers, and folding chairs, and wheeled them down onto the docks. Carpenters and electricians scrambled up masts and over the decks of the boats, tacking long strands of Christmas lights to everything in sight. College boys scrubbed the decks and polished the portholes. Caterers minced their way in between. The bay itself was a cold gray; promising wind.

Ellen was alone inside the *Mach 10*. Cases of champagne and Smirnoff were stacked haphazardly around the cabin. She sat on the floor in the middle of them. She wore a camel-colored pair of slacks and a sweater to match, but her hair had gone limp and the face, so confident and chic the last time I saw her, had slipped into an unwanted softness. She looked like a little girl who had lost her first beau. She was crying softly. It was a sad, hopeless bleating. She seemed glad to have company. It didn't matter who it was.

"I hate these goddamn boat parades. Five whole nights of it. Fifty guests at a time. I spend all day getting the boat cleaned up. Food. Liquor. Flowers. Try to keep the guest lists straight. Very Important People. Pretend I'm witty and charming. The boats are decked out with enough wattage to light up a city. Up one side of the bay and down the other. Three endless hours of it. Try not to get drunk until the people leave." She looked for a handkerchief. I handed her mine.

"My father is Ernie Davidson. When I was a kid, he and I strung the lights up ourselves. A single strand up along the mast and out to the end of the boom. There were only about twenty boats. The first one pulled a Christmas tree in a skiff behind it.

"Most of the houses around the bay were empty. Dark. We made a circle around the island and went up to the turning basin. Just this little armada of boats huddled together in the dark. Everybody singing carols. Watching the lights sparkle back from the black, black water. It was so beautiful . . ."

She started crying again. She was right about the parade. It was bloated now. Big fat power boats gussied up like overblown women with too many diamonds. Hundreds of them. Charging up the bay like gangbusters. Confusion. Noise. Thousands of people crammed onto the island and the peninsula. Even so, I guessed it wasn't the boat parade that made her cry.

"Your father asked me to come."

She looked up at me for the first time, a terrible, fierce hope in her eyes.

"You're Chandler Cairns."

"I haven't seen David. I checked with some of my friends at school. They've been asking the students. No one has seen him."

The hope blinked off as quickly as it had come.

A man from Beach Liquor wheeled a cart up the gangway outside and piled a dozen cases of something on the deck. Ellen didn't move. After a minute I sat on the floor with her.

Up close she was just a middle-aged woman whose life was beginning to unravel. She was a typical California girl from the time when California girls were rare and before everybody else in the world had moved in and taken it away from them. The apple of her father's eye. Schooled at Westridge and then Stanford. Idealist. Taught to believe in happy endings. Love conquers all. The triumph of justice. It was a measure of California girls that they held on to their illusions long past the time their counterparts from the East had given them up. Stubbornly refused to believe what their intelligent eyes told them until it was too late to do anything about it. I could never decide whether they were the true tragic figures in the urbanization of California or if they were the lucky ones to have lived in paradise so long.

"I thought maybe David had gone to you."

"Why would he do that?"

"Bill and he had a fight. David accused his father of terrible things. Of destroying a city, a whole way of life for his own gain. Of coercing the police into arresting you for the murder of Sven. Of buying people, buying his way into society by giving to its pet charities. Bill said that was the way business was done.

Everyone understood the rules. That only idealists and fools believed otherwise.

"I took my husband's side. It was a mistake. David was very upset. We could all feel how much you had influenced him. He felt torn between the two of you. Like it was a battle between good and evil. Right and wrong." She paused.

I wasn't the one who had influenced the boy. It was the books I had thrown at him. But I would never be able to convince her of that. I didn't try.

"He loves his father, you know."

There was a tinge of regret in the way she said it. I remembered the two of them, David and McIan, coming down the steps from the Tower, the son measuring his step to his father's, his head thrown back in that confident way. The camaraderie between the two. I wondered if they had shut her out, too.

"David's here in the city. At least he was this morning." I took the weather forecast out of my pocket and showed it to her. "Do you have any idea what this means?" She shook her head.

"Somebody shoved it under the door. David's handwriting was on the envelope."

She took the piece of newsprint in her hand and held it to her thin chest, smoothing the folds against her.

"David is too much like me," she said. "He tries to emulate his father. He worships him. But he's soft like me. Too sensitive. He doesn't care about money. It isn't his game."

"What would he do if he thought his father had done something wrong?"

"I don't know." There was a look of anguish on her face. "He would try to stop him. But if that didn't work, I just don't know. He wouldn't send his father to jail."

208

"Even for murder?"

"Especially then. Not if it was already done. Not if it wouldn't bring the dead man back.

"Please find him, Chandler. He trusts you. He has a car. Credit cards. He could be anywhere. But I don't think he's gone off to an island somewhere in the Caribbean. He's hiding somewhere. In some terrible little hole-in-the-wall in Costa Mesa or down at the beach. He's trying to decide between the two of you." The tears rolled down her cheeks. The skin underneath was thin as parchment.

"Tell him . . . whatever he decides, it's all right. Tell him I love him."

She stood up. The mask settled back on her face. She opened one of the boxes and started stashing the bottles beneath the bar. The rings tinkled against each other on her fingers. I watched her for a minute and then left.

I spent the rest of the morning looking for David. I started at the high school. David didn't have many friends. I found his two closest ones on their way to the pool. McIan had contacted both of them. Neither of them had seen David. They were worried about him. On a hunch I went up into Barr Hall and passed by the AP English classroom. David's seat at the table was empty.

Melissa Nussbaum, who had sat next to him before he'd dropped the class, was also absent.

Melissa was a tall, thin, quiet girl with a pale classic beauty that went mostly unnoticed by her peers. She wore no makeup. Her blond, almost white, hair was long and straight. Under the exterior she had a sharp, rather extraordinary way of looking at the world. I had discovered the love affair by accident.

I had found the note under the table after they had gone for the day. The shock was not so much in what it said but in what it implied. It was an assignation of a deeply intimate nature and clearly not the first. Rather than embarrass them I'd thrown it away. But on occasion, glancing at the two of them, sitting side by side as cool and detached from each other as books on a shelf, I wondered if, with all that self-possession, they had ever been children at all.

Rosenberg, the man who had taken over my AP classes and was now sitting at my desk, pretended not to notice when I stopped by the English department office and looked Melissa's address up in the file.

Melissa lived in one of the duplexes just off Ocean Boulevard on the peninsula, a block from the beach. Originally it had been one cottage, but the owner had added an outside stairway and divided it into two separate apartments. There was a rental sign in the window. The screens on the windows were rusted through. The little patch of yard had been cemented over. A couple of toys lay abandoned around the front step. A pipe with a broken shower head dripped water onto the side of the house. The sign on the mailbox indicated that Melissa's mother, Catherine Nussbaum, lived upstairs.

No one answered the door. I heard a faint movement and then silence as someone switched off a radio. I knocked again, but if the two of them were inside they were not going to let me know. I scribbled a note to Melissa, asking her to call me, and slipped it under the door. Then I walked out onto the beach and stood there for a while where I could watch the stairway.

Catalina was a long brown smudge on the horizon. The smog seemed to be moving down the coast from LA. It squatted there, thick and ugly, like the thing that was bothering me. I wondered idly if there was going to be a Santa Ana this late in the season. No one came in or out of Melissa's apartment in the next few minutes. I found a phone booth and tried to get McIan. He wasn't at home or in his office.

It took an hour and a half to drive the last ten miles from Santa Ana to the beach. By five the freeway leading into the city was bumper to bumper, moving about a mile an hour. The cars, thousands of them, were gridlocked on Coast Highway, funneling, two at a time, onto the peninsula for the boat parade. The roads as far inland as the airport were locked tight as a vise. I tried to find a way around the jam. Finally I gave up and inched along with everybody else.

Kate was waiting for me. She was sitting on the steps in the dark. The pup was sniffing around for something under the bougainvillea.

"We have to talk."

We left the pup in the yard, locked the gate and walked down to the harbor.

The bay down at the tip of the peninsula was deserted. We saw the parade coming from a distance, out of the dark, the long line of lights winding their way down from the Pavilion. The music came first, small and human-sized, across the water and then suddenly the parade was on top of us. The boats bore down the bay like behemoths. Lights towered over the docks. Searchlights raked the shore. Christmas carols and Santas ho-ho-hoing, amplified, loud, blared out over the water and reverberated from the houses. The line of boats doubled back on itself so that the sound and light filled the bay on both sides. And then, as suddenly as it had come, the parade was gone, around the islands, up toward the turning basin. The sound drifted back to us faintly. The last light disappeared into the dark.

Kate was tense and preoccupied beside me. We waited until the waves had rippled themselves out against the dark peninsula and the bay was silent again.

"McIan's lawyers called. They've threatened to sue over the publication. The city is evicting me from the gallery. McIan has donated an auditorium to one of the elementary schools. In return the school board is going to terminate your license to teach."

"Is that all?"

Usually she laughed. This time she didn't.

"McIan wants the dunes. In return we can have our lives back."

"Whew! That's a relief." I waited for the smile. Resigned myself to the knowledge that it wasn't going to come.

"We can't do it."

"Do what?"

212

"Sell to McIan." Her voice was firm. Brave. If she was trembling it was because of me. Because she was not sure of what I'd do.

"We could sell to someone else. Davidson will give us market value. Do you know how much that is?"

She nodded. In the dark I could feel the closeness of her body. Smell the sweet mysterious warmth.

"We could buy any house we wanted, Kate. One for each of us. Hire McIan's lawyers away from him. Spend the rest of our lives traveling. Donate to causes." I wanted to make sure she understood what it was she would be giving up. But of course she had considered all the possibilities and rejected them. Kate's strength had always been the fine intelligence that informed her decisions.

Across the bay the towers of Pacific Plaza glittered on the hillside. A million lights winked down from the city that surrounded and was about to smother the little beach town.

"Do you ever wonder what McIan sees, standing by the window in his tower, looking down at us, at the town? It must look like a giant computer game with all these thousands of little squares. Only it's real money he's playing with. Real people he's moving around. It must be the most exciting game in the world. Like gambling. Moving stocks, buying, selling. Monitoring the boards in Tokyo. Anticipating Bonn. A giant game of monopoly with land as the bargaining chip. Better than sex. A higher high than cocaine. Imagine all that male energy and drive channeled into the game. City-council takeovers and company skirmishes as the substitute for war. The power when you win. It's not the Mercedes and the baccarat and the pretentious little houses that the players care about. It's the game that counts. Playing Monopoly with grown-up toys. Real people getting hurt."

Across the bay and up along the cliffs above Mesa del Mar the cars were starting home. Red taillights rimmed the bay, inching toward Coast Highway. Kate moved away from me and then back again. I could see her small fine head framed against the dark. I waited for her to go on, to finish what she had started.

"We can't do it, Chandler. All those years Sven held on to the lots, paid the taxes, left the dunes for the reeds and the gulls and kids who played in them."

I sighed. It was my turn.

"That, I suppose, is why he left it all to us. To a redheaded Welsh girl who can't be bribed or corrupted or frightened into doing something she doesn't believe in and to a middle-aged English teacher who loves her." I hadn't meant to say it. I wished I could take it back.

Kate slipped her hand in mine as if to comfort me.

"Thanks, Chandler," she whispered.

Her lips brushed lightly past mine and then she turned away and we went home.

Kate's art gallery burned down sometime after midnight.

I heard someone shouting in the yard and then she was pounding on my door. We drove in silence, about sixty-five in a twenty-five-mile zone, all the way up the peninsula and across the bridge to the Heights, but no one stopped us.

The blaze was out by the time we got there. The street was cordoned off and half a dozen fire trucks stood there blinking red lights into the dark. Police cars stood guard at both ends of the street. About ten spectators, nearby residents, peered over the barricade. I recognized one of them. Intense. Pale. Todd Van Damm. Firemen in soot-splashed slickers ran back and forth, wetting down hot spots, pulling down walls that were about to collapse, stringing yellow tape around the lot. Canvas hoses snaked back and forth across the road. A truck with a thirty-five-foot turret was pouring water into the black mess that was all that was left of most of Kate's life.

The entire place was gone. It had taken about twenty minutes. Canvases. Prints. The plates for the book she was illustrating. Everything. Some of the paintings, her favorites, went back to the days when we had lived together and were for display only. A black stream of ashes washed it all away down the gutter. Kate tried to run inside but the firemen held her back. She broke away from them, screaming at them as though they were the culprits, that it was her studio and she had to save the oils. But the ashes were still hot and they held her back until I could get to her and lead her back to the car.

The investigator was a short squat man with a clipboard and a no-nonsense face. He asked a few questions and then he let us go. He had a copy of the report from the city that had condemned the electrical system in the gallery. In the morning he was going to blame it on the wiring.

Kate was white-lipped. In shock. I wrapped a car blanket around her and drove her home. I took her into the house and helped her upstairs. She screamed at me to leave her alone and lunged away every time I came near her. I got her to drink some brandy and put her in Sven's old bed. When I pulled the blankets up over her she started shivering. Her whole body shook as though her bones had come loose. I lay next to her and held her until she stopped shaking. Then I pulled a chair up beside the bed and sat there listening to her breathe.

She cried in her sleep like a child. I held her hand and stroked her head, and finally, toward morning, she shouted something into the darkness and slipped off into a deep and terrible sleep.

The wind reversed direction about dawn. It came down out of the high deserts through the canyons, bringing with it the cold, bitter taste of the mountains. It gathered speed in the long passes between San Bernardino and El Tejon, Santa Ana and Trabuco. By the time it hit the beaches it had picked up enough static to start a fire.

Out at the airport the planes reversed direction. I saw the first plane banking out over the sea, about a mile out from the jetty, then descending for its approach up the estuary. I let the puppy out into the yard and stood with him for a few minutes in the cold. The fronds in the palm trees shifted along the alley like ghosts. I could almost feel everything around me drying out.

Kate was still asleep. I pulled the blinds down over the window and fed the puppy. I left a note on the kitchen table in case she woke before I got back.

The sand on the beach was blowing away. It went down the peninsula in great sheets that rose and fell like parachutes billowing as they broke loose and took flight. The waves came into the beach at an angle. The wind tore the tops off them and flung them backward so that they broke, headless, and were swept immediately back into the sea. Seabirds, thousands of them, sat offshore, beyond the surfline, eyeing the land suspiciously as it dissolved in front of them.

The street where Melissa lived was quiet. Everyone was sleeping off the effects of the night before. Curtains were pulled over the windows. Newspapers lay where they'd been tossed against picket fences and across doorsteps. I found a place out of the wind and sat down to wait.

David came out about seven-thirty. I followed him around the corner, past the bank, the shell shop, and across the street to Winchell's Doughnuts. He bought a box of doughnuts and two coffees. When he turned to leave the window, he bumped into me.

I tried to stop him. The coffee spilled over both of us. He sprinted off down the street in the direction from which he had come.

"David!" But he didn't stop. I ran after him for a block and then I gave up. It was enough to know where David was staying and that he was safe. I bought two cinnamon rolls from Bon Appetit and took them home to Kate.

Miss Silver Bells was on edge. It wasn't like her. Maybe it was the time of the month. More likely McIan suddenly had a few other things on his mind beside tea and crumpets and an afternoon tryst with a less-than-platinum English lady.

"Mr. McIan is out." This was said primly.

"Would you ask him to call Chandler Cairns? I have something urgent to tell him. It concerns his son."

"I'll leave a message, sir." Technically she was perfect. There was just the hint, almost subliminal, of disdain.

No one had any idea where Ellen McIan was hiding. I talked to half a dozen keepers of the flame at the Yacht Club, the Los Coyotes Country Club, the pro at the Tennis Club. Jean Louis the hairdresser hadn't seen her. She wasn't at Le Chic. They all conscientiously repeated my name and phone number and promised to pass them on in the case that she made an appearance. As a last resort I went by the Bay Club. The *Mach 10* was locked tight. Five cases of liquor were stacked on the dock next to it. I wrote a note and jammed it down the hatch cover.

Todd Van Damm's housemates were still sitting where I had last seen them on the porch, staring through the dirt-encrusted glass panes at the sand blowing down the street. Little piles of sand were accumulating along the sills and against the front-door steps. No one bothered to get up. I let myself in.

Van Damm wasn't in his room. The door was locked. I opened it with my VISA card. The bed had recently been slept in and hastily abandoned. The clock was set for about twenty minutes ago. Shaving stuff, encased in a plastic baggie, had been tossed onto the sheets with a pair of black silk pajamas. The backpack had gone with him.

I went through the papers that lay loose on his desk. He was neat and methodical about his classwork, so it wasn't difficult. The faint odor of paint thinner came from his closet. A single empty can sat beside a paint box full of oils.

It wasn't until I was ready to go that I gave a cursory glance at the paintings. Now, when it was too late, they leapt out at me from the walls. What Kate had called the boy's wet dreams were composed of fire. The gushing fountains and bleeding gates were erected in flames. The funeral pyre was only the most obvious of them. The other oils were renderings of flames writhing and licking and exploding against a background of pure black hatred. Sexual repression poured onto canvas by that pale intense face that stared out of the crowd as the unexpected flash of the fire truck swept across it.

There was a sound on the stairs. One of Van Damm's housemates looked into the room and gave me a distinctly unfriendly stare.

"You looking for something in particular?"

"No."

My heart was ticking away like a clock. He stood in the hallway and watched me go.

He wasn't the one I was afraid of.

Thurber was on the phone when I got back to the house. I told him about Kate and then about Van Damm. He promised to call a pal of his at the courthouse and ask him to run a check on the name. While he was at it he said he might as well run the whole list. I read them out to him and he wrote them down.

I tried again to get McIan and his wife. Miss Silver Bells was out to lunch. A more promising voice answered for her. She assured me that there was a note on the desk in front of her for McIan and that it was marked "urgent." He had not called in yet. I took the ferry across to the island and parked on Collins. Davidson's big old beach house was surrounded by sandbags. It was beginning to resemble the Maginot Line.

No one answered the door. I heard the phone inside. It rang about a dozen times and finally stopped. I left a note in his mailbox and went to find Kate.

The investigator was still poking around the ashes when I got there. He reminded me of a stolid little beagle sniffing the ground for bodies underneath. The yellow power truck was parked at the curb with its conning tower clamped up against the top of the utility lines. Kate was sitting on an upended crate that someone had placed there, carefully filling out a fistful of forms.

The place where Kate's Gallery had stood looked like a bomb site. A charcoal rim stood at the edges where the walls had burned and then splintered. Mounds of ash lay in the center. The wind blew the ashes off in giant spirals and sent them gusting, like smoke, toward the peninsula. One of the neighbors had brought out his hose and stood, trying futilely to water the ashes down.

"It's arson."

Kate had taken a shower and washed her hair. It clung to her fine-boned skull in small wet wine-colored curls. Her face was pale and composed. The strength that I had never doubted for a moment was back again.

"The Edison Company turned off the electricity Wednesday afternoon."

The investigator poked with his long metal rod in the center of a pile of ash like a diviner looking for gold. It struck metal. He stopped, cleared away the ashes with quick little strokes. Inserted the wand into the handle of what had once been a gasoline can and held it up to the light.

I told him about Van Damm.

We took the ferry across to the island. Kate stood in the forward end, braced against the wind. The blunt prow caught the chop and the spray hit her full in the face. She didn't seem to feel it. The ferry slid sideways in the wind. The diesel motor churned to keep it headed upstream toward the dock. The bay, usually placid as a pond, was slate-gray, broken into a thousand tiny whitecaps whipping down the channel.

We docked hard. The ferry hit the boards at an angle, slid awkwardly into the slot. Before it had quite stopped, Kate stepped off onto the dock. I followed her up the gangway onto the bayfront walk.

The whole island vibrated like a wind chime. The boats, thousands of them, rang like bells. Lines banged against steel and wood masts, slapped along poles, tugged at copper buoys. Each mast had a different sound, all of them clinking and clanging and pealing away like a percussion section. Strings of Christmas lights lurched dangerously in wide arcs. Island residents peered anxiously out of bay windows, consulted barometers, kept their doors shut tight against the wind. Occasionally a boat owner hurried out to the end of his dock, blown drunkenly against the rail. Checked and rechecked the lines that secured his boat to the float, tied down the strings of lights with an extra length of cord. Returned to the house to make yet another call to the White's Bay Chamber of Commerce to see if the boat parade for that night had been canceled or if it was still on hold.

Kate hurried ahead of me and I struggled to keep up. It was the way we always traveled—she moving ahead like a sail, billowing out and circling back, pulling me forward. It was Kate who always drove me out of doors in a rainstorm to see the waves tear boulders out of the jetty and hurl them into the sea; Kate who insisted on waking in time for the first pale light of the eclipse, drove out to the desert at midnight so that we could lie together on the sand and watch stars raining down as a meteor crashed into the atmosphere. Kate who showered my life with beautiful things. Forced me to feel. It had often struck me that I possessed nothing to offer her in return. It was no wonder that she had left me. Watching her, that awful longing lodged tight in my throat like a stone.

"Kate!" She stopped, came back to me. She stood in front of me like a child while I pulled the hood up over the soft copper fuzz, tied it securely under her chin. Only the eyes showed under the hood, slate-gray, reflecting the bay, a few freckles, the sharp nose, the generous mouth. In the old days I'd have bent forward and kissed her. Licked the salt off her lips. Now I tucked the end of the drawstring inside the hood, snapped the collar shut.

"Thank you." Her eyes were clear and grave.

I shrugged.

"I'm very grateful. It would have been terrible without you."

She wiped impatiently with the back of her hand at the tears that sprang into her eyes, despite her. A gust of wind blew down the bay from the north, smoothing it, fan-shaped, leaving a print like a hand pressed into the water and then released. Every mast in the bay leaned and then jerked upright. I heard the blast of the ferry behind us. It hurtled past with the faint smell of exhaust.

I waited. Kate was probably the only person in the world I could never anticipate. Who invariably came out with the unexpected.

"Sven was right. We belong together. All that arguing over principle. What a waste! Me, turning my life into second-rate watercolors. And you in your pulpit, preaching. Trying to change a world that does not want to be changed."

She stood without moving on the sidewalk in front of me, gallant, grave, honest Kate.

"Let's save something from life. Make it up to each other. Oh, Chandler, I'm sorry. Love me . . ."

I didn't answer. I held her tight against the wind and the cold and the bitter years ahead. Felt that warm, beloved body shaking against me, her heart beating like a bird inside my jacket. The wind whipped past us. Set the boat lines clanking against each other like angry bell claps. Tried to pry us apart.

The two of us held fast.

The wind held. Poinsettias, watered in the morning, dried out and wilted in their pots by nightfall. Shingled beach cottages creaked and shrank back into themselves, tinder-dry. Palm fronds came loose and fell like great feathered darts onto the streets and parking lots. If it hadn't been Saturday night, which always the biggest night of the parade, the Chamber of Commerce would have called it off. They dithered back and forth, cast anxious looks at the bay from their perch atop Pacific Plaza. In the end they gave a tentative go-ahead and issued a warning for parade participants to leave twice the normal distance between their boats and the ones ahead.

By 5 P.M. all the roads in and out of the harbor area were jammed tight. Night came down with the finality of a fire curtain and trapped us all behind it. The sky, scoured clean by the wind, was an unaccustomed black. Stars winked down on the bay like unexpected guests.

Thurber's boat charged down the bay toward us like a riderless horse, twenty minutes late as usual. He missed the dock the first time around. Kate and I leapt aboard as he slid past for the second try.

The boat was a PC 44, *Vivace*, a beautiful old wood-hulled sloop that his father had sailed in the bay in the forties, winning every competition in its class. It was no match for the lightweight fiberglass tubs that raced today, but Thurber wouldn't part with it. Kate and Thurber had spent Thursday rigging the lines with tiny clear Christmas lights. Thurber stood at the helm all bundled up in a peacoat and with wool scarves up to his eyes, serene and happy as Captain Hornblower.

There were six of us huddled in the cockpit. Three of Thurber's lawyer pals gossiped and guffawed and kept us all in light spirits. An enormous thermos of hot mulled wine sat between us.

Thurber approached the formation area cautiously. About a hundred boats milled around in front of the Pavilion like overweight fireflies, trying to form some kind of order out of chaos. Some stood dead in the water. Others backed and filled. The ferry, loaded with enough passengers and cars to sink the *Queen Mary*, dodged between them. Boats scattered to either side and then reassembled in its wake. For a few moments before we plunged in, we were onlookers. The noise drifted across the water in spurts and snatches out of the dark. Shouts, sharp as pistol shots, hurtled past in the cold dry air. Individual words. Names. A few good-natured warnings. Laughter. From somewhere up in the Heights came the distant wailing of sirens. Kate shivered and leaned tight against me.

The sudden blast of wind hit the *Vivace* broadside and sent it skittering back down the bay. Kate and I clung to the railing and Thurber shouted to everyone to hold tight. Up by the Pavilion all hell broke loose. We heard the smack of hulls colliding, the shouts of passengers. Lights came loose and went out or trailed like fishing lines, blinking wanly just under the surface of the water. The lights, thousands of them, reflections multiplied in the dark water, bobbed up and down like horses in a carousel that has gotten out of control.

At the dot of seven the *Pavilion Queen,* the biggest boat in the harbor, replica of a river steamboat, backed out of its slip, blue lights high atop the helmsman's tower, and moved grandly up the bay. One by one the boats, some of them now limping, a few minus their lights, fell obediently into line behind her. Thurber waited for a space between two slow-moving yachts and then slipped into the parade.

Thurber handed over the helm to Kate, who was the best sailor of all of us, and came to sit beside me. The lights swirled around us dizzyingly while he fished in his pockets for the list and came up triumphant.

"Well, it's a damned funny list, Cairns. You were right. They all have arrest records. Some of them have served time in jail. The others were put on probation or remanded to hospital wards."

"Drugs?"

"Guess again."

"Arson." I didn't even add a question mark.

225

"Two of them." Thurber got out his glasses and held the list up under the lights. "Ned Burroughs. Fifty-four years old. Caucasian. Address in Santa Ana. Has a child-bride and two children. Burned down a liquor store in Fountain Valley. It was assumed, though never proved, that the owner of the store paid him four hundred dollars to do it. The money was found in his pocket. Burroughs was caught three blocks from the fire with the gas cans still in the back seat. Currently serving time at Soledad."

"And the other?"

"Huynh Nguyen. Vietnamese immigrant. A survivor. Clever as they come. Arrested for setting an incendiary device in a Vietnamese grocery store in Garden Grove. The blast blew the entire block of stores apart. He beat the rap. Everyone, even the defense attorney, thought he was guilty as hell."

"What about Van Damm?"

"Pyromaniac."

I glanced up at Kate. She had her back to us, straight and tall at the helm. She gave no sign that she heard us.

"Pyros. They're the dangerous ones. They don't do it for money. They just want to see the flames licking the sky and hear the fire trucks screaming through the streets." My eyes went up across the bay to the hospital and the place where Kate's Gallery had stood.

"Assuming that David got this list from his father, why would McIan have a list of pyros?"

"Beats me."

"No one would hire them to burn something down. They get caught. Tell who paid them. Turn evidence for a lighter sentence. McIan couldn't take the risk."

"But they don't need to be paid, do they? Don't even need to see your face. Just a telephone call. A suggestion. A word or two whispered into a receiver.

like an obscene telephone call." I remembered McIan standing at the helm. Giving me his theory of the perfect crime—crazies. "You don't have to do anything. You just sit back and wait for the poor son of a bitch to do it for you."

We were in the turning basin now. The *Pavilion Queen* had gotten out of line and was sitting in the center of the bay while all the other boats made a wide circle around her and headed back down the bay again. Diners sat in the candlelit windows of the Rusty Pelican and Cano's. They spilled onto the docks with drinks in hand, waving and shouting as the boats passed. Somewhere a radio phone began to squawk. I didn't know Thurber had one. It was buried below in one of the bunks in a pile of canvas cushions and probably hadn't been used since Old Sven had refitted the boat. Thurber uncovered it and stared at it in amazement. Sven had made him install it and showed him how to use it in case of emergency. Now he looked at it helplessly.

"Just leave it. The damn thing never went off before. It's got to be a foul-up." One of the lawyers pulled the right switch and spoke into the box. The call was for me.

It was McIan. The son of a bitch had ignored my messages all day and taken this moment to return my call. I could see the *Mach 10* across the turning basin, lit up like a shopping mall. It looked like a hundred people were crowded onto it. I supposed McIan was up in the pilot room with a drink in his hand and a few chosen admirers to watch him place his phone call. He sounded high as a kite. Elated almost. It was difficult to hear anything. I gave him my news and then I had to repeat it twice. The last time he got it. "David is with Melissa Nussbaum on the peninsula." I gave him the address.

The static disappeared and the parade sudden[l]
was put on hold. I heard McIan as clearly as thoug[h]
he were standing in front of me. He uttered a sound[,]
high-pitched and clear. And then the radio wen[t]
dead. We saw the *Mach 10* veer out of line and lea[p]
with a sudden surge of power back down the bay. I[t]
came about thirty miles an hour across the turnin[g]
basin and bore straight down at us. In a moment o[f]
panic I thought the boat was going to ram us. I[t]
charged straight at us, scattering the boats on eithe[r]
side of us, all of them scrambling to get out of th[e]
way, and then at the last moment it slipped betwee[n]
the *Vivace* and the boat ahead of us, with only inche[s]
to spare, and sped on down the bay. For a momen[t]
the passengers on the *Mach 10* were close enough t[o]
touch. They held to the rails and screamed in deligh[t]
as though they were on a joy ride. I didn't see McIan[.]
The only face that looked, unseeing, into the spac[e]
between us and seemed frightened belonged to Elle[n]
McIan. Maybe she had just guessed what was about t[o]
happen.

The fire started at the west end o[f]
the peninsula. By the time we saw the flames, the[y]
had engulfed the entire block of tinder-dry building[s.]
A second fire, a tiny prick of red flame, started thre[e]
blocks to the east. It was like igniting a gas main. Th[e]
wind fed it, tossed it upward, licked it along the ro[w]
of shingle houses.

It took a few minutes for everyone to realize wha[t]
was happening. The bay became a madhouse. Boa[t]

piled out of line, scrambling for shore. The bay reverberated with shrieks of terror. Sirens, stuck in the bot-
tleneck of traffic, were wailing, static, futile. Two city
fire-patrol boats came screaming up the bay and posi-
tioned themselves as close to shore as the crowd
would let them and spewed great fountains of water
inland. It reached only the first line of houses. The
fire could not have started at a worse place. The two
access roads merged into one. Ocean Boulevard was
blocked. Every alley was filled with stalled cars and
panicked drivers. The peninsula was effectively cut
off from help.

Thurber turned the *Vivace* back toward the center
of the peninsula and his own home. While we moved
down the channel a third fire started, closer to the
midsection of the peninsula. It could have been
started by any one of the arsonists on McIan's list. I
was betting on Van Damm.

Thurber tried to bring the boat close into shore and
found it impossible. People were diving off into the
water, loading boats with their belongings. Cars were
lined up for a mile at the ferry. A single fire truck had
made it to the launch dock and was being loaded into
the ferry from the island to the peninsula side, where
it would be stuck again. I dived into the water and
swam ashore.

The fourth fire had been set in the Bookstore.
There was nothing to stop it, and already the wind
was blowing it in long red tongues down the street.
Thurber's house was completely engulfed. A block
away flames were spurting out of the apartment
where I'd seen David. They came out of the top-story
windows and flared fifty feet into the sky. McIan was
already there. Melissa appeared in the doorway. She
tottered onto the front steps and collapsed. McIan

shouted something at her. She didn't answer. He shook her. I ran to stop him.

"Is David in there?"

She nodded. The words came out like wind in a bellows. "He won't leave."

McIan tried to get in through the front porch and was beaten back by the flames. I ran around to the side and kicked in the kitchen door. McIan followed me. McIan clawed his way to the stairs. He had his coat over his head so that he could breathe and was unable to see anything but his feet. It didn't make much difference. The smoke was so thick you couldn't see anything anyway. We never heard the boy die. The entire back part of the house collapsed. McIan was caught under the stairway. I pulled him free and dragged him outside. By then one of the fire trucks had arrived and was pouring water into the place. The flames leapt up into the sky. A gust of wind blew them across the alley and set fire to the next block.

I caught a glimpse of McIan before I left. He was trying to fight his way out of the restraining grip of the firemen to run back into the house and failed. I heard him scream. I looked back once more. He stared weeping into the smoke and the flames where the body of his son, pride of his life, flesh of his flesh, was slowly burning into ash.

It would have been difficult to halt the fire at any time. With the Santa Ana blowing down the bay, it was all but impossible. Van Damm went ahead of us down the peninsula, lighting his little fires in the most vulnerable places. Thin batten boards, tinder-dry shingles, beach cottages leapt instantly into flame. The light from the blaze had turned to the blackness of smoke. From Pacific Plaza and the hillsides behind Mesa del Mar it would look like one huge bonfire one out of control. Here, in the streets, there was nothing but blackness, an awful choking dark.

The disaster brought out the best in everyone. They routed people out of their homes and loaded tourists onto boats. They held hoses and swung buckets of water. Those who had homes on the peninsula went to save their property. All the others swarmed to the docks to pick up refugees, ferried them in boatloads across to the island. They herded the old and the confused out onto the beaches, away from the boardwalk to the water's edge, and kept them there, wrapped in blankets, while the wind blew the ashes over them and into the sea.

The fire was only thirty minutes old. A fifth of the peninsula was an inferno. The police were swarming over the Pavilion and the fun zone by the time I got there, looking for the maniac who was setting the fires. The crowd was jammed around the merry-go-round and down to the dock trying to get away from the holocaust and onto the ferry. I saw Van Damm in the crowd. The glow of fire played over his face. It was alight, bathed in a crazed ecstasy. He saw me and ducked down behind the shoulders of the man ahead of him.

I shouted for help and rammed my way into the crowd. By the time I got past the first two onlookers, Van Damm was gone. I caught a glimpse of him streaking down the alley toward the far end of the peninsula. The roads were still jammed tight with cars. Most of them had been abandoned. Van Damm was on foot. He was fleet and he knew the peninsula as well as he knew his own tortured mind. He darted into the courtyard of the Coast Inn and out through a passageway into the street. I could hear nothing but the roar of the fire. It was like a great wind, flame consuming wood, tiles crashing to the ground, walls splintering, china breaking. It came over the peninsula in great waves and rendered my senses numb.

In small sheltered pockets between the houses, the flames reflected off the smoke so that it was as light as though it were noon. In other passages the smoke blew along the ground, thick as a night fog. Sometimes I saw Van Damm running ahead of me. Most of the time I didn't. He had nothing in his hands, only a small backpack over his shoulder. If there were explosives somewhere, they had already been planted along the route.

I lost him on the beach. It was almost impossible to breathe. The smoke was so thick I thought I would choke on it. It blew past in terrible thick gusts. Ashes mixed with sand blew against my face and neck so that I felt I was being abraded by sandpaper. I went down to the shoreline. I couldn't tell where the sand ended and the water began. One moment I was standing on the beach and the next a black wave was swirling around my waist. There was no sky, no ground, no water. Just a terrible bone-choking blackness. It was like stepping off the edge of the world.

Somewhere above me I heard the *thwunk-thwunk* of helicopters coming up the beach from Pendleton Marine Base. A vague patch of light, no more than a faint glow, passed overhead but the smoke was too thick and the searchlight didn't reach the ground.

A sudden flame flared out about twenty feet from where I was standing knee-deep in water. I saw a single pole of the pier and the black-clad figure of Van Damm. He had attached something to the lee side of the piling and set it alight. The flame flared out in the wind like the fire of a welder's torch and then it began to climb. The underside of the pier caught and the blaze spread out into the blackness. The water underneath turned rust and then a blood-gold.

He didn't see me. He set the backpack down and stepped away from the pier to watch. The flame climbed to the underpinnings and began to spread along the length of the pier. He must have wired it, night after night, climbing up beneath the struts and pilings. We weren't at war. There were no guards stationed there to stop him. Who would want to blow up an old pier, used only, in the winter, by a few Vietnamese fishermen and a couple of skateboarders. The fire spread quickly in the wind. The flames shot out around the pilings, and blew to the east so that the pier wavered like the skeleton of a ship plowing, masts aflame, stark and black across the horizon.

It was a mistake to stop and watch. There were more fires to set but Van Damm couldn't take his eyes from the spectacle. It pulled him like a magnet, his handiwork. Flame against darkness.

I got him from behind. He was stronger than he looked. The pale compact body was rock-hard. A dancer's body. We went down together in the sand. I shouted for help but I didn't expect any. One more cry in an entire peninsula shouting for help.

I was not a fighter. I hated contact sports and I was no contest for a kid half my age. But I held on. Van Damm struggled to get away but I had my head rammed into his back and my arms clamped around his chest and I held on. It wasn't as difficult as it might have been. I thought of David and Old Sven and Kate's watercolors, Thurber's files burned to ash, and I crushed him like a butterfly. He tried to get me off, and when that didn't work he dragged me behind him through the sand. He yelled and shouted at me and tried to break my fingers, but I didn't waste my breath on pain, just concentrated on holding on, on not letting go, on squeezing with every last bit of strength I owned. When he turned back toward the water and a wave came in and knocked him down, I had won. The water was my medium. In the first shock of surprise I got a lifeguard's grip on him and held him under until I felt his breath go and the first shuddering gasp of sea into his lungs.

The helicopter found us. They came in to douse water over the pier. The light caught Van Damm spread out on the sand and my own form bent over him breathing life back into him. A couple of marines jumped out to help and I turned him over to them.

The wind now, when it was too late, stopped. For a few minutes the smoke rose straight up into the sky. I could see the flames along the beach, great walls of them, over the cottages that burned like a hundred campfires, lighting the windows from within, leaping over the weathered shingled roofs, arching from the palm trees and the electric lines. Above the fun zone I could see the Ferris wheel, alight, turning against the sky. A single seat had caught fire and it spun eerily over the peninsula, circling low over the water and then up again into the incredibly black sky. Behind us the flames had reached the end of the pier. The wood frame blazed out over the water like a long series of flaming crosses. Waves reached up out of the black, turned gold in the light beneath it, smashed against the pilings, where the fires at the base sputtered and went out. For a moment the pier hung there, vaulted like a cathedral, veteran of storms, tides, generations, blazed brightly for one last glorious moment, and then collapsed into the sea.

The lower half of the peninsula was dark. All electricity had been cut off. Everyone had been evacuated. I waited for the flames to cross the fun zone, lick the deep eaves of the Pavilion, play leapfrog unhindered along the docks and the small, well-lived-in old homes, burn the summer cottages down to the dunes, sweep clear to the jetty and leave the entire peninsula razed, devalued, ready for the earth movers to move in and begin pouring the foundations for McIan's hotels.

But the line held. It was partly because the firemen, outnumbered, outclassed, had performed heroically, had made their Maginot Line and refused to be driven one step behind it. And partly it was because Van Damm had stopped to admire his handiwork and not quite completed McIan's scheme. But mostly it was thanks to the Santa Ana winds, which died as they had come. One last cold gust blew off the desert floor, whipped down through the canyons and then fell in a whirl of ash on the sand. Somewhere outside the channel islands, the balance shifted. The moist sea air crept back across the channel, crawled up the beach and spread over what was left of the little beach town. I waited for the police to come and take Van Damm away and then I went home to find Kate.

Christmas week was a cold and bitter one. Kate opened Sven's house to a dozen refugees from the burned-out area of the peninsula and tended them as lovingly as though they were her own relatives home for the holidays. Thurber moved in with me and after the shock wore off, set about amassing a new library, ordering files, sending away for book catalogues, preparing lists for the Library of Congress and second-hand bookstores.

Van Damm was held in prison without bail where, according to Thurber's friends at the courthouse, he confessed daily and in great detail to the crime of which he stood accused. He maintained, and was adamant about it, that no one had paid him to commit arson. It was his own idea. It had come to him, he said, when he received, by mail, a copy of the plan, prepared by the Office of Emergency Preparedness, for the evacuation of the peninsula in case of a disaster. Accompanying it had been a warning of the fire hazard in beach communities during Santa Ana wind conditions in combination with peak traffic hours. He never inquired why the documents, which were not for general distribution, had been sent to him. He had thrown his copy away as soon as he received it. There had been a telephone call on the morning of the fire, a recording, giving wind conditions and warning against lighting fires but it had only confirmed him in what he had already decided to do. Van Damm was shown photographs of McIan, Sylvus, Erik, even Lawrence. He had never seen any of them.

We celebrated the New Year, Kate, Thurber, and I, sitting together out at the end of a dock on the bay. At midnight a few shouts and the subdued honking of horns rose from the dark peninsula behind us. A single skyrocket arched up over the bay and fell somewhere in the darkness of the estuary. Thurber wept. Kate and I sang "Auld Lang Syne" in voices that trembled and promised that from now on everything would change.

The recall election was held in White's Bay during the first week in January. The turnout, unusually high for a special election, voted overwhelmingly to recall McIan's four council members and to replace them with the slate which Kate's organization had backed. An environmentalist, a lawyer who was born and raised in the city, an engineer, and the harbor area PTA president were elected to fill out their terms. Even the yuppies up on the Heights, sensing disaster threatening their newly established way of life, voted against the developers. The catchword, which everyone professed to be worried about, was "traffic." The subtler and more devastating changes, the erosion of values, the loss of a sense of camaraderie, of honesty, a certain idealism, passed unnoticed.

It was, said Kate, only a holding action.

I was still under indictment for the murder of Sven and his son-in-law. A couple of days before my first court appearance, I tried one last time to see Sheila.

Sven's daughter was wearing a turquoise pantsuit. Her hair was clean and blow-dried into a soft golden halo. I saw, for a moment only, a resemblance to the little girl in the photo that Sven had kept on his mantel. She peered out suspiciously and kept the screen door locked between us.

"Kate and I are selling the house."

"I heard." Something flickered across her face. I couldn't tell whether it was disappointment or something else.

"You can have whatever's left. There won't be much. Most of it will go for lawyers' bills. We've made a trust for Duck Island and the dunes property along the beachfront. The Friends of the Bay will hold the deed. That way it will take two hundred signatures to change the trust. Including Kate's and mine."

"I suppose that's why he didn't leave it to me."

I detected something unexpectedly complicated inside that smooth, unwrinkled face. I wasn't sure what it was. Bitterness? Envy? It had never occurred to me that she might think I had taken her place in Sven's life. For the first time I felt sorry for her.

I tried to tell her how much Sven had loved her.

"You were always about five years old for him. The curls. The big bow on your head. He talked about how he used to sit you in the prow of the skiff and row up and down the bay so everybody could see you."

Two tears worked their way out from under the mascara and ran down her cheeks. She sniffed and then wiped them away with her hand.

"He worried all the time that Sylvus would hurt you. Hurt the children. He used to drive up here at night, just to see the lights on. See the car in the drive."

"Go away. I'll call the cops."

I realized with a sense of surprise that she hated me. Despised me enough so that she would be glad to see me spend the rest of my life in jail for a murder I did not commit.

I stared in through the screen at her. She shrank back into the house. The bitterness and anger surrounded her in the dark.

"Your husband and your brother were running drugs for McIan, weren't they? Sven caught them. He went back to the *Flyaway*, late in the afternoon and found the two of them loading the cocaine into Sylvus' van. Old Sven stole it out of the van. Hid it beneath the sink where it would harm no one. Just Old Sven trying to protect his son. Protect you. Isn't that right?"

Sheila turned her face away as though she hadn't heard, didn't want to hear.

"You know who killed Sven, don't you, Sheila?"

She didn't answer.

"Was it Sylvus?"

She stared back at me with a malevolence that turned the soft face into a caricature of a Barbie Doll.

"Did McIan tell him to do it?"

She came back out of the darkness, up to the screen. Her body pressed against it, her lips close to the mesh, angrily, as though she were in a confessional against her will.

"No one told him to do it. It was his own idea." Her voice hissed through the screen, stung my ear.

"McIan tried to buy the beachfront lots from Dad. Dad threw him out of the house, so he came to me."

She hung her head.

"And you agreed. Signed away your inheritance for a million dollars. Only you couldn't collect until Sven was dead."

All the starch went out of her. As though she'd known it all so long, she'd lost interest. She spoke in a low voice without expression.

"Sylvus went out alone. He took the car. When he came back he was soaking wet and he had bloodstains all over his clothes. He told me what he'd done. Followed Dad up the bay. Waited until Dad had gone. Shot Dad with his own gun. And then propped it up between his knees like he'd shot himself. He was afraid to put the clothes in the trash. We drove over to Glendora the next morning and left them in the dump."

"Did you know he was going to kill me?"

She stared at me. "I knew."

"And you let him . . ."

She shrugged.

"That's all I know. Now go away."

"Will you tell the court?"

Sheila stared at me through the screen, her pudding face empty. The beautiful blue eyes as clear and meaningless as glass.

"I already did. This morning."

She closed the door and turned the latch.

I was free.

It was several months before I went to see McIan. Miss Silver Bells had been replaced by a French mannequin. The brass plate with McIan's name was gone from the door of the president's office. The new one said "Tom Campbell." The young woman seemed surprised that I had never heard of him. He came from a big concrete-manufacturing firm in Ohio. On the way out of the building I passed a new crop of eager young men. They were pressed and shined and ready to go to work for the new boss.

No one answered the door of the big house on the hill. There was a lockbox over the door and weeds coming up in the drive. The sprinkler hadn't been turned on for a couple of weeks and the grass was drying out in spots. The azalea leaves had burned to a deep brown in the sun. I heard the sound of a radio and followed it around the drive to the back. McIan was alone beside the pool. There was some ice in a pitcher and bottles of gin and tonic water on the glass-topped table in front of him. He didn't look around when I announced myself. It was almost as though he was expecting me.

"Sit down, Cairns."

He hadn't shaved. He wore a swim suit that had faded several shades and a pair of go-aheads on his feet. A thin layer of dust had settled on the surface of the pool. Behind the pool was a cement-and-stone deck that extended out over the edge of the hill. Beyond that was an unobstructed view of the bay and the city. They shimmered beneath us in the sun. The sea itself stretched, immense, a hot white glare, to the horizon. Hundreds of small white sails, mere dots, drifted out through the channel and up and down the coast.

"I suppose you've come to join the wake."

"Which wake?"

McIan gestured in a circle that included the house, himself, and the city below us. He didn't mention his son.

It was eleven o'clock in the morning.

"Pour yourself a drink, Cairns."

I filled a glass with ice and got some water from the cooler.

I waited for McIan to speak. He didn't seem to be in a hurry. I walked out over to the edge of the deck and looked down. The houses marched down the hill in staggered lots. Each one had its own pool. A new highway was being gouged out of the hillside halfway down. The high whine of earth movers filled the summer air. I tried to find the place on the peninsula where the fire had razed the houses. It was too far away to tell. Already new foundations were being laid.

I went back to McIan. He hadn't moved.

"Van Damm's been found innocent by reason of insanity."

McIan shrugged.

"There were only two people killed in the fire. The jury decided the old woman died of natural causes.

241

Van Damm was acquitted of that charge. The other one—" I was hesitant to say David's name out loud. McIan's jaw tightened in anticipation. I let it go. "The other death was the direct result of the fire. Van Damm's been locked away in a hospital for psychiatric treatment."

McIan lifted his glass to his lips, found it empty. He set it down again.

"The assassination theory worked. You got away with it."

"Did I?"

"If the wind hadn't stopped all those hotels would be going up right now. All those houses burned and only the land, leased land, sitting under them. The whole peninsula ripe for redevelopment. All the old-timers who couldn't afford to build again, moving out. The leases coming back to Davidson. A man like you, he knows ways to get hold of deeds held by his father-in-law. If the wind hadn't stopped, McIan, you'd be thumbing your nose at Barkdahl, the man who threw you out, instead of sitting up here alone, drinking yourself to death."

"I admit nothing, Cairns. I didn't pull the trigger. Hell, I don't even own a gun. I never met Van Damm. No money changed hands."

"David held you responsible."

"David is dead." He said it with a terrible finality.

"He figured it out, didn't he? Heard you talking in your study or found it by accident on the computer. It was just an accident that he knew Old Sven. And then he tried to stop you and when that didn't work, turned to me."

For a moment we both were silent.

"Which one of us killed him, McIan? Did you do it or did I?"

McIan stared across the table at me. It was the look

of a burned-out man. A man too tired to do anything, even hate.

"You killed him, Cairns. All that talk about moral commitment. Adherence to principle. Daniel Berrigan and *The Trial of the Catonsville Nine*. He believed in you. In all that crap. Peace marchers throwing themselves down in front of tanks. Greenpeace sailors sailing into the South Pacific to prevent atomic testing." For a moment he was roused and then, just as suddenly, he was spent again. I finished it for him.

"So he staked himself out on the peninsula. Like a sacrificial goat, tethered to the stake. He made a moral commitment. To you, McIan. He loved you that much. He thought you'd never hurt him. Thought he'd save the town from being razed. Save your soul from damnation."

McIan's hands were trembling. He tried to open the bottle of gin and failed, knocked it over instead.

"But you didn't get the message. He was so certain that I would find him and that I would tell you. But you weren't answering your phone. And when you did find out it was too late. You can't stop a crazy man. You can look the other way. But you can't pull him back once he's been set loose."

McIan's face sank in on itself. It was hard to remember how, less than a year ago, the two of them, father and son, handsome, virile, had strode confidently down the steps from his office, aglow with masculine camaraderie and the pride they took in each other.

McIan hadn't moved or changed expression. Tears were coursing down his face. Finally he spoke again.

"Didn't he know? Did he think in those last minutes—that I would have gone ahead? That I would have let him die?" The words were wrung out of McIan. It was the reason he'd hoped I'd come. Had waited for me here. It was the question he needed answered.

"He'd seen you do it to others. To Sven. To me."

"I loved him. Why did he do it, Cairns? When he saw it was too late to save the peninsula, why did he stay in that room and let himself be burned to death?"

He wanted to know. I hesitated.

"It was for you. Retribution."

McIan sank back into himself. He didn't speak. After a while he got up and went into the house. Ellen wouldn't be there. She had left him and gone back to live with her father on the island. I wondered if Miss Silver Bells was around somewhere. He was alone in a big house without gardeners or maids or anyone to answer the phone. I waited outside by the pool for him to come back. After about five minutes I heard a shot. It wasn't much. Just a little pop that echoed through the empty house. And then quiet. There was a phone on a stand beside the pool. I picked it up and called the police.

T he lawyers' bills stopped coming and we kept the house.

We spent our honeymoon in Old Sven's attic bedroom. If the years had taught us anything, it was to expect nothing. The result was a series of unexpected gifts. They piled, one on top of the other, an embarrassment of riches. Rainbows chasing rainbows. We took a fierce joy in each other. Even randy Old Sven would have approved. Kate was more beautiful than when she was young, made richer and more dangerous by experience, her body all tans and coppers and dark shadows. She spread herself for me like a fine lace quilt, a red-haired Sargasso Sea. Seduced me utterly and without mercy.

We took long walks along the beaches and out on the rocks. The storms passed over, one by one, on their way from the North Pacific to the Sierras. Each one left a surprise for us on the beach. Thousands of butterfly shells with translucent wings that caught the slightest breeze and skimmed across the water like tiny toy sailboats. A new species of bird. Deep gouges in the sand. The carcass of a shark. They seemed to us unaccountably wonderful.

In the fall the birds came back to the beach. Gulls. An army of them stood one-eyed, wary, kept watch from the sand. Pelicans. Carved out of the rocks like harsh modern sculptures. Long-necked. Awkward. Occasionally one of them made a solo flight out over the water, paused in midflight, plummeted like a rock into the sea. Bands of sandpipers ran on thin stilts ahead of us along the beach.

Kate and I went for long healing swims in the ocean. Threw ourselves headlong into the waves. Felt the first shock of cold, a birth slap. A quickening of blood. Rush of life. Sharpening of the senses. The waves broke over us. We dived into the coolness. Sliced through the blue, the green. Dived beneath the surface into the twilight, emerged triumphant, dripping water into the sun. We felt as quick and sleek as seals. Alive as a nest of eels.

Today we swim out beyond the buoy until the beach, sun-drenched, shimmers indistinctly in the distance. The water is clear. Patterns of sunlight and shadow play across the sand twenty feet below us. The lines move and change like a fishnet cast against the sun, loose-woven, continuously moving. Kate dives down beneath me, slides up along the length of my body, clings with arms and legs, tastes of salt. It is the happiest moment of my life. It pays for all the others. Below us two shadows move across the sea floor. They hover, coalesce, take up a guarded watch behind us.

TOUGH STREETS

The grit, the dirt, the cheap cost of life—the ongoing struggle between the law...and the lawbreakers.

BIG TIME TOMMY SLOANE
James Reardon
_____ 90981-0 $3.95 U.S.   _____ 90982-9 $4.95 Can.

TIGHT CASE
Edward J. Hogan
_____ 91142-4 $3.95 U.S.   _____ 91143-2 $4.95 Can.

RIDE A TIGER
Harold Livingston
_____ 90487-8 $4.95 U.S.   _____ 90488-6 $5.95 Can.

THE RIGHT TO REMAIN SILENT
Charles Brandt
_____ 91381-8 $3.95 U.S.   _____ 91382-6 $4.95 Can.

THE EIGHTH VICTIM
Eugene Izzi
_____ 91218-8 $3.95 U.S.   _____ 91219-6 $4.95 Can.

THE TAKE
Eugene Izzi
_____ 91120-3 $3.50 U.S.   ._____ 91121-1 $4.50 Can.

Seattle is a city paralyzed by fear. A serial killer is loose on its streets. And as each new victim surfaces, the tide of panic rises.

UNDERCURRENTS
RIDLEY PEARSON

"ONE HELL OF A WRITER.
HE GRABS. HE TWISTS.
HE TIGHTENS THE SCREWS...
A SUPERB READ!"
— CLIVE CUSSLER,
author of TREASURE